HIS & HERS

HIS & HERS

ALICE FEENEY

THORNDIKE PRESS
A part of Gale, a Cengage Company

LIBRARY OF CONGRESS CIP DATA ON FILE.
CATALOGUING IN PUBLICATION FOR THIS BOOK
IS AVAILABLE FROM THE LIBRARY OF CONGRESS

ISBN-13: 978-1-4328-8117-7 (hardcover alk. paper)

Published in 2020 by arrangement with Macmillan Publishing Group, LLC/Flatiron Books

Printed in Mexico
Print Number: 01   Print Year: 2020

For Them

Two sides, one story.
Who will you believe?

It wasn't love at first sight.

I can admit that now. But by the end, I loved her more than I thought it was possible to love another human being. I cared about her far more than I ever cared about myself. That's why I did it. Why I had to. I think it's important that people know that, when they find out what I've done. If they do. Perhaps then they might understand that I did it for her.

There is a difference between being and feeling alone, and it is possible to miss someone and be with them at the same time. There have been plenty of people in my life: family, friends, colleagues, lovers. A full cast of the usual suspects that make a person's social circle, but mine has always felt a little bent out of shape. None of the relationships I have ever formed with another human being feel real to me. More like a series of missed connections.

People might recognize my face, they may

even know my name, but they'll never know the real me. Nobody does. I've always been selfish with the true thoughts and feelings inside my head; I don't share them with anyone. Because I can't. There is a version of me I can only ever be with myself. I sometimes think the secret to success is the ability to adapt. Life rarely stays the same, and I've frequently had to reinvent myself in order to keep up. I learned how to change my looks, my life . . . even my voice.

I also learned how to fit in, but constantly trying to do so is more than just uncomfortable now, it hurts. Because I don't. Fit. I fold my jagged edges inside myself, and smooth over the most obvious differences between us, but I am not the same as you. There are over seven billion people on the planet, and yet I have somehow managed to spend a lifetime feeling alone.

I'm losing my mind and not for the first time, but sanity can often be lost and found. People will say that I snapped, lost it, came unhinged. But when the time came it was — without doubt — the right thing to do. I felt good about myself afterward. I wanted to do it again.

There are at least two sides to every story:

Yours and mine.

Ours and theirs.

His and hers.

Which means someone is always lying.

Lies told often enough can start to sound true, and we all sometimes hear a voice inside our heads, saying something so shocking, we pretend it is not our own. I know exactly what I heard that night, while I waited at the station for her to come home for the last time. At first, the train sounded just like any other in the distance. I closed my eyes and it was like listening to music, the rhythmic song of the cars on the tracks getting louder and louder:

Clickety-click. Clickety-click. Clickety-click.

But then the sound started to change, translating into words inside my head, repeating themselves over and over, until it was impossible not to hear:

Kill them all. Kill them all. Kill them all.

HER:
ANNA ANDREWS

Mondays have always been my favorite day.

The chance to start again.

A clean enough slate with just the dust of your own past mistakes still visible — almost, but not quite wiped away.

I realize it's an unpopular opinion — to be fond of the first day of the week — but I'm full of those. My view of the world tends to be a little tilted. When you grow up sitting in life's cheap seats, it's too easy to see behind the puppets dancing on its stage. Once you've seen the strings, and who pulls them, it can be hard to enjoy the rest of the show. I can afford to sit where I want now, choose any view I like, but those fancy-looking theater boxes are only good for looking down on other people. I'll never do that. Just because I don't like to look back doesn't mean I don't remember where I came from. I've worked hard for my ticket and the cheap seats still suit me fine.

I don't spend a lot of time getting ready in the mornings — there is no point putting on makeup, just for someone else to take it off and start again when I get to work — and I don't eat breakfast. I don't eat much at all, but I do enjoy cooking for others. Apparently, I'm a feeder.

I stop briefly in the kitchen to pick up my Tupperware carrier, filled with homemade cupcakes for the team. I barely remember making them. It was late, definitely after my third glass of something dry and white. I prefer red but it leaves a telltale stain on my lips, so I save it for weekends only. I open the fridge and notice that I didn't finish last night's wine, so I drink what is left straight from the bottle, before taking it with me as I leave the house. Monday is also when my trash gets collected. The recycling bin is surprisingly full for someone who lives alone. Mostly glass.

I like to walk to work. The streets are pretty empty at this time of day, and I find it calming. I cross Waterloo Bridge and weave my way through Soho toward Oxford Circus, while listening to the *Today* program. I'd prefer to listen to music, a little Ludovico perhaps or Taylor Swift depending on my mood — there are two very different sides to my personality — but instead I endure the dulcet tones of middle-class Britain, telling me what they think I should know. Their voices still feel foreign to my ears, despite sounding like my own. But then I didn't always speak this way. I've been presenting the *BBC One O'Clock News* bulletin for almost two years, and I still feel like a fraud.

I stop by the flattened cardboard box that has been bothering me the most recently. I can see a strand of blond hair poking out the top, so I know she's still there. I don't know who she is, only that I might have been her had life unfolded differently. I left home when I was sixteen because it felt like I had to. I don't do what I'm about to do now out of kindness; I do it because of a misplaced moral compass. Just like the soup kitchen I volunteered at last Christmas. We rarely deserve the lives we lead. We pay for them however we can, be it with money, guilt, or regret.

I open the plastic carry case and put one of my carefully constructed cupcakes down on the pavement, between her cardboard box and the wall, so that she'll see it when she wakes. Then, worried she might not like or appreciate my chocolate frosting — for all I know she could be diabetic — I take a twenty-pound note from my purse and slide it underneath. I don't mind if she spends my money on alcohol; I do.

Radio 4 continues to irritate me, so I switch off the latest politician lying in my ears. Their over-rehearsed dishonesty doesn't fit with this image of real people with real problems. Not that I'd ever say that out loud or on-air during an interview. I'm paid to be impartial regardless of how I feel.

Maybe I'm a liar too. I chose this career because I wanted to tell the truth. I wanted to tell the stories that mattered most, the ones that I thought people needed to hear. Stories that I hoped might change the world and make it a better place. But I was naïve. People working in the media today have more power than politicians, but what good is trying to tell the truth about the world when I can't bear to be honest about my own story: who I am, where I came from, what I've done.

I bury the thoughts like I always do. Lock them in a secure secret box inside my head, push them to the darkest corner right at the back, and hope they won't escape again anytime soon.

I walk the final few streets to Broadcasting House, then search inside my handbag for my ever-elusive security pass. My fingers find one of my little tins of mints instead. It rattles in protest as I flip it open and pop a tiny white triangle inside my mouth, as though it were a pill. Wine on my breath before the morning meeting is best avoided. I locate my pass and step inside the glass revolving doors, feeling several sets of eyes turn my way. That's okay. I'm pretty good at being the version of myself I think people want me to be. At least on the outside.

I know everyone by name, including the cleaners still sweeping the floor. It costs almost nothing to be kind and I have a very efficient memory, despite the drink. Once past security — a little more thorough than it used to be, thanks to the state of the world we have curated for ourselves — I stare down at the newsroom and it feels like home. Cocooned inside the basement of the BBC building, but visible from every floor, the newsroom resembles a brightly lit red-and-white open-plan warren. Almost every available space is filled with screens and tightly packed desks, with an eclectic collection of journalists sitting behind each one.

These people aren't just my colleagues, they're like a dysfunctional surrogate family. I'm almost forty years old, but I don't have anyone else. No children. No husband.

Not anymore. I've worked here for almost twenty years but, unlike those with friends or family connections, I started right at the bottom. I took a few detours along the way, and the stepping-stones to success were sometimes a little slippery, but I got where I wanted to be, eventually.

Patience is the answer to so many of life's questions.

Serendipity smiled at me when the previous news anchor left. She went into labor a month early, and five minutes before the lunchtime bulletin. Her water broke and I got my lucky break. I'd just come back from maternity leave myself — earlier than planned — and was the only correspondent in the newsroom with any presenting experience. All of which was overtime and overnight — the shifts nobody else wanted — I was that desperate for any opportunity that might help my career. Presenting a network bulletin was something I had been dreaming of my whole life.

There was no time for a trip to hair and makeup that day. They rushed me on set and did what they could, powdering my face at the same time as they miked me up. I practiced reading the headlines on the teleprompter, and the director was calm and kind in my earpiece. His voice steadied me.

I remember very little about that first half-hour program, but I do recall the congratulations afterward. From newsroom nobody to network news anchor in less than an hour.

My boss is called the Thin Controller behind his slightly hunched back. He's a small man trapped inside a tall man's body. He also has a speech impediment. It prevents him from pronouncing his *R*s, and the rest of the newsroom from taking him seriously. He has never been good at filling gaps on rosters so, after my successful debut, he decided to let me fill in until the end of that week. Then the next. A three-month contract as a news anchor — instead of my staff position as a correspondent — swelled into six; after that it was extended to the end of the year, accompanied by a nice little pay raise. Viewing numbers went up when I started presenting the program, so I was allowed to stay. My predecessor never returned; she got pregnant again while on maternity leave and hasn't been seen since. Almost two years later, I'm still here and expect my latest contract to be renewed any day.

I take my seat between the editor and the lead producer, then clean my desk and keyboard with an antibacterial wipe. There is no telling who might have been sitting here overnight. The newsroom never sleeps, and sadly not everyone in it adheres to my preferred level of hygiene. I open up the running order and smile; it still gives me a little thrill to see my name at the top:

News Anchor: Anna Andrews.

I start writing the intros for each story. Despite popular opinion, we don't just *read* the news, we write it. Or at least *I* do. News anchors, like normal human beings, come in all shapes and sizes. There are several who have crawled so far up their own asses I'm amazed they can still sit down, let alone read a teleprompter. The nation would be appalled if they knew how some of their so-called national treasures behaved behind the scenes. But I won't tell. Journalism is a game with more chutes than ladders. Getting to the top takes a long time, and one wrong move can land you right back down at the bottom. Nobody is bigger than the machine.

The morning breezes by just like any other: a constantly evolving running order, conversations with correspondents in the field, discussions with the director about graphics and screens. There is an almost permanent line of reporters and producers waiting to talk to the editor beside me. More often than not, to request a longer duration for their package or two-way.

Everyone always wants just a little more time.

I don't miss those days at all: begging to get on-air, constantly fretting when I didn't. There simply isn't time to tell every story.

The rest of the team are unusually quiet. I take a quick look to my left, and notice that the producer has the latest roster up on her screen. She closes it down as soon as she sees me looking. Rosters are second only to breaking news when it comes to influencing stress levels in the newsroom. They come out late and rarely go down well, with the distribution of the most unpopular shifts — lates, weekends, overnights — always cause for contention. I work Monday to Friday now, and haven't requested any leave for over six months, so, unlike my poor colleagues, there is nothing roster-shaped for me to worry about.

An hour before the program, I visit makeup. It's a nice place to escape to — relatively peaceful and quiet compared with the constant noise of the newsroom. My hair is blow-dried into an obedient chestnut bob, and my face is covered with HD-grade foundation. I wear more makeup for work than I did for my wedding. The thought forces me to retreat inside myself for a moment, and I feel the ridge of indentation on my finger, where my ring used to be.

The program goes mostly according to plan, despite a few last-minute changes while we are on-air: some breaking news, a delayed TV package, a camera with a mind of its own in the studio, and a dodgy feed from Washington. I'm forced to wrap up an overenthusiastic political correspondent in Downing Street, one who regularly takes up more than their allotted time. Some people like the sound of their own voices a little too much.

The debrief begins while I'm still on set, waiting to say good-bye to viewers after the weather segment. Nobody wants to hang around any longer than absolutely necessary after the program, so they always start without me. It's a gathering of correspondents and producers who worked on the show, but is also attended by representatives of other departments: home news, foreign news, editing, graphics, as well as the Thin Controller.

I swing by my desk to collect my Tupperware carrier before joining everyone, eager to share my latest culinary creations with the team. I haven't told anyone that it's my birthday today yet, but I might.

I make my way across the newsroom

toward them, and stop briefly when I see a woman I don't recognize. She has her back to me, with two small children dressed in matching outfits by her side. I notice the cute cupcakes my colleagues are already eating. Not homemade — like mine — but shop-bought and expensive-looking. Then I return my attention to the woman handing them out. I stare at her bright red hair, framing her pretty face with a bob so sharp it could have been cut with a laser. When she turns and smiles in my direction it feels like a slap.

Someone passes me a glass of warm prosecco, and I see the drinks trolley that management always orders from catering whenever a member of staff leaves. It happens a lot in this business. The Thin Controller taps his glass with an overgrown fingernail, then he starts to speak, strange-sounding words tumbling out of his crumb-covered lips.

"We can't wait to welcome you back . . ."

It's the only sentence my ears manage to translate. I stare at Cat Jones, the woman who presented the program before I did, standing there with her trademark red hair, and two beautiful little girls. I feel physically sick.

". . . and our thanks to Anna, of course,

for taking the helm while you were away."

Eyes are turned and glasses are raised in my direction. My hands start to tremble and I hope my face is doing a better job of hiding my feelings.

"It was on the roster, I'm so sorry, we all thought you knew."

The producer standing next to me whispers the words but I'm unable to form a reply.

The Thin Controller apologizes too, afterward. He sits in his office, while I stand, and stares at his hands while he speaks, as though the words he is struggling to find might be written on his sweaty fingers. He thanks me, and tells me that I've done a great job filling in for the last . . .

"Two years," I say, when he doesn't appear to know or understand how long it has been.

He shrugs as though it were nothing.

"It is *her* job, I'm afraid. She has a contract. We can't sack people for having a baby, not even when they have two!"

He laughs.

I don't.

"When does she come back?" I ask.

A frown folds itself onto the vast space that is his forehead.

"She comes back tomorrow. It's all on

the . . ." I watch as he tries and fails to find a substitute for the word "roster," like anything beginning with the letter *R*. ". . . it's all on the *woster,* has been for some time. You're back on the correspondent desk, but don't worry, you can still fill in for her, and present the program during school holidays, Christmas and Easter, that sort of thing. We all think you did a *tewwific* job. Here's your new contract."

I stare down at the crisp white sheets of A4 paper, covered in carefully constructed words from a faceless HR employee. My eyes only seem able to focus on one line:

News Correspondent: Anna Andrews.

As I step out of his office, I see her again: my replacement. Although I suppose the truth is that I was only ever hers. It's a terrible thing to admit, even to myself, but as I look at Cat Jones with her perfect hair and perfect children, standing there chatting and laughing with *my* team, I wish she was dead.

HIM:
DETECTIVE CHIEF INSPECTOR JACK HARPER

Tuesday 05:15

The sound of my phone buzzing wakes me from the kind of dream I don't wish to be woken from. One in which I am not a fortysomething-year-old man, living in a house with a mortgage I can't afford, a toddler I can't keep up with, and a woman who is not my wife but nags me anyway. A better man would have got his shit together by now, instead of sleepwalking through a loaned-out life.

I squint at my phone in the darkness and see that it is Tuesday. It is also stupidly early, so I'm relieved that the text doesn't appear to have woken anyone else. Sleep deprivation tends to have terrible consequences in this house, though not for me — I've always been a bit of a night owl. I shouldn't feel excitement about what I read on the screen, but I do. The truth is, since I left London, my job has been as dull as a nun's underwear drawer.

I'm head of the Major Crime Team here, which sounds exciting, but I'm based in deepest, darkest Surrey now, which isn't. Blackdown is a quintessential English village less than two hours from the capital, and petty crime and the occasional burglary tend to be as "major" as it gets. The village is hidden from the outside world by a sentinel of trees. The ancient forest seems to have trapped Blackdown — and its inhabitants — in the past, as well as permanent shadow. But its chocolate-box beauty could never be denied. Blackdown is filled with an abundance of thatched cottages, white picket fences, an above-average number of elderly residents, and a below-average crime rate.

It's the kind of place people come to die, and somewhere I never thought I'd find myself living.

I stare at the message on my phone, practically drooling over the words as I drink them down:

Jane Doe discovered in Blackdown Woods overnight. MCT requested. Please call in.

Just the idea of a body being found *here* feels like it must be a mistake, but I already know it isn't. Ten minutes later, I'm sufficiently dressed, caffeinated, and in the car.

My latest secondhand 4 × 4 looks like it could do with a wash, and I realize — a little too late — that I do too. I sniff my armpits and consider going back inside the house, but I don't want to waste time or wake anyone. I hate the way they both look at me sometimes. They have the same eyes, filled with tears and disappointment a tad too often.

I'm a little overenthusiastic perhaps, to get to the crime scene before everyone else, but I can't help it. Nothing this bad has happened here for years, and it makes me feel good — optimistic and energized. The thing about working for the police for as long as I have, is that you start to think like a criminal without being seen as one.

I turn on the engine, praying it will start, ignoring the glimpse of my own reflection in the rearview mirror. My hair — which is now more gray than black — is sticking out in all directions. There are dark circles beneath my eyes, and I look older than I remember being. I try to console my ego; it's the middle of the bloody night, after all. Besides, I don't care what I look like, and other people's opinions matter even less to me than my own. At least that's what I keep telling myself.

I drive with one hand on the steering

wheel, while the other feels the stubble on my chin. Maybe I should have at least shaved. I glance down at my crumpled shirt. I'm sure we must *own* an ironing board, but I've no idea where it is or when I last used it. For the first time in a long time, I wonder what other people see when they see me. I used to be quite the catch. I used to be a lot of things.

It's still dark when I pull into the National Trust parking lot and I can see that — despite the fact that I came straight here — everyone else appears to have beaten me to it. There are two police cars and two vans, as well as unmarked vehicles. Forensics are already on the scene, as is Detective Sergeant Priya Patel. Her career choice hasn't managed to grind her down yet; she's still shiny and new. Too young to let the job make her feel old, too inexperienced to know what it will do to her eventually. What it does to us all. Her daily enthusiasm is exhausting, as is her perpetually cheerful disposition. My head hurts just from looking at her, so I tend to avoid doing so as often as it is possible when you work with someone every day.

Priya's ponytail swings from side to side as she hurries toward my car. Her tortoise-shell glasses slip down her nose, and her big

29

brown eyes are a bit too full of excitement. *She* doesn't look as if she's been dragged from her bed in the middle of the night. Her slim-fit suit can't possibly be keeping her petite body warm, and her freshly polished brogues slide a little on the mud. I find it strangely satisfying to see them get dirty.

I sometimes wonder whether my colleague sleeps fully dressed, just in case she needs to leave the house in a hurry. She put in a special request to transfer here to work under me a couple of months ago, though god knows why. If there was ever a time in my life when I was as eager as Priya Patel, I can't remember it.

As soon as I step outside the car, it starts to rain. An instant heavy downpour, saturating my clothes in seconds, and assaulting me from above. I look up and study the sky, which thinks it is night even though it is now morning. The moon and stars would still be visible, had they not been covered with a blanket of dark clouds. Torrential rain is not ideal for preserving outdoor evidence.

Priya interrupts my thoughts and I slam the car door without meaning to. She rushes over, trying to hold her umbrella over my head, and I shoo her away.

"DCI Harper, I —"

"I've told you before, please call me Jack. We're not in the army," I say.

Her face experiences a freeze frame. She looks like a chastised puppy, and I feel like the miserable old git I know I've become.

"The Target Patrol Team called it in," she says.

"Is anyone from the TPT still here?"

"Yes."

"Good, I want to see them before they leave."

"Of course. The body is this way. Early indications show that —"

"I want to see it for myself," I interrupt.

"Yes, boss."

It's as though my first name is simply a word she can't pronounce.

We pass a steady stream of staff I vaguely recognize — people whose names I've forgotten, either because I didn't learn them in the first place, or I haven't seen them for so long. It doesn't matter. My small but perfectly formed Major Crime Team is based near here, but covers the whole county. We work with different people every day. Besides, this job isn't about making friends, it's about not making enemies. Priya has a lot to learn about that. The hushed quiet we walk in might be uncom-fortable for her, but not for me. Silence is

31

my favorite symphony; I can't think clearly when life gets too loud.

She shines a flashlight on the ground a little way ahead of our footsteps — irritatingly efficient as always — as we crunch over a dark carpet of fallen leaves and broken twigs. Autumn has been and gone, a guest appearance this year before shying away to make room for an overconfident winter. The top button is missing from my coat, so it no longer does up all the way. I overcompensate for the gap with a Harry Potter–style scarf displaying my initials — a gift from an ex. I've never quite managed to part with it, a bit like the woman who gave it to me. It probably makes me look like a fool, but I don't care. There are some things we only hold on to because of who gave them to us: names, beliefs, scarves. Besides, I like the way it feels around my neck: a cozy personalized noose.

My breath forms clouds of condensation, and I shove my hands a little deeper into my coat pockets trying to keep dry and warm. I'm pleased to see that someone thought to put up a tent around the body, and I step inside the white PVC door. My fingers find the shape of a child's dummy in my pocket at the exact moment my eyes see the corpse. I grip the pacifier so hard that the plastic cuts into my palm. It causes a small burst of pain, the kind I sometimes need to feel. It isn't as though I haven't seen a dead person before, but this is different.

The woman is partially covered by leaves, and quite a distance from the main path. She would have been easy to miss in this dark corner of the woods, were it not for the bright lights the team have already set up around her.

"Who found the body?" I ask.

"Anonymous tip-off," says Priya. "Someone called the station from a pay phone down the lane."

I am grateful for an answer that is as short as the person who gave it. Priya is prone to being a talker, and I am prone to impatience.

I take a step closer, and lean down toward the dead woman's face. She's in her late thirties, slim, pretty — if you like that kind of thing, which I suppose I do — and her general appearance suggests three things to me: money, vanity, and self-control. She has the kind of body that has been taken care of with years of gym visits, diets, and costly creams. Her long, expertly bleached blond hair looks as though she might have just brushed it before lying down in the mud. Strands of gold in the grime. No sign of a struggle. Her bright blue eyes are still wide open, as though shocked by the last thing that they saw, and from the color and condition of her skin, she has not been here long.

The corpse is fully clothed. Everything this woman is wearing looks expensive: a woolen coat, a silky-looking blouse, and a black leather skirt. Her shoes appear to be the only thing missing — not ideal for a walk in the woods. It's impossible not to notice her small, pretty feet, but it's the blouse I find myself staring at. Like the lace bra underneath, I can see that it used to be white. Both are now stained red, and it's clear from the frenzied pattern of flesh and torn fabric that she was stabbed multiple times in the chest.

I have a curious urge to touch her, but don't.

That's when I notice the victim's fingernails. They've been roughly cut to the quick, and that isn't all. I loathe being seen wearing glasses, but my eyesight isn't what it used to be, so I find the nonprescription pair I keep for emergencies and take a closer look.

Red varnish has been used to spell letters on the nails of her right hand:

T W O

I look at the left hand and it's the same,

but the letters spell a different word:

F A C E D

This wasn't a crime of passion; this murder was planned.

I tune back into here and now, and realize that Priya hasn't noticed yet; she's been too busy reading me her notes and telling me her thoughts. I generally find she tends to talk unless specifically asked to stop. Her words trip over themselves, rushing out of her mouth and into my ears. I try to look interested, translating her hurried sentences as she says them.

". . . I've initiated all standard golden-hour procedures. There's no CCTV in this part of town, but we're gathering footage from the high street. I'm guessing she didn't walk here barefoot in the middle of winter, but without any ID or vehicle registration — the parking lot was completely empty — I can't issue an ANPR . . ."

People rarely say what they mean under stress, and all I hear is her desperation to prove to me that she can handle this.

"Have you seen a dead body before?" I ask, interrupting.

She stands a little straighter and sticks out her chin like a disgruntled child.

"Yes. In the morgue."

"Not the same," I mutter beneath my breath.

There are so many things I could teach her, things she doesn't know she needs to learn.

"I've been thinking about the message the killer wanted to send," Priya says, staring back down at her notepad, where I can see the beginnings of one of her many lists.

"They wanted people to know that the victim was two-faced," I reply, and she looks confused. "Her fingernails. I think someone cut them and wrote a message."

Priya frowns then bends down to get a closer look. She stares up at me in wonder, as though I'm Hercule Poirot. I guess reading is my superpower.

I avoid her gaze and return my attention to the face of the woman lying in the dirt. Then I instruct one of the forensics team to take pictures of her from every angle. She looks like the kind of person who enjoyed having her photo taken, wearing her vanity like a badge. The flash blinds me, and I'm reminded of another time and place: London a few years ago, reporters and cameras on a street corner, clamoring to get a shot of something they shouldn't want to see. I bury the memory — I can't stand the press — then I notice something else.

36

The dead woman's mouth is ever so slightly open.

"Shine your flashlight on her face."

Priya does as I ask, and I get down on my knees again to take a closer look at the body. Lips that were once pink have turned blue, but I can see something red hiding in the dark space between them. I reach to touch it, without thinking, as though under a spell.

"Sir?"

Priya interrupts my mistake before I make it. She is uncomfortably close to me; so much so that I can smell her perfume, along with her breath: a light whiff of recently drunk tea. I turn and see an old frown form on her young face. I would have thought this whole experience — finding a body in the woods for the first time — might have fazed her, unnerved her a little, but maybe I was wrong. I try to remember how old Priya is — I find it so hard to tell with women. If I had to guess I'd say late twenties or early thirties. Still hungry with ambition, confident of her own potential, unscarred by the disappointments that life has yet to hit her with.

"Shouldn't we wait for the pathologist to examine the body before we touch anything?" she asks, already knowing the answer.

Priya sticks to the rules the way good liars stick to their stories. She says "pathologist" like a kid who just learned a new word in school, one who wants people to hear them use it in a sentence.

"Absolutely," I reply, and take a step back. Unlike my colleague, I've seen plenty of dead bodies before, but this is not like any case I have previously worked on. I zone out a little again while Priya starts to speculate about the identity of the woman. It feels like this is the start of something big, and I wonder if I'm up to the task. No two murders are the same, but it's been years since I handled a case even remotely like this, and a lot has changed since then. The job has changed, I've changed, and it isn't just that.

This is different.

I've never worked on the murder of someone I know before.

And I knew this woman well.

I was with her last night.

HER

Tuesday 06:30

We all have secrets; some we won't even tell ourselves.

I don't know what woke me, or what time it is, or where I am when I first open my eyes. Everything is pitch-black. My fingers find the bedside lamp, which sheds some light on the matter, and I'm pleased to see the familiar sight of my own bedroom. It is always a relief to know that I made it home when I wake up feeling like this.

I am not one of those women that you read about in books, or see on TV dramas, who frequently drink too much and forget what they did the night before. I'm not an amateur alcoholic and I'm not a cliché. We're all addicted to something: money, success, social media, sugar, sex . . . the list of possibilities is endless. My drug of choice just happens to be alcohol. It can take a while for my memories to catch up with me,

39

and I might not always be happy or proud about what I've done, but I do always remember. *Always.*

That doesn't mean I have to tell the whole world about it.

Sometimes I think I am the unreliable narrator of my own life.

Sometimes I think we all are.

The first thing I remember is that I lost my dream job, and the memory of my worst nightmare coming true seems to physically wound me. I switch off the light — I no longer wish to see things so clearly — then lie back down on the bed, burrowing beneath the covers. I wrap my arms around myself and close my eyes as I recall walking out of the Thin Controller's office, then leaving the newsroom mid-afternoon. I took a taxi home, feeling a little too unsteady on my feet to walk, then I phoned my mother to tell her what had happened. It was foolish, but I couldn't think of anyone else to call.

My mother has become a bit forgetful and confused in recent years, and phone calls home only make me feel guilty for not visiting more often. I have my reasons for never wanting to go back where I came from, but they are better forgotten than shared. It's easier to blame the miles for the distance that exists between some parents and their children, but when you bend the truth too far it tends to break. It sounded like Mum at first, on the other end of the line, but it wasn't really her. After I poured my heart out, she was completely silent for a moment, then she asked whether eggs and fries for tea would cheer me up after my bad day at school.

Mum doesn't always remember that I'm thirty-six and live in London. She frequently forgets that I have a job, and that I used to have a husband and a child of my own. She didn't even seem to know that it was my birthday. There was no card this year, or last, but it's not her fault. Time is something my mother has forgotten how to tell. It moves differently for her now, often backward instead of forward. Dementia stole time from my mother, and stole my mother from me.

Reaching back inside my memories for a source of comfort was understandable given the circumstances, but I shouldn't have stretched as far back as my childhood; it's a bit too hit-or-miss.

When I got home, I closed all the curtains and opened a bottle of Malbec. Not because I was scared of being seen — I just like drinking in the dark. Sometimes even I don't like to see the me that I become when nobody else is looking. After my second glass, I got changed into something less conspicuous — some old jeans and a black jumper — then I went to pay someone a visit.

When I returned a few hours later, I stripped out of my clothes in the hallway. They were covered in dirt, and I was filled with guilt. I remember opening another bottle and lighting the fire. I sat right in front of it, wrapped in a blanket, gulping down the wine. It took me forever to warm up after being out in the cold for so long. The logs hissed and whispered as though they had secrets of their own, and the firelight cast a series of ghostly shadows that danced around the room. I tried to get *her* out of my head, but even with my eyes squeezed shut, I could still *see* her face, *smell* her skin, *hear* her voice, crying.

I remember seeing the dirt beneath my fingernails, and scrubbing myself clean in the shower before I went to bed.

My phone buzzes again and I realize that must be what woke me. It's early morning now, still as dark outside the apartment as it is inside, and eerily quiet. Silence is a fear I've learned to feel, rather than hear. It creeps up on me, often lurking in the loudest corners of my mind. I listen but there is no sound of traffic, or birdsong, or life. No rumble of the boiler, or murmurs from the network of ancient pipes that try and fail to heat my home.

I stare at my mobile — the only light in the shadows — and see that it was a breaking-news text that woke me. The screen casts an unnatural glow. I read the headline about the body of a woman being found in the woods, and wonder whether I am still dreaming. The room seems a shade darker than it did before.

Then my phone starts to ring.

I answer it, and listen as the Thin Controller apologizes for calling so early. He wonders whether I might be able to come in and present the program.

"What happened to Cat Jones?" I ask.

"We don't know. But she hasn't turned up for work, and nobody can get hold of her."

The little pieces of me I got broken into yesterday start to creep and crawl back together. Sometimes I get lost in my own thoughts and fears. Trapped within a world of worry, which, deep down, I know only exists inside my head. Anxiety often screams louder than logic, and when you spend too long imagining the worst, you can make it come true.

The Thin Controller asks more questions when I fail to answer the first.

"I'm *weally* sorry to *wush* you, Anna. But I do need to know now if possible . . ."

His speech impediment makes me hate him a little less. I know exactly what I am going to say — I rehearsed this moment in my imagination.

"Of course. I'd never let the team down."

The tangible relief on the other end of the line is delicious.

"You're a lifesaver," he says, and for a moment I forget that the opposite is true.

It takes longer than usual to get myself ready; I'm still drunk, but it's nothing some prescription eye drops and a cup of coffee can't rectify. I drink it while it's still too hot, so that it scalds my mouth; a little pain to ease the hurt. Then I pour myself some cold white wine from one of the bottles in the fridge — just a small glass, to soothe the burn. I head for the bathroom and ignore the bedroom door at the end of the corridor, the one I always keep closed. Sometimes our memories reframe themselves to reveal prettier pictures of our past, something a little less awful to look back at. Sometimes we need to paint over them, to pretend not to remember what is hidden underneath.

I shower and choose a red dress from my wardrobe, one with the tags still attached. I'm not a fan of shopping, so if I find something that suits me, I tend to buy it in every color. Clothes don't make the woman, but they can help disguise the cloth we are cut from. I don't wear new things right away; I save them for when I need to feel good, rather than feel like myself. Now is a perfect time to wear something new and pretty to hide inside. When I'm satisfied with who I look like, I wrap her up in my favorite red coat — getting noticed isn't always a bad thing.

I take a cab to work — eager to get my old self back to my old job as soon as possible — and pop a mint in my mouth before stepping into reception. It's been less than twenty-four hours, but when I stare down at the newsroom it feels like coming home.

As I make my way toward the team, I can't help noticing how they all turn to look up at me, like a group of meerkats. They exchange a series of anxious expressions, neatly carved into their tired-looking faces. I thought they would look happier to see me — not all news anchors pull their weight the way I do to get a bulletin on-air — but I fix my unreturned smile, and grip the metal banister on the spiral staircase a little tighter than before. It feels like I might fall.

When I reach for my chair, the editor stops me, putting her icy-cold hand on top of mine. She shakes her head, then looks down at the floor, as though embarrassed. She's the kind of woman who regularly prays for a fat bank account and thin body, but God always seems to muddle up her prayers. I stand in the middle of the seated team, feeling the heat of their stares on my flushed cheeks, trying to guess what *they* know that *I* don't.

"I'm *so* sorry!" says a voice behind me. It seems ludicrous to describe it as brushed velvet, but that's exactly how it sounds: a luxurious, feminine purr. It's a voice I did not expect or want to hear. "The nanny canceled at the last minute, my mother-in-law agreed to step in but managed to crash her car on the way over — nothing too serious, just a bump really — and then, when I *finally* managed to settle the girls and leave the house, my train was delayed *and* I realized I'd forgotten my phone! I had no way of letting you know how late I was going to be. I can't tell you how sorry I am, but I'm here now."

I don't know why I believed Cat Jones was gone for good. It seems silly now, but I suppose I had imagined a little accident of

46

some sort. Just something to prevent her from presenting the lunchtime bulletin ever again, so that I could step back into her shoes, and be the person I want to be. I am redundant now that she is here, and I can already feel myself start to crumple and fold into someone small and invisible. An unwanted and unnecessary spare part in a newly refurbished machine.

She tucks her bright red hair behind her ears, revealing diamond studs that look far more genuine than the person wearing them. Her hair color can't possibly be natural, but it looks perfect, just like her figure-hugging yellow dress, and the set of pearly white teeth revealed when she smiles in my direction. I feel like a frumpy fraud.

"Anna!" she says, as though we are old friends, not new enemies. I return the smile like an unwanted gift. "I thought you'd be at home with your own little one on your first day of freedom, now that I'm back! I hope motherhood is treating you well. What age is your daughter now?"

She would have been two years, three months, and four days old.

I've never stopped counting.

I guess Cat remembers me being pregnant. It appears nobody ever told her what happened a few months after Charlotte was

47

born. Everything seems very still and silent in the newsroom all of a sudden, with everyone staring in our direction. Her question sucks the air from my lungs and nobody, including me, seems able to answer it. Her eyebrows — which I'm quite certain have been tattooed onto her face — form a slightly theatrical frown.

"Oh my goodness, did they call you in because of me? I'm *so* sorry again — you could have had a nice morning off for a change, stayed at home with your family."

I hold on to the news anchor's chair for balance.

"It's fine, honestly," I say, and manage a smile that hurts my face. "I'm looking forward to being a correspondent again to be honest, so I'm delighted you're back. I actually miss getting out of the studio and covering real stories, meeting real people, you know?"

Her expression remains neutral. I interpret her silence as a way of saying that either she doesn't agree, or doesn't believe me.

"If you're so excited to get out and about again, maybe you should take a look at that murder that broke overnight? The body in the woods?" Cat replies.

"That's not a bad idea," says the Thin Controller, appearing by her side and smiling like a monkey with a new banana.

I feel myself start to shrink.

"I haven't seen the story," I lie.

I think now might be a good time to pretend I'm sick. I could go home, lock myself away from the world, and drink myself happy — or at least less sad — but Cat Jones continues to speak, the whole team appearing to hang on her every word.

"A woman's body was found overnight in a place called Blackdown, a sleepy Surrey village according to the wires. It might turn out to be nothing, but you could go check it out maybe? In fact, I insist we find you a camera crew. I'm sure you don't want to just . . . hang around here."

She glances over at what we call the taxi rank — the corner of the newsroom where the general correspondents sit, waiting to be deployed on a story, often not getting on-air at all.

Journalists with specialist subjects — like business, health, entertainment, crime — all sit in offices upstairs. Their days tend to be busy and satisfying, their jobs relatively safe. But things are very different for a humble general correspondent. Some had quite promising careers at one time, but probably pissed off the wrong person, and have been gathering unaired stories like dust ever since.

There is a lot of deadwood in this newsroom, but the tough varnish of media unions can make it tricky to carve out. It is hard to imagine a more humiliating seat in the newsroom for a former news anchor than correspondent corner. I've worked too hard for too long to disappear. I am going to find a way to get myself back on-air again, but this is the one story I don't want to cover.

"Is there *anything* else?" I ask.

My voice sounds strange, as though the words got strangled.

The Thin Controller shrugs and shakes his head. I notice the light dusting of dandruff on the shoulders of his ill-fitting suit, and he sees me staring at it. I force a final smile to dispel the latest awkward silence.

"Then I guess I'm on my way to Blackdown."

We all have cracks, the little dents and blemishes that life makes in our hearts and minds, cemented by fear and anxiety, sometimes plastered over with fragile hope. I choose to hide the vulnerable sides of myself as well as I'm able at all times. I choose to hide a lot of things.

The only people with no regrets are liars.

The truth is, even though I'd rather be anywhere but here right now, Blackdown is the one place I don't ever want to go back to. Especially not after last night. Some things are too difficult to explain, even to ourselves.

Killing the first one was easy.

She looked as though she didn't want to be there when she stepped off the train at Blackdown Station. I could relate to that. I didn't really want to be there either, but at least I was properly dressed for the cold in an old black sweater. Not like her. It was the last service from Waterloo, so she'd already had a late night, but clearly still had plans for the evening with her red lips, blond hair, and black leather skirt. It looked like the real deal, not fake like the woman wearing it. Her career choice always seemed so selfless and compassionate to others — running a homeless charity — but I knew she was far from being a saint. More like a sinner trying to make up for her wickedness.

Sometimes we all do good things because we feel bad.

Blackdown was deserted, just as it always is at that time of night, so she was the only passenger to get off and walk down the lonely little platform. It's a sleepy variety of town, where people go home and go to bed early on weeknights, shrouded in a cloak of middle-class manners and conformity. A place where if something bad does happen, people remember how to forget surprisingly quickly.

The station itself is a listed building constructed in 1850, as the stone carving above the double doors proudly declares. A picturesque and quaint village railway stop, despite Blackdown swelling into a town several years earlier. It's like going back in time and stepping into a scene from a black-and-white film. Due to its heritage, it is protected from all unnecessary forms of modernization. There are no security cameras, and only one way in and one way out.

I could have killed her there and then.

But her phone rang.

She talked to the person who called all the way from the platform to the parking lot, so even if nobody had seen, someone might have heard.

I watched as she slid into her Audi TT, a company car she had decided the charity could pay for, along with other things, including a designer coat, a trip to New York, and highlights in her hair. I'd seen the yearly statements filed by her accountant. Found them in

53

her home office — the desk drawer wasn't even locked. She was regularly stealing money from the charity and spending it on herself, and it would have been a crime to let her keep getting away with it.

She drove the short distance from the station to the woods, and it wasn't far for me to have to follow. I watched as she got out of her own car and into another. Then she tucked that beautiful blond hair behind her ears and went down on the driver. It was little more than an appetizer, something to whet her appetite maybe, before hitching her skirt up and her underwear down for the main event.

I noticed how she liked to keep her clothes on, slapping away the hands that tried to help her out of them. It didn't matter; the most beautiful part of her was still on show: her collarbones. I've always found them to be one of the most erotic parts of a woman's body, and hers were so striking. The shape of the cavities between her shoulders and her clavicles, where her fragile bones protruded from her snow-white skin, was simply exquisite. Looking at them made me ache. I liked her shoes too; so much so that I decided to keep them. They are far too small for my feet to be able to wear — more of a souvenir, I suppose.

I saw how her face changed when someone was inside her. Then I closed my eyes, and listened to the sounds two people make when they know they shouldn't be fucking each other but can't stop. Like animals in the forest. Fulfilling a basic need without considering the consequences.

But there are always consequences.

I liked the way her face looked afterward: shiny with sweat despite the cold, some color on those pale cheeks, and her perfect mouth open a fraction, where she had been literally panting like a Best in Show dog. Lips parted just wide enough to slip a little something inside.

Most of all, I enjoyed the look in her pretty blue eyes just before I killed her. It was an expression I had never seen her face wear before — fear — and it suited her very well. It was as though she already knew that something very bad was about to happen.

HIM

This is very bad.

If anyone ever finds out, they're going to think it was me, but I'm reasonably confident nobody knew about our little arrangement. Every time I see the victim's body lying in the dirt today, I think about being inside her last night.

Sometimes it felt like I was watching her do the things she did to me from a distance, as if she were doing them to someone else. I often struggled to believe our affair was real, as though this beautiful woman being interested in me was too good to be true. I guess now, given what has happened, it was. She got into the car, then unzipped my fly without a word and went down on me. After that, she let me do whatever I wanted, and I did, enjoying the little sounds that came out of that perfect mouth.

I had imagined doing those things to her

for a very long time.

She was so far out of my league — I suppose deep down I knew it would have to end one day — but from the moment our late-night liaisons began a few months ago, she let me do *anything* to her. It made little sense to me given how beautiful she was, but I stopped questioning our incompatibility after a while. She was like a drug: the more of her I had, the more I needed in order to get high.

When a woman like that grabs your attention, they rarely give it back. She came and went like the tide, and I knew sooner or later she'd leave me washed up, but I enjoyed the ride while it lasted.

We both got what we wanted out of the arrangement — sex without the strings. It didn't mean anything and I think that's why it worked. No dinners, no dates, no unnecessary complications. She told me she got divorced a few months earlier, said he cheated on her. The man was clearly a fool, but then so was I, kidding myself that I was anything more than someone she used in order to feel better about herself. I didn't mind knowing that was all I was to her. She had a reputation for looking good but being bad; beautiful people do tend to get away with far more than the rest of us. Most of the time. I thought if nobody knew about what we were doing, then nobody could get hurt. I was wrong.

"Say my name" was the only thing she ever said during sex, so I did.

Rachel. Rachel. Rachel.

"You all right, sir?"

Priya is staring at me, and I wonder if I've been talking to myself again. Even worse, she appears to be looking at the scratch on my face, where Rachel left her mark. I've never understood why women do that during sex, scratching with their fingernails like feral cats. Hers were always the same: long and pink with fake-looking white tips. I didn't mind marks on my back that nobody could see, but she caught me on the face last night. I stare down at Rachel's fingers again now, the nails roughly cut to the quick, and the two words painted on them: TWO FACED. Then I look back at Priya. Seeing my colleague staring at the faint pink scar on my cheek makes me want to run, but I turn away instead.

"I'm fine," I mumble.

I make my excuses and sit in my car for a while, pretending to make calls while trying to warm up and calm down. I turn and stare at the backseat, quickly double-check the floor, but there are no visual signs of Rachel being in here, even though her prints must be everywhere. I lost count of the times and ways we did it in this car. Frankly, it's as filthy as we were. I'll get it cleaned later, inside and out, when a suitable time presents itself.

I don't know what I was thinking getting involved with a woman like her. I *knew* she was trouble, but perhaps that's why I couldn't say no. I guess I was flattered. Meeting up with Rachel was always preferable to going home; there was nothing much *there* to look forward to after a long day at work. But if people found out, I could lose everything.

It's still raining. The constant pitter-patter on the windshield sounds like drums inside my ears. I have a headache at the base of my skull, the kind that can only be cured with nicotine. I'd kill for a cigarette right now, but I gave up smoking a couple of years ago, for the child, not wanting to inflict my poor life choices on an innocent human being. A nice glass of red would make the pain go away too, but drinking before lunchtime is something else I gave up. I consider my options and realize that I have none — best to stick to the plan.

Priya knocks on the window. I contemplate ignoring her, but think better of it and get out of the car, back to cold and wet reality.

"Sorry to interrupt, sir. Were you talking to someone?"

Just myself.

"No."

"The big boss said he couldn't get through on your phone," she says.

If she meant the words to sound like an accusation, she was successful. I take out my mobile and see eight missed calls from the deputy chief constable.

"Nothing showing. Either he's calling the wrong number or I've got a bad signal," I lie, slipping it straight back inside my pocket. Lying is something I'm pretty good at, to myself as well as others; I've had plenty of practice. "If he calls back just tell him everything is under control, and I'll update him later." Having some hotshot superior officer, who is half my age, shit all over my show is the last thing I need right now.

"Okay, I'll let him know," Priya says.

I see her add that to the invisible list of things to do she always writes inside her head. There is clearly something else she wants to tell me, and her face lights up like a pinball machine when she remembers what it is.

"We think we've got a print!"

What?

"What?"

"We think we've got a print!" she repeats.

"Finger?" I ask.

"Foot."

"Really? In this mud?"

The rain has already made a series of mini rivers across the forest floor. Priya beams at me like a kid who wants to show a parent their latest painting.

"I think Forensics are super excited to be allowed out of the lab. It looks like a large recent boot print, right next to the body, initially hidden by dead leaves. They've done an incredible job! Do you want to see?"

I briefly stare down at my own muddy shoes before I follow her.

"You know, even if they *have* managed to find a footprint, I predict it might belong to one of the team. The whole scene should have been properly cordoned off straightaway, as soon as you arrived," I say. "Including the parking lot. Any tracks we come across now will be worthless in court."

The smile fades from her face and I breathe a little easier.

I don't think anyone knows I was here, or

has any reason to suspect my involvement with the murder victim. So as long as it stays that way, I should be fine. My best course of action is to act normal, do my job, and prove that someone else killed Rachel before anyone can point the finger at me. I try to clear my head a little, but my mind is too busy and my thoughts are too loud. The one I hear the most plays on repeat, and right now it's true: I wish I'd never come back to Blackdown.

HER

I don't see the point in trying to get out of going back to Blackdown. It would just raise more questions than I have answers for, so I go home and pack a bag. I don't intend to stay overnight, but things don't always go according to plan in this business. It might have been a while, but I haven't forgotten the drill: clean underwear, non-iron clothes, waterproof jacket, makeup, hair products, a bottle of wine, a few miniatures, and a novel I already know I won't have time to read.

I put my little suitcase in the back of the car — a red Mini convertible I bought when my husband left me — then climb in and fasten my seat belt; I'm a very safe driver. I was worried I might still be over the limit after last night, but I have my own breathalyzer in the glovebox for occasions such as these. I take it out, blow in the tube, and wait for the screen to change. It turns green,

63

which means I'm good. I don't need to turn on the GPS, I know exactly where I'm going.

The journey down via the A3 is relatively painless — it's still rush hour, and the majority of drivers on the road at this time of day are hurrying toward London, not away from it — but minutes feel like hours with nothing except the same views and anxieties for company. The radio does little to drown them out, and every song I hear seems to make me think about things I'd rather forget. Covering this story is a bad idea, but since I can't explain that to anyone it doesn't feel like I have a choice.

The uncomfortable feeling in the pit of my stomach worsens as I take the old familiar turnoff and follow the signs for Blackdown. Everything looks just the same as it always did, as though time stands still in this little corner of the Surrey Hills. A lifetime ago this was the place I called home, but when I look back now, it feels like someone else's life, not my own. I'm not the same person I was then. I've changed beyond recognition, even if Blackdown and its residents haven't.

It's still beautiful, despite all the ugly things that I know have happened here. As soon as I turn off the highway, I find myself navigating a series of narrow country roads. The sky soon disappears from view, courtesy of the ancient forest that seems to swallow me whole. Trees that are centuries old lean across a network of sunken lanes, with steep banks of exposed roots on either side. Their gnarly branches have twisted together up above, blocking out all but the most determined shards of sunlight. I focus hard on the road ahead, steering myself through unwanted thoughts, as well as the shadowy tunnel of trees toward the town.

When I emerge from the canopy of leaves, I see that Blackdown still wears its Sunday best every day of the week. Pretty, well-looked-after Victorian cottages stand proud behind neat gardens, moss-covered dry-stone walls, and the occasional white picket fence. The window boxes on neighboring properties compete with one another all year round, and you won't find any litter on these streets. I pass the village green, the White Hart pub, the crumbling Catholic church, then I pass the imposing exterior of St. Hilary's. Seeing the girls' grammar school causes me to step on the accelerator. I keep my eyes on the road again, as though if I don't look directly at the building, then the ghosts of my memories won't be able to find me.

I pull into the National Trust parking lot, and see that my cameraman is already here. I hope they've assigned a good one. All the BBC crew vehicles are exactly the same — a fleet of estate cars with an arsenal of filming equipment hidden in the trunk — but cameramen, and women, are all different. Some are better than they think they are at the job. Several are considerably worse. How I look on-screen very much depends on who is filming me, so I can be a little fussy about who I like to work with. Like a carpenter, I think I have a right to choose the best tools with which to cut and shape and craft my work.

I park next to the crew car, still unable to see who is sitting inside. The driver's seat is fully reclined, as though whoever it is has decided to take a nap. It's not a great sign. It has been a long time since I was on the road, and staff turnover is high in news, so chances are it could be someone I've never worked with. This career path is steep and a little pointy, with very little room at the top. The best people often move on when they realize they can't move up. I consider the possibility that it might be someone new, but when I get out of my car and take a look inside theirs, I can see that it isn't.

The window is down — despite the cold

and rain — and I see the familiar shape of a man I used to know. He's smoking a roll-up and listening to eighties music. I decide it's best to get the awkward reunion out of the way, if that's what this is going to be. I prefer leaving people I have a history with in the past, but that can be tricky when you work with them.

"Those things will kill you, Richard," I say, getting into the passenger seat and closing the door. The car smells of coffee and smoke and him. The scent is familiar, and not altogether unpleasant. My other senses are less impressed. I ignore my instinctive urge to clean away all the mess that I can see — mostly chocolate bar wrappers, old newspapers, empty coffee cups, and crumpled Coke cans — and I try not to touch anything.

I notice that he is wearing one of his trademark retro T-shirts and a pair of ripped jeans, still dressing like a teenager despite turning forty last year. He looks like a skinny but strong surfer, even though I know he has a fear of the sea. His blond hair is long enough to be tied back, but hangs in what we used to call "curtains" when I was at school, haphazardly tucked behind his pierced ears. He is a Peter Pan of a man.

"We all have to die of something," he says, taking another drag. "You're looking well."

"Thanks. You look like shit," I reply.

He grins and the thick ice is at least cracked, if not broken.

"You know, you don't always have to tell it like it is. Especially in the morning. You might have a few more friends if you didn't."

"I don't need friends, just a good cameraman. Know any?"

"Cute," he says, then taps the ash from his cigarette out of the window, before turning to stare at me. "Shall we just get this done?"

There is a slightly menacing look in his eyes, one that I do not remember. But then he gets out of the car, and I realize he just meant the job. I watch while Richard checks his camera — he might not be a perfectionist when it comes to hygiene, but he takes his work seriously — and I feel a wave of gratitude and relief that I'll be working with him today, for so many reasons. Firstly, he can shoot the shit out of any story, and make me look good even when I feel bad. Secondly, I can be myself with him. Almost.

Richard and I slept together a few times when I was a correspondent. It isn't something that anyone else knows — we both had good ring-shaped reasons on our fingers

68

to keep it that way — and it isn't something I'm terribly proud of. I was still married, just, but I was a bit broken. Sometimes I find the only way to ease the worst forms of pain is to damage myself in a different way. Distract my attention from the things that can and will break me. A little hurt to help me heal.

I'd never defend infidelity, but my marriage was over long before I slept with someone I shouldn't have. Something changed when my husband and I lost our daughter. We both died a little bit when she did. But like ghosts who don't know they are dead, we carried on haunting ourselves and each other for a long time afterward.

This is a stressful job at the best of times, and in the worst of times we all take comfort where we can. Most news is bad news. There are things I have seen because of my job that have changed me, as well as my view of the world and the people in it. Things I can never unsee. We are a species capable of horrific acts, and incapable of learning from the lessons our own history tries to teach us.

When you witness the horror and inhumanity of human beings close up, every single day, it permanently changes your perspective. Sometimes you just need to look the other way, and that's all our affair was: a shared need to remember what it is like to feel something. It is not unusual for people in my line of work — half the newsroom seems to have slept with each other — and I sometimes struggle to keep up with the latest staff configurations.

Richard pulls on his coat, and I see a glimpse of a toned stomach as his arms reach for his sleeves. Then he drops his cigarette, extinguishing what is left of it with the sole of his large boot.

"Coming?" he asks.

He leaves the tripod behind and we walk toward the woods, no need for sticks in the mud here. I do my best to avoid all the puddles, not wanting to ruin my shoes. We don't get far. Aside from a couple of snappers, we are the only press to have arrived, but it's soon made clear that none of us are welcome.

"Please stay behind the police tape," says a petite young woman.

Her clothes are too neat, her vowels are too pronounced, and she reminds me of a disillusioned class prefect. She waves her badge — a little self-consciously, I note — when we don't respond, as though used to being mistaken for a schoolgirl and having to show ID. I manage to read the name "Patel," but little else before she puts it back in her pocket. I smile, but she doesn't.

"We'll be setting up a wider cordon soon. For now, can I please ask that you stay back down in the parking lot. This is a crime scene."

The woman has clearly had a charisma bypass.

I can see the lights that have been set up behind her, along with a small army of people dressed in forensics suits, a few of them crouched down over something on the forest floor in the distance. They've already put up a tent around the body, and I know from experience that we won't get another chance to get this close again. Richard and I exchange a silent glance, along with an unspoken conversation. He hits Record on the camera and swings it up onto his shoulder.

"Of course," I say, and accompany my off-white lie with a wide smile.

I do whatever I need to do to get the job done. Upsetting the police is never ideal, but sometimes unavoidable. I don't like to burn bridges, but there tends to be another one — further upstream in this case, I suspect.

"We'll just get a couple of quick shots and then get out of your way," I say.

"You'll get out of the way now, and go back to the parking lot like she asked you."

I take in the sight of the man who has come to stand beside the female detective. He looks like he hasn't slept in a while, appears to have gotten dressed in the dark, and is wearing a Harry Potter–style scarf around his neck. A modern-day Columbo, minus the charm. Richard keeps filming and I stay exactly where I am. This is a familiar dance and we all know the moves — it's the same steps for any breaking news: get the shot, get the story.

"This footpath is a public right of way. We are perfectly entitled to film here," I say.

It's the best line I can come up with, a stalling tactic to allow Richard to zoom in and get a few more close-ups of the scene.

The male detective takes a step forward and covers the lens with his hand.

"Watch it, mate," Richard says, taking a step back.

"I'm not your *mate*. Fuck off back to the parking lot or I'll have you arrested."

The male detective glares at me before turning back toward the tent.

"We're just doing our jobs, no need to be an asshole," says Richard over his shoulder as we retreat.

"Did you get the shot?" I ask.

"Of course. But I don't like people touching my camera. We should make a complaint. Get that guy's name."

"No need, already got it. His name is DCI Jack Harper."

Richard stares at me.

"How do you know that?"

I think for a second before answering.

"We've met before."

It's the truth, just not the whole of it.

HIM

Seeing Anna winds me, not that I plan on telling anyone the truth about that. I replay the encounter in my mind, until it becomes an irritating rerun I could quote line for line, and take my frustration out on everyone around me. I wish I had handled it better, but I'm already having the mother of bad days, and *she* shouldn't be here. There is a brand-new shirt inside my wardrobe that I could have worn today, had I known I was going to see her. It's been hanging in there for months, but still has the creases from the packet it came in. I don't know what I'm saving it for — it isn't as though I ever go anywhere since I moved down here — and now she's seen me looking like *this,* with crumpled clothes and a jacket older than some of my colleagues. I pretend not to care, but I do.

The place is swarming with satellite

74

trucks, cameramen, and reporters. I have no idea how the press got hold of the details so soon, including *her.* It makes no sense. Even if they knew about a body being found, there are several entrances to these woods — which stretch for miles across the valley and surrounding hills — half of which I don't even know, and there are more than a handful of parking lots. So I don't understand how they knew to come to this one, and Anna was pretty much the first to arrive.

I spot her talking to Priya away from the rest of the press, and resist the urge to march over and interrupt. She's always known how to make friends out of enemies. I just hope DS Patel isn't naïve enough to trust a journalist, or say something she shouldn't, on or of the record. She hands Anna something. The two women smile and I have to strain to see what it is: blue plastic shoe covers. Anna leans on a tree trunk as she pulls them over her high heels. She looks in my direction and waves, so I pretend not to see and turn away. She must have asked to borrow a pair from the forensics team, so as not to get her pretty reporting shoes dirty in the mud. Unbelievable.

"I think I know who she is," says Priya, appearing by my side and interrupting my internal monologue.

At least, I hope it was internal.

I am aware that I've started to actually talk to myself out loud recently. I've caught people staring at me in the street when it happens. It mostly seems to occur when I'm overly tired or stressed, and as a middle-aged detective, living with a perpetually unhappy woman and a two-year-old child, I'm pretty much always both. I try to remember if anyone on the team smokes — perhaps I could just bum one, calm myself down.

Priya is staring at me as though waiting for some kind of response, and I have to rewind my mind to remember what she said.

"She's a TV news anchor, that's probably why you recognize her."

My words are in too much of a hurry to leave my mouth and trip over themselves. I sound even more ill-tempered than I feel. Priya — who rides my mood swings as though they are her favorite thing in the playground — won't let the conversation slide.

"I meant the victim, boss. Not Anna Andrews." Hearing someone say her name out loud winds me a second time. I've no idea what face I am pulling, but Priya seems to feel the need to defend herself from it. "I do watch the news," she says, doing that strange thing again where she sticks out her chin.

"Good to know."

"In terms of the victim, I don't know *her* name, yet, but I have seen her around town. Haven't you?"

Seen her, smelled her, fucked her . . .

Thankfully Priya doesn't pause long enough for me to answer.

"She's hard to miss, don't you think? Or was, with the blond hair and fancy clothes. I'm sure I've seen her walking along the high street with a yoga mat. Listening to the rest of the local team, it sounds like she was from here, born and raised in Blackdown. They seem to think she still lived here too, but that she worked in London. For a homeless charity. Nobody seems to remember her name."

Rachel.

She didn't just work for a homeless charity, she ran it, but I don't correct Priya, or tell her that I already know almost everything there is to know about the victim. Yoga was something else that Rachel turned to after her husband turned to someone else. She became a bit obsessed with it, going four or five times a week, not that I minded. That particular hobby had benefits for us both. Apart from meeting me in parking lots or the occasional hotel — we never visited each other's homes or met in public — she didn't seem to do a lot of socializing unless it was for work. She posted pictures of herself on Instagram with alarming regularity — which I enjoyed looking at when I was alone and thinking of her — but for someone with thousands of so-called friends online, she had surprisingly few in real life.

Maybe because she was always too busy working.

Or perhaps because other people were jealous of her perceived success.

Then again, it might have been because below the beautiful exterior, she had an ugly streak. One that I chose to ignore but couldn't fail to see.

We've established a wide cordon around this particular pocket of the woods now, but it's as though we've put up fly tape, the way the press insists on buzzing around, trying to get a better view. I've been told by higher up the food chain that *I* should give a statement on camera, and have received a torrent of phone calls and emails — from people I've never heard of at HQ — wanting me to approve a line of copy for a police social media account. I don't *do* social media, except to spy on women I'm sleeping with, but lately it feels as though the powers that be think it is more important than the job. The next of kin haven't even been informed yet, but apparently, *I'm* the one who needs to work on my priorities. My stomach rumbles so loudly I'm sure the whole team hears it. They all seem to be staring at me.

"Almond?" asks Priya, waving what looks like a packet of bird seed in my direction.

"No. Thank you. What I want is a bacon sandwich or a —"

"Cigarette?"

She produces a packet from her pocket, which is unexpected. Priya is one of those fancy vegetarians — a vegan — and I've never seen her pollute her body with anything more dangerous than a single slab of dark chocolate. She's holding my old favorite brand of smokes in her little hand, and it's like catching a nun reading a Victoria's Secret catalog.

"Why do you have those?" I ask.

She shrugs. "Emergencies."

I dislike her a little less than I used to and take one.

I snap it in half — an old habit of mine that makes me think this little stick of cancer will only be half as bad for me — then I let her light it. She's so small I have to bend down, and I choose to ignore the way her hands tremble as she holds a match in one, and shelters it from the wind with the other. I've met former smokers who say that the smell of cigarettes now makes them feel sick. I am not like them. The first cigarette to touch my lips for two years is nothing less than ecstasy. The temporary high causes my face to accidently smile.

"Better?" Priya asks.

I notice that she didn't have one.

"Yes. Much. Organize that press conference. Let's give the hacks what they want, and hope they all sod off afterward."

She smiles too, as though it is contagious.

"Yes, boss."

"I'm not your . . . never mind."

Twenty minutes later, minus my Harry Potter scarf, I'm standing in the parking lot in front of ten or more cameras. I haven't had to do anything like this for a while, not since I left London. I feel out of practice, as well as out of shape, and unconsciously suck my stomach in before I start to speak. I try to silently reassure my anxious ego that nobody I know will see this. But I'm not as good at lying to myself as I am at lying to others, and the thought brings little comfort. I remember the crumpled clothes I'm wearing; I knew I should have at least shaved this morning.

I clear my throat and am about to speak when I see her, pushing her way to the front. The other journalists look disgruntled until they turn and recognize her face. Then they step aside and let her through, as though reporter royalty has arrived. I've experienced enough on-camera press conferences and statements in my time to know that most on-screen talent gets treated the same as everybody else. But Anna exudes confidence, even though I know the person on the inside doesn't match the version she presents to the rest of the world.

Everyone else here seems to be dressed in muted shades of black or brown or gray — as though they deliberately color-coordinated their clothes with the murder scene — but not her. Anna is wearing a bright red coat and dress, and I wonder if they are new; I don't recognize them. I avoid looking in her direction; it's distracting. Nobody here would ever guess that we know each other, and it is in both our interests to keep it that way.

I wait until I have their full attention and the rabble is silent once more, then I deliver my preprepared and preapproved statement. Detectives are no longer permitted to speak for themselves. At least, I'm not. Not after the last time.

"Early this morning, police received a report of a body being found in Blackdown Woods just outside the village. Officers attended and the body of a woman was discovered not far from the main parking lot. The woman has not yet been formally identified, and the death is currently unexplained. The area is cordoned off while investigations continue. There will be no further statements from this location, and I will not be answering any questions at this time."

I would also like to take this opportunity to remind you that this is a crime scene, not an episode of whatever bullshit detective box set you're watching on Netflix.

I don't say the last line. At least I hope I didn't. I start to turn away — we are deliberately not sharing very much with the press or public at this stage — but then I hear *her.* I've always loved listening to the way different people speak — it can tell you so much about them. I don't just mean accents, I mean everything: the tone, the volume, the speed, as well as the language. The words they choose to use, and how and when and why they say them. The silences between the sentences, which can be just as loud. A person's voice is like a wave — some just wash right over you, while others have the power to knock you down and drag you into an ocean of self-doubt. The sound of her speaking makes me feel like I'm drowning.

Anna clearly didn't hear the part about no questions. Or, knowing her, just chose to ignore it.

"Is it true that the victim was a local woman?"

I don't even turn to face her.

"No comment."

"You said that the death was currently being treated as unexplained, but can you confirm that this is a murder investigation?"

I'm aware that the cameras are still rolling, but start to walk away. Anna is not a woman who likes to be ignored. When she doesn't get an answer to her last question, she asks another.

"Is it true that the victim was found with a foreign object inside their mouth?"

Only now do I stop. I slowly turn to face her, a hundred questions colliding inside my mind as I take in the green eyes that appear to be smiling. The only two people who know about something being found inside the victim's mouth are DS Patel and me. I deliberately haven't told anyone else yet — it's the sort of thing that will leak before I want it to — and Priya is as tight-lipped as a clam. Which leaves me with yet another question I can't answer: How did Anna know?

HER

I ignore the stares from the other journalists and hurry back to my car. I've forgotten what it is like to stand in the cold for hours on end, and I regret not wearing more layers. Still, at least I look good. Better than Jack Harper at any rate. As soon as I'm inside the Mini, I turn on the engine and crank up the heating to try to warm myself. I want to make a phone call without the whole world listening in, so have asked Richard to grab a few extra shots.

It's strange to imagine the *One O'Clock News* team all sitting in the newsroom without me, everything carrying on as normal, as though I were never there. I think I can persuade the Thin Controller to let me get on-air with what I've already got. Then at least this won't have been a complete waste of time. Best to go straight to the top for an answer, I think; today's program editor suffers from chronic indecision.

Finally, after listening to the phone ring for longer than it ever should when calling a network newsroom, someone answers.

"One O'Clock News," she purrs.

The sound of Cat Jones's velvety voice causes mine to malfunction.

I picture her sitting in what, only yesterday, was my chair. Answering my phone. Working with my team. I close my eyes and can see her red hair and white smile. The mental image doesn't make me feel sick, it makes me feel thirsty. My fingers come to the rescue, and automatically start to search inside my bag for a miniature whiskey. I open it, twisting the screw cap with my one free hand — I've had practice — and down the bottle.

"Hello?" says the voice on the other end, in a tone resembling the polite preempt people use before hanging up when nobody answers.

My reply gets stuck in my throat, as though my mouth has forgotten how to form words.

"It's Anna," I manage, relieved that I can still remember my own name.

"Anna . . . ?"

"Andrews."

"Oh, god, I'm *so* sorry. I didn't recognize your voice. Did you want to speak to —"

"Yes. Please."

"Of course. Let me put you on hold and see if I can grab his attention."

I hear a click before the familiar BBC News countdown music starts to play. I've always rather liked it, but right now it's deeply irritating. I glance outside the window at the rest of the press still standing around. Some of the faces are familiar and everyone seemed genuinely happy to see me, which was nice. I remember that a few of them shook my hand, and reach inside my handbag again, this time in search of an antibacterial wipe for my fingers. I'm about to hang up — tired of being kept on hold — when the sound of shouting in the newsroom replaces the music.

"Can someone else try answering the goddamn phones when they *wing*? It *weally* isn't difficult, and probably won't cause *we-petitive stwain* injury as none of you do *it vewy* often. Yes, who is it?" the Thin Controller snaps in my ear.

Despite the job title and bluster, he is a man who is rarely in control of anything. Including his speech impediment. I have often suspected that the newsroom is allergic to his imagined authority, and the

87

chorus of phones still ringing unanswered in the background reinforces the theory.

"It's Anna," I say.

"Anna . . . ?"

I resist the urge to scream; forgetting me is clearly contagious.

"Andrews," I reply.

"Anna! Apologies, it's chaos here this morning. How can I help?"

It's a good question. Yesterday I was presenting the program; now it feels like I'm cold calling to beg to be on it for a minute or two.

"I'm at this murder scene in Blackdown —"

"Is it a murder? Hang on . . ." His voice changes again, and I realize he is speaking to someone else. "I said no to a *pwe-pubescent* political *weporter* I've never heard of on the PM stowy — it's the bloody lead. Well, tell the Westminster editor to pull her head out of Downing Street's arse for five minutes . . . I don't care what they are doing for other outlets, *I* want a *gwown*-up correspondent on my bulletin, so get me one. You were saying?"

It takes a moment to realize he is speaking to me again. I'm too busy imagining him in a physical, rather than verbal, fight with the five-foot-two Westminster editor. She would end him.

"The murder you sent me to . . ." I persevere.

"I just thought you'd *wather* be there than here, given what happened this morning. I did glance at the wires after the police statement a little while ago. But everything I *wead* just said it was an unexplained death . . ."

"That's all the police are saying at the moment, but I know there's more to it than that."

"How do you know?"

It's a difficult question to answer.

"I just do," I say, and my reply sounds as weak as I feel.

"Well, call me back when you've got something on the *wecord,* and I'll see if we can squeeze you in."

Squeeze me in?

"It's going to be a big story," I say, not ready to give up yet. "It would be good to get it on-air before anyone else does."

"I'm *sowy,* Anna. Trump's latest tweet is causing a meltdown, and it's already a *weally* busy news day. Sounds to me like this body in the woods might just be a local news *stowy,* and I don't have *woom.* Call if that changes, okay? Got to go."

"It's not a —"

I don't bother to finish my sentence, because he has already hung up. I disappear inside my own darkest thoughts for a while. It's like Halloween every day in this business — grown adults wearing scary masks, pretending to be something they're not.

Someone knocks on my window and I jump. I look up, expecting to see Richard standing outside my car, but it's Jack, and he's wearing his best disgruntled detective face. He looks just as angry with me as he did the last time we saw each other. I step out to join him, and smile when Jack looks over his shoulder to check if anyone is watching us. He always was a little paranoid. He's standing so close that I can smell the stale smoke on his breath. I'm surprised because I thought he had given it up.

"What the fuck are you doing?" he asks.

"My job. It's nice to see you too."

"Since when does the BBC send a news anchor to a story like this?"

I regularly tell myself that I don't care what this man thinks of me, but I still don't want to tell him that I no longer present the program. I don't want to tell anyone.

"It's complicated," I say.

"Things always are with you. What do you know and why did you ask that last question after the press conference?"

"Why didn't you answer it?"

"Don't play games with me, Anna. I'm not in the mood."

"You never were a morning person."

"I'm serious. Why did you ask that?"

"Is it true then? Was there something inside the victim's mouth?"

"Tell me what you think you know."

"You know I can't do that. I always protect my sources."

He takes a step closer; a little too close.

"If you do anything to jeopardize this investigation, I will treat you the same way as I would anyone else. This is a murder scene, not Downing Street or some red-carpet film premiere."

"So, it *is* murder."

His cheeks turn a little red when he realizes his own mistake.

"A woman we both know has died, show some respect," he whispers.

"A woman we both know?"

He stares at me as though he thought maybe I already knew.

"Who?" I ask.

"It doesn't matter."

"Who?" I ask again.

"I don't think it's a good idea for you to cover this story."

"Why? You just said it was someone we

91

both knew, so maybe *you* shouldn't be investigating it."

"I've got to go."

"Sure. Run away like you always do."

He starts to leave, but then turns back and gets so close his face is right in front of mine.

"You don't have to behave like a bitch every time we see each other. It doesn't suit you."

The words sting a little. More than I would like to admit, even to myself.

He walks away and I fix a smile on my face until he is completely out of view. Then something strange and unexpected happens: I cry. I hate the way he can still get under my skin, and loathe myself for letting him.

The sound of the car parked next to mine being remotely unlocked startles me.

"Sorry to interrupt."

Richard opens the trunk, carefully laying his camera inside. I wipe beneath my eyes with the back of my hand, and damp smears of mascara stain my fingers.

"You okay?" he asks. I nod and he successfully interprets my silence as a sign that I do not want to talk about it. "Do we need to package for lunchtime? If so, we should get on with —"

"No, they don't want anything unless the

story develops," I say.

"Right. Well, back to London then?"

"Not yet. There's more to this story, I just know it. There are some people in town I want to talk to, on my own; your camera will just scare them. I'll take my car. There's a nice pub down the road called the White Hart, they do a great all-day breakfast. Why don't I meet you there a bit later?"

"Okay," he says slowly, as though buying time while still selecting his next words. "I know you said that you had met the detective before. Did something happen between you once upon a time?"

"Why? Are you jealous?"

"Am I right?"

"Well, you're not wrong. Jack is my ex-husband."

HIM

Tuesday 09:30

My ex-wife knows more about this than she is letting on.

I don't understand how, but then I lived with the woman for fifteen years, was married to her for ten of them, and still always struggled to tell the difference between her truth and her lies. Some people build invisible walls around themselves in the name of self-preservation. Hers were always tall, solid, and impenetrable. I knew we were in trouble long before I did anything about it. Truth in my work is everything, but truth in my personal life can feel like a bright light I need to turn away from.

Nobody here knows that I was married to Anna Andrews. Just as I expect nobody she works with knows about me. Anna has always been intensely private, a condition she inherited from her mother. Not that there's anything wrong with that. Don't ask,

94

don't tell works for me too when it comes to my life away from the job.

Like a lot of people who have been in a relationship for a long time, we would regularly say "I love you." I don't remember exactly why or when it started to lose its meaning, but those three little words turned into three little lies. They became more of a substitute for "good-bye" — if one of us was leaving the house — or "goodnight" — when we were going to sleep. We dropped the "I" after a while; "Love you" seemed sufficient, and why waste three words when you could express the same empty sentiment with two? But it wasn't the same. It was as though we forgot what the words were supposed to mean. My stomach rumbles loudly and I remember how hungry I am.

When I was a child my mother didn't let us eat between meals, and sweets were banned from the house. She worked as a receptionist at the local dentist and took tooth decay very seriously. The other kids would all take snacks to school — chips, candy bars, biscuits — I got an apple, or, on special occasions, a little red box of Sun-Maid raisins. I remember the rush of anger I felt whenever I found them in my packed lunch — the box said the raisins came all the way from California, and I realized that even dried fruit had a more interesting existence than eight-year-old me. The most I could hope for was a Golden Delicious, which was a misleading description because in my opinion those apples were neither.

The only time I ever tasted chocolate as a child was when my grandmother came to visit. It was our little secret, and it tasted like a promise. Nothing else I remember from my childhood gave me more unadulterated pleasure than those little brown squares of Cadbury Dairy Milk melting on my tongue.

I eat a chocolate bar every day now. Sometimes two if things are bad at work. No matter which one I buy, or how much it costs, it never tastes as good as the cheap chocolate bars my grandmother used to bring. Even they don't taste the same. I think when we finally get what we think we want, it loses its value. It's the secret nobody ever shares, because if they did, we would all stop trying.

Anna and I got what we thought we wanted.

It wasn't a never-ending supply of chocolate bars, or a private island in the sun. First it was an apartment, then a car, then a job, then a house, then a wedding, then a baby. We followed the same safe paths that older generations had carved out for us, trampled into permanence by so many previous footsteps that it was only too easy to follow. We were so certain we were headed in the right direction, we left tracks of our own, to help future couples find their way. But we didn't discover a pot of golden happiness at the end of the rite-of-passage rainbow. When we finally got where we thought we wanted to be, we realized that there was nothing there.

I think it's the same for everyone, but as a species we are preprogrammed to pretend to be happy when we think we should be. It is expected of us.

You buy the car you always wanted, but in a couple of years you want a new one. You buy the house of your dreams, but then decide that your dreams weren't big enough. You marry the woman you love, but then you forget why. You have a baby because that's next on your list of things to do. It's what everybody else does, so maybe it will fix the thing that you've been pretending wasn't broken. Maybe a child will make you happy.

And she did for a while, our daughter.

We were a family and it felt different. Loving her seemed to remind us how to love each other. We had somehow made the most beautiful living thing that my eyes had ever seen, and I would often stare in wonder at our baby, amazed that two imperfect people could somehow produce such a perfect child. Our little girl saved us from ourselves for a short while, but then she was gone.

We lost a daughter and I lost my wife.

The truth is that life broke us, and when we finally acknowledged that we didn't know how to fix each other, we stopped trying.

"The body has been moved, sir," says Priya.

I don't know how long I have been standing outside the tent in a world of my own. Even if nobody else finds out about last night, I can't help worrying that Anna somehow knows something. She could always see through my lies.

We both ran away from what happened. She hid inside her work, and I came back here — to a place where I knew she wouldn't follow me — not because I wanted to, but because I couldn't bear the way she looked at me anymore. Anna never actually blamed me for what happened, at least not out loud. But her eyes said all the things she didn't. Full to the overflowing brim with hurt and hate.

"Sir?" says Priya.

"That's good, well done."

I had deliberately asked the team to move the body from the scene while I was giving the press conference. There are some things that should never be captured on camera.

Priya is still waiting beside me, I'm not sure what for. When I don't speak, she does, and I find myself staring at her rather than listening. She always looks the same to me: ponytail, old-fashioned hair clips pinning any stray strands off her face, glasses, shiny lace-up shoes, and ironed blouses or whatever it's called when a woman wears a shirt. She's like a walking Marks & Spencer catalog; lamb dressed as mutton. Not like my ex-wife, who is always so stylish. Anna looks even better now than when we were together, unlike me.

I think maybe solitude suits her. She's lost some weight, I notice, not that I ever minded. She was never *big*, even when she thought she was. She used to say that she was a size eleven — always somewhere between a ten and a twelve. Christ knows what she is now . . . an eight perhaps. Loneliness can shrink a person in more ways than one. Unless perhaps she isn't lonely.

I always used to wonder about the cameramen Anna went on trips with. She was sometimes away for days at a time, staying in hotels, covering whatever story she had been deployed on as a correspondent. Her job always came first. Then what happened happened. Anna was broken; we both were. But when she got her lucky break and started presenting, things were better between us for a while. She worked more regular hours, and we spent more time together than we had before. But something was missing. Someone. We could never seem to fully find our way back to each other.

It was Anna who asked for the divorce. I didn't feel like I had any right to argue. I knew she still blamed me for the death of our daughter, and that she always would.

"I don't understand how she knew."

"Sorry, sir?" Priya asks, and I realize that I said the words out loud without meaning to.

"The object inside the victim's mouth. I don't understand how Anna could have known about that."

DS Patel's eyes look even bigger than normal behind her tortoise-shell glasses, and I remember seeing her and Anna talking before the press conference.

"Please tell me that you didn't tell a

journalist something which I specifically told you not to?"

"I'm so sorry, sir," she says, sounding like a child. "I didn't mean to. It just sort of slipped out. It was as though she already knew."

I don't blame Priya, not really. Anna always found the right questions to ask in order to get the right answers. It still doesn't explain why she is really here though.

I start walking back toward the parking lot. Priya practically runs beside me, trying to keep up. She's still apologizing, but I've tuned out again. I'm too busy watching Anna talk to her cameraman, and I don't like the way he looks at her. I know men like him; I used to be one. She climbs into the red Mini convertible she bought after the divorce — probably because she knew I'd hate it — and I'm surprised to see that it looks as if she is going to leave. I have never known her to give up easily on a story or anything else. Which makes me wonder where she is going.

I walk a little faster toward my own car.

"Are you okay?" DS Patel asks, still chasing after me.

"I'd be a lot better if other people did their jobs properly."

"Sorry, boss."

101

"For Christ's sake, I'm *not* your bloody boss."

I search inside my pockets for my keys as the Mini disappears toward the parking lot exit. Priya stares at me, in silence for a change, with a hint of defiance in her eyes that I don't think I've seen before. For a moment I worry that even she knows more than she should.

"Yes, sir," she says in that tone of hers that makes me feel old and awful all at once.

"I'm sorry, I didn't mean to snap at you. I'm just a little tired. The kid kept me up half the night," I lie.

I live with a different woman and child now, but unlike me, the kid never has any trouble sleeping. Priya nods, but still looks unconvinced. I get in the car before she has time to ask where I'm going, willing the damn thing to start as I turn on the engine. I don't know what I'm doing or why I am doing it. Instinct, I suppose; that's how I will justify this to myself later. I don't make a habit of following my ex-wife, but something tells me I should on this occasion. More than that, it feels like I must.

There are always unanswered questions when it comes to Anna.

Why is she really here? Does she already know who the victim is? How did she know the exact location of the murder scene before we told the press? Does she miss me? Did she ever really love me in the first place?

The one about our little girl is always loudest.

Why did she have to die?

There are so many unanswered questions keeping me awake at night. Insomnia has become a bad habit I can't break. Every day seems to start backward — I wake up tired and go to bed feeling wide awake. It isn't the guilt about killing Rachel — it started long before that, and nothing I do seems to help. The sleeping pills the doctor gave me are a waste of time, and I get terrible headaches if I take them with alcohol, which of course I find hard not to do. Wine is always the most reliable crutch when it feels like I might fall.

I do my best to completely avoid doctors if I can, anyway. Hospitals are filthy places, and no amount of sanitizer, or handwashing, ever seems to remove the stench of illness and death from my skin after visiting one. Medical establishments are filled with germs and judgment, and I find the people who work in them always ask the same questions, so I always give the same answers: no, I've never smoked and yes, I do drink, but in moderation.

There is no law I know of saying that you have to tell your doctor the truth.

Besides, lies told often enough can start to sound true.

My mind tends to wander most when I am in the car, but that's nothing new, I have always been prone to daydreaming. Not that I'm a danger to myself or others in that regard. I'm a very safe driver, I just do it on autopilot sometimes, that's all. The roads are mostly empty around here anyway. I wonder if that will change now? It will initially, of course — the police, the media circus — but I wonder what will happen afterward. When the show is over and all the . . . mess has been cleared away. Life will surely return to normal for most of the locals. Not those directly affected, of course, but grief is always sharpest at the point of impact. I wonder whether the coach-loads of tourists will still come to visit in the summer months? No bad thing if they don't, if you ask me. Popularity can spoil a place just like it can spoil a person.

I don't worry about my lack of remorse, but I do question what it means. I wonder whether I am fundamentally a different person from the one I was before I killed her. People still seem to look at me the same way they did yesterday, and when I stare in the mirror, I can't see any obvious change.

But then maybe that's because it wasn't really my first time.

I've killed before.

I bury the memory of what I did that night because it still hurts too much, even now. One wrong decision resulted in two ruined lives, not that anyone ever knew what really happened. I never told a soul. I'm sure plenty of people could understand my reasons for killing Rachel Hopkins if they knew the truth about her — some might even thank me — but nobody would ever understand why I killed someone I loved so much.

And they never will because I'll never tell them.

HER

There are so many things I never tell people about myself.

Too many.

I have my reasons.

It's raining again, so hard that it is almost impossible to see the road ahead. Angry, fat drops of water relentlessly slap the windshield before crying down the glass like tears. I continue to drive until it feels like there is enough distance between me and the crime scene, as well as me and my ex-husband, then I pull over into a turnoff and sit there for a moment, transfixed by the sight and sound of the wipers:

Swish and scrape. Swish and scrape. Swish and scrape.

Leave this place. Leave this place. Leave this place.

I check ahead and then behind in the rearview mirror. When I'm satisfied that the road is empty, I down another miniature whiskey. It burns my throat and I'm glad. I savor the taste and the pain for as long as I dare, then toss the empty bottle in my bag. The sound of it clinking with the others reminds me of the windchime that used to hang outside my daughter's nursery. Alcohol doesn't make me feel better; it just stops me feeling worse. I pop a mint, then blow into the breathalyzer, and when my routine self-loathing and self-preservation are complete, I carry on.

On my way back to town I pass the school I used to go to. I see a few girls standing outside, wearing the familiar St. Hilary's uniform that I always hated so much: royal blue with a yellow stripe. They can't be more than fifteen years old, and they look so young to me now, even though I clearly remember how old I *thought* I was at their age. Funny how often life seems to work in reverse. We were children masquerading as adults and now we are adults acting like children.

I feel a little bit sick as I pull up outside the house, but that's not because of the drink. I park the Mini a little farther down the street so as not to be seen; I'm not sure why. She's going to know that I'm here eventually. The guilt over how long it has been since I visited this place seems to trap me inside the car. I try to remember when exactly it was that we last saw each other . . . more than six months this time I suppose.

I didn't even visit last Christmas. Not because I had other plans — Jack and I were divorced by then and he was already living with someone else — but because I felt like I couldn't. I needed to be alone. So, after an afternoon volunteering at a soup kitchen on Christmas Eve, I spent three days locked inside my apartment, with nothing but wine bottles and sleeping tablets for company.

When I woke up on December 28, I didn't feel any better, but I did feel able to carry on. Which was both a good thing and my best-case scenario. There was a plan B if I hadn't managed to feel differently about the future, but I flushed that option away and I'm glad. Christmas used to be my favorite time of year, but now it is something that needs to be got through, not celebrated. And the only way I know how to do that is alone.

Sometimes it feels as though I live just below the surface, and everyone else lives above. When I try to be, and sound, and act like they do for too long, it feels like I can't breathe. As though even my lungs were made differently, and I'm not able, or good enough to inhale the same air as the people I meet.

I lock the car and look up and down the old familiar street. Nothing much has changed. There is a bungalow that has morphed into a house, and a yard that has become a driveway a little farther down the road, but otherwise, everything looks just like it used to. Like it always has. As though perhaps the last twenty years were a lie, a figment of my tired imagination. The truth is, I feel like I've been teetering on the edge of crazy town for a while now, but have yet to fully cross the border.

My feet come to a standstill at the last house on the lane, and it takes me a while to look up, as though I am scared of making eye contact. When I do turn to stare at the old Victorian cottage, it looks exactly the same as it always did. Except for the peeling paint on the window frames and aging front door. The place looking old is new to me. The yard is what shocks me the most: an overgrown jungle of uncut grass and heather. The two lines of lavender bushes on either side of the path have also been neglected; crooked, woody stems reach out like twisted, arthritic fingers, as though to prevent anyone from going in.

Or getting out.

I stare down at the gate and see that it is broken and hanging off its hinges. I lift it to one side and navigate my way to the front door, hesitating before ringing the bell. I needn't have bothered. It doesn't work, so I knock instead. Three times, just like she taught me all those years ago, so she would know it was me. For a long time, she wouldn't let anyone else into the house.

When nobody answers, I stare down at the faded welcome mat and see that it is upside down. It's as if it isn't for visitors at all, but there instead to welcome her into the real world, should she ever decide to step outside and rejoin it. I silently scold myself and try to put the unkind thoughts to bed, tucking them in as tightly as possible. Then I see what I'm looking for: a cracked terra-cotta flowerpot on the doorstep. I lift it up and am a little surprised that she still keeps a key hidden underneath.

I let myself inside.

HIM

I lost her at the second roundabout — she has always driven faster than she should — but it didn't matter. I had already guessed by then where she was going. I'll be honest, I was surprised, after all this time. As soon as I see her car on the street, confirming my suspicions, I pull over a little farther down, turn off the engine, and wait.

I'm good at waiting.

Anna looks different from earlier this morning. Still beautiful, with her shiny brown hair, big green eyes, and little red coat, but smaller. As if this place has the power to physically do that to her. She looks more fragile, easy to break.

My ex never did like coming back here, even before our daughter died, not that she would ever talk about it or explain why. After it happened, she stopped going anywhere except the newsroom. Even shopping

112

was something that she would only do online, so that she rarely left the apartment except for work.

She couldn't even bear to say our little girl's name, and was furious if I ever did, covering her ears as though the sound of it offended them. There are things that have happened in my life — mistakes I have made, people I have hurt — that I seem to have almost completely deleted from my mind. It's as though the memories were too painful to hold on to, and needed to be erased. But, despite my guilt, my daughter isn't one of them. I sometimes still whisper her name inside my head. Unlike Anna, I don't want to forget. I don't deserve to.

Charlotte. Charlotte. Charlotte.

She was so small and so perfect. Then she was gone.

When you find out you're allergic to something, the logical thing to do is to avoid it. And that's what Anna did with her grief. She kept busy at work in public, and in private spent all of her time hiding at home, trying to protect herself from the rashes of fear that seeing other people inflicted on her. She's learned to hide her anxiety from others, but I know worry makes her world go round.

My stomach starts to grumble and I realize I still haven't eaten anything today. I usually have a few sugary snacks in the car. If my dead mother knew, I'm sure she would haunt me with a ghostly toothbrush. I open the glove compartment, but instead of the chocolate bar or forgotten biscuits I'd been hoping to find, I see some black, lacy underwear. I'm guessing it must have belonged to Rachel — women taking their clothes off in my car is not a regular occurrence — though I've no idea how it got in there.

I reach inside the glove compartment again and spot some Tic Tacs. They remind me of Anna — she always had little boxes of mints — and while they won't do much to satisfy my hunger, they're better than nothing. I shake the small plastic box, then flip open the lid and tip a few out. But the white shapes are *not* mints. I stare at the thick fingernail clippings on the palm of my hand and think I'm going to be sick.

A car door slams down the street. I throw the underwear and the Tic Tac box back inside the glove compartment, slamming it closed seconds afterward, like a nervous echo. As though if I can't see them, they were never really there.

Someone knows I was with Rachel last night, and now they are fucking with me.

114

I can think of no other explanation, but who?

I stare out of the window and watch Anna's every move. She took her time getting out of the car, despite her rush to get here. I can't help thinking it's because she is afraid of what she might find behind closed doors. I sympathize with that because she is right to be.

I know what is waiting for her inside that house, because I go there all the time.

I even had my own key cut.

Not that either of them knew.

HER

I should have known it would be like this.

There is a pile of unopened mail behind the door, making it difficult to open. I close it behind me as soon as I've managed to squeeze through the gap, but discover it's just as cold inside the house as it was out on the street. My eyes try to adjust to the gloom — it is difficult to see — but the thing I notice first, and most, is the smell. It's as though something has died in here.

"Hello?" I call, but there is no answer.

I hear the familiar murmurs of a television at the back of the house, and don't know whether to feel happy or sad about it. The roman blinds are all down, with just a sliver of winter sun trying to backlight their elderly cotton edges. I remember that they were all homemade, over twenty years ago. I try the light switch but nothing happens, and when I squint up into the darkness, I

116

can see that there is no bulb.

"Hello?" I call again.

When nobody answers a second time, I pull the cord on the blind to raise it just a little, and am engulfed in a cloud of dust, a million tiny particles dancing in the beam of light that floods the room. I turn to see that what was once a homely living room is now empty, except for cardboard boxes. Lots of them. Some are stacked precariously high and leaning to one side, as though they might topple over at any moment. Each has been labeled with what looks like a thick black felt-tip pen, and my eyes are drawn to the box in the farthest corner that says ANNA'S THINGS.

Coming here always feels wrong, but none of this feels right.

It doesn't make any sense — my mother would rather die in this house than leave it — it's something we used to frequently argue about before we stopped talking altogether. My hands start to shake, just the way they did when I lived here. Not that any of that was *her* fault; she didn't even know. I was a different version of myself then, one that I doubt many people would like or recognize. Home is not always where the heart is. For people like me, home is where the hurt lives that made us into who we are.

My mother was always fond of boxes, but not all of them were real. When I was a little girl, she taught me how to build them in my head, and hide my worst memories inside. I learned to fill them with the things I most wanted to forget, so that they were locked away and hidden in the darkest corners of my mind, where nobody, including me, would ever look. I tell myself the same thing I always do when I come here:

You are more than the worst thing you've ever done.

I feel a familiar pain in the back of my head, which starts to throb in time with my heartbeat. It's the kind of fast-accelerating agony that can only be cured with alcohol, and the need to do so takes over everything else. I reach inside my bag and find a half-empty blister pack of painkillers. I pop two inside my mouth, then search for a miniature to wash them down with.

They're not as hard to come by as they used to be — miniatures — and I no longer have to steal them from flights or hotels. I have my favorites: Smirnoff vodka, Bombay Sapphire gin, Bacardi, and, for a special sweet treat, Baileys Irish Cream. But quality scotch tends to be my number one choice, and there are a wide variety of those available in teeny-tiny bottles now — even with next-day delivery online. All small enough to fit discreetly inside any pocket or purse. I twist the lid off the first one I find in my bag and drink it down like medicine; vodka this time. I don't bother popping a mint afterward. Parents know their children, even the bad ones.

"Mum!" My voice sounds just the same as it did when I was a child when I say her name.

But there is still no answer.

"Plenty big enough for the two of us" was how she described this tiny cottage when I was still here. As though she had forgotten that there used to be three of us living in the house. I can still hear her saying it now inside my head, along with all the other lies she told to try to stop me from leaving.

It's a brick-built Victorian two-up two-down, with an extension tagged on the end like a twentieth-century afterthought. Our house always used to look like a nice home, even when it stopped feeling like one. Not anymore. I squeeze past the stacks of boxes, until I reach the door that leads to the rear of the building. It squeaks in protest when I open it, and the smell is considerably worse. It hits the back of my throat, and I gag when

119

my mind speculates on what might be causing it.

I pass the stairs, walk through what still resembles a dining room — despite the boxes on the table — and do my best not to trip over anything in the dark. I spot Mum's old record player on the dresser in the corner, covered in a thick layer of dust. Even when I tried to introduce her to cassettes and CDs, she insisted on sticking with vinyl. I caught her sometimes, dancing around the room with her arms held out, as though she were waltzing with an invisible man.

I reach the kitchen, turn on the light, and my hand automatically comes up to cover my mouth. Dirty plates coated in uneaten food, along with half-drunk cups of tea, litter every available surface. There are a couple of lazy-looking flies, buzzing around what might once have been a microwavable lasagna. It is not like my mother to eat ready meals. She rarely ate anything we didn't grow in our own garden and would rather go hungry than eat fast food.

The smell is a little overwhelming now. When I manage to look up from all the filth and mess in the kitchen, I see the glow of the TV out in the sunroom right at the back of the house. It's the place where she always most liked to sit, with the best view of her beloved garden.

I see her then, sitting in her favorite armchair in front of the television, a bag of knitting on the floor by her side. My mother always preferred making things herself: food, clothes, me. Years ago, she helped me knit a Harry Potter scarf for Jack. It was strange and surreal to see him still wearing it today.

I take a step closer and see that she is smaller than I remembered, as though life has made her shrink. Her gray hair has thinned and there are hollow shapes where there used to be rosy cheeks. The clothes she is wearing look dirty and too big, and the buttons on her cardigan are done up incorrectly, so that one side of the white bobbled material looks longer than the other. It's covered in faded embroidered bees, and I remember buying it for her a long time ago — a last-minute birthday present. I'm surprised she still has it. I glance at the TV screen and see that she has been watching the BBC News Channel, as though hoping to catch a glimpse of me in the background. I knew she did that, but to *see* it makes me feel even worse than before.

She isn't watching now.

Her eyes are closed and her mouth is slightly open.

121

I take a step closer, and memories I locked away a long time ago start to stir. I shake my head, as though trying to silence them before they get too loud. It isn't just the mess in the kitchen that stinks, it's her. She smells of body odor, piss, and something else I can't quite put my finger on. Or am choosing not to.

"Mum?" I whisper.

She doesn't answer.

Memories are shapeshifters. Some bend, some twist, and some shrivel and die over time. But our worst ones never leave us.

"Mum?" I say her name a little louder, but she still doesn't answer or open her eyes.

I have rehearsed my mother's death in my imagination for years. Not because I wanted her to die; it was just something that happened from time to time inside my head. I don't know whether other daughters do that too — it isn't the sort of thing people talk about — but now that it might be happening for real, I know I'm not ready.

I reach out, then hesitate before touching her hand. When I do, her fingers are icy cold. I lean down, until my face is next to hers, trying to see whether she is breathing. Despite the pills, the pain in my head is so bad now that I briefly close my eyes, and it feels as though I fall back in time.

I hear a scream and it is several seconds before I realize that it is my own.

HIM

Tuesday 10:10

My own memories of this place in the past invade my present.

I watch Anna stand outside the house she grew up in, and it's as though the years fall away and I'm seeing a little girl. I could get out of the car right now and stop her, but I don't. Sometimes you have to let things play out, no matter how unpleasant. I already know what she is going to find inside, and I feel horrible about it. I also know that she has her own key, but watch as she bends down to take the spare one from under the flowerpot, before disappearing behind the peeling front door.

The cottage used to be beautiful, but, a bit like the woman inside, it has not aged well. Anna's mother was a woman who knew how to make a house a home, and it was always by far the nicest cottage on the lane. Picture perfect. At least on the outside.

124

People used to actually stop and take photos because it looked like a doll's house with its pretty little front yard, window boxes, and white picket fence. Nobody stops to take photos of it anymore.

But, back then, she was so good at cleaning, tidying, and making a place feel cozy, that she did it for a living. Anna's mum cleaned for half the village for over twenty years — including the house where I live now — and she didn't just clean. She'd buy little scented candles and flowers and leave them in people's homes. Occasionally she'd bake a bunch of brownies and leave them on the kitchen table. She even babysat my sister from time to time too. Sometimes, it was just the way she made the bed, or plumped the pillows, but you always knew when Mrs. Andrews had paid a visit. She was never short of work or references.

I wait in the car. When nothing happens, I wait a little longer, but then the familiar mix of boredom and anticipation distracts me, and I get out to stretch my legs. I walk along the street, keeping an eye on the house, then stop to examine Anna's Mini. There is nothing out of the ordinary about it — aside from the garish red color — there are no dents, no marks, no scratches. I don't even know why I'm doing this. I guess sometimes in my line of work — as well as in life — you don't always know what you're looking for until you find it.

And then I do.

I see a pay-and-display parking lot ticket with a familiar National Trust logo on the floor of the passenger seat. Discarded and a little crumpled, the small square of printed white paper doesn't seem like anything of significance at first. I know she parked outside the woods this morning — I was there, I saw her. But I'm surprised that anyone in the media would have paid any attention to the parking meter, given the circumstances. I'm sure the National Trust was far more concerned with a body being found on its property than a few people forgetting to pay and display.

I stare at it a little longer, without knowing why, as though my eyes are patiently waiting for my brain to catch up with what they have seen. Then I check my watch before looking back at the ticket one last time. The date. It isn't today's. I push my face right up against the car window, squinting inside until I am absolutely sure of what I see. According to that little square of black-and-white paper, Anna visited the parking lot where the body was found *yesterday*.

I look up and down the street as though wanting to share this information with another human being, to have them verify that it is real.

Then I hear a woman scream.

HER

Tuesday 10:15

I stop screaming when my mother opens her eyes.

She looks as terrified as I feel at first, but then the creases in the skin around her mouth stretch into a smile, her face lights up in recognition, and she starts to laugh.

"Anna? You scared me!"

Her voice is the same as it always was, as though she is still the middle-aged mum I remember, not the old woman sitting in front of me now. I find it disorienting, how what I see and what I hear don't match. My mother is only seventy, but life ages some people more quickly than others, and she was on a fast track for a long time. Fueled by drink and long periods of depression I never acknowledged or understood. There are things children choose not to see in their parents; sometimes it is best to walk past a mirror without stopping to look at your reflection.

She continues to laugh, but I don't. I feel like a child again and can't seem to find any words to fit the scenario. I am shocked by the state of her and the house, and have a terrible urge to turn around, walk out, and leave this place forever. And not for the first time.

"Did you think I was dead?"

She smiles and pulls herself up and out of the chair. It looks as though it requires considerable effort.

I let her hug me. I'm a little out of practice when it comes to affection — I can't remember the last time someone held me — but I try not to cry and eventually remember to respond. It is a long time before either of us lets go. Despite the general chaos, there are still photos of me as a child dotted everywhere around the house. I feel them looking down at us, from the walls and dusty shelves, and I know all those earlier versions of myself would not approve of the me I am now. Every single picture that she ever framed is of me aged fifteen or younger. As though I stopped aging in my mother's head after that.

"Let me look at you," she says, though I doubt her misty eyes can see me like they used to.

We share an unspoken conversation about the number of months it has been since we last saw each other. All families have their own version of normal, and long periods of absence without explanation are ours. We both know why.

"Mum, the house . . . the mess . . . the boxes. What is going on?"

"I'm moving out. It's time. Would you like some tea?"

She shuffles past me, out of the sunroom and into the kitchen, somehow finding the kettle among all the dirty cups and plates. She turns on the tap to fill it, and the elderly pipes rattle in protest. They make a strained noise, as though they are as tired and broken as she looks to me now. She places the kettle on the hob, because she thinks gas is cheaper than electricity.

"Take care of the pennies and the pounds will look after themselves," she says with a smile, as though reading my mind.

I instantly think of myself as the bad penny who just turned up, and wonder if she is thinking the same. The silence is stretched and awkward while we wait for the kettle to boil.

My mother wasn't always a cleaner, but everything about her and our home was always neat and tidy, spick-and-span, *clean.*

It was as though she was allergic to dirt, and I think I may have inherited her OCD approach to hygiene. Though looking around now, that has clearly changed.

My parents bought this house so that we would be in the right catchment area for a good school. When I still didn't get a place at a decent public one, they decided to pay for a private education, even though we couldn't really afford it. My dad was away for work even more than before after that, but it was what they both wanted: to give me the start in life that neither of them had. For me, it was the start of a lifetime of not fitting in.

I was fifteen when he disappeared for good. That's more than old enough to walk home alone from school, but Mum said she would pick me up that day. When she wasn't there, I was furious. I thought she had just forgotten about me. Other people's parents didn't forget. Other people's parents turned up on time, in their fancy cars, wearing their fancy clothes, ready and waiting to take their offspring back to their fancy houses to eat their fancy dinners. I seemed to have little in common with the other children at my school.

I walked home in the rain that day, with

my backpack, gym clothes, and art portfolio. It was all so heavy that I had to keep swapping which hand carried what. There was no hood on my coat, and it wasn't possible to carry an umbrella as well as everything else, so I was completely drenched before I was even halfway. I remember the rain trickling down the back of my neck, and the tears running down my cheeks. Not because of the bags, or the rain, but because earlier that day Sarah Healey had said, in front of the whole class, that I had a Jewish nose. I didn't know what that meant or why it was a bad thing, but everyone had laughed at me. I planned to ask my mother about it as soon as I got home.

As a teenager, all I wanted was to be the same as everyone else. It's only now that I realize how dull my life might have turned out if I was.

I reached the top of the hill, soaked to the skin and out of breath, and had to put everything down and rest for a moment. I looked at the pattern of ugly red grooves on my cold fingers — temporary scars from all the bags — and rubbed the palms of my hands together, trying to make the lines disappear and warm myself up at the same time. Then I turned onto our lane, the highest in Blackdown. You could see for miles from up there in those days, before they started building the big fancy houses on the hill. There were uninterrupted views of the village below, the woods surrounding it, and the patchwork quilt of countryside in the distance, unfolding all the way to the blue haze of the sea on a clear day. It was the perfect spot to look down at all the people who normally looked down on us.

Our house might have been the smallest, but it was also the prettiest, tucked away all by itself at the dead end of the lane. In summer there were coachloads of tourists that came to visit what is still often described as England's most quintessential village. They walked to the top of the hill for the views, but sometimes they took pictures of our cottage too while they were there. Not that my mother minded. She would spend hours in the front yard, planting and pruning, as well as painting our front door every spring. She made the place look shiny and new, despite it being over one hundred years old.

I didn't bother to look for my key; there was always one hidden under the pretty flowerpot on the porch. Even before I slotted it into the lock that day, I could hear the television, and suspected my mother had fallen asleep in front of it. I stepped inside before deliberately slamming the door behind me.

"Mum!"

I shouted her name like an accusation, before dropping my wet coat and bags on the floor, literally dripping onto the carpet. I thought about not removing my school shoes — that would have really upset her — but instead I dutifully untied my laces and left them by the door. My socks were wet, so I took them off too.

"Mum!"

I called her again, irritated that she hadn't already answered and acknowledged my existence. I stomped through to the living room and saw that she'd put up the Christmas tree. The fairy lights were twinkling like stars, but they didn't hold my attention for long. There were no presents underneath, just my mother, lying facedown on the floor and covered in blood.

There was a trail of muddy footprints on the carpet behind her, as though she had crawled in from the garden. I tried to whisper her name again, but the word got stuck in my throat. When my brain caught up with what my eyes were seeing, I fell down onto the floor beside my mother's broken body, and tried to turn her over. Her hair had been stained red with blood, and was stuck to the side of her battered and bruised face. Her eyes were closed, her clothes were torn, and her arms and legs were covered in cuts and scratches.

"Mum?" I whispered, afraid to touch her again.

"Anna?"

Her head turned and her right eye opened a little; the left one was swollen shut. I didn't know what to do. The twisted sound of her rasping voice seemed to hurt my ears, and I had a terrible urge to run away. She looked over my shoulder then, at the old cream rotary phone on the coffee table. I leapt up, hurrying toward it.

"I'll call the police —"

"No," she said.

It was clear from the look on her face that speaking — even a single word — was causing enormous pain.

"Why not?"

"No police."

"I'll call an ambulance then," I said, dialing the first nine.

"No."

She started to crawl toward me, and it was like something from a horror film.

"Mum, please. I have to call someone. You need help. I'll call Dad. He'll know what to do and he'll come home and —"

She reached toward me with a trembling,

bloody hand. Then took hold of the phone, and ripped it right out of the wall before collapsing back onto the floor.

I started to cry, and thought of maybe going to find a neighbor who could help.

"No neighbors," she croaked, as though reading my mind the way she often did. "No police, no anybody. Promise me."

She stared at me with her good eye until I nodded that I understood, then rested her head back down on the floor.

"I'll be okay. I just need to rest," she said, her voice so faint I could barely hear it.

She seemed determined to make the decision for me, but I still wasn't convinced it was the right one.

"Why can't I at least call Dad?"

She let out a breath, as though the silence were a note she'd been made to hold too long.

"Because Dad is the one who did this to me."

Him

Tuesday 10:15

Sometimes this job is all about making decisions. I've learned over the years that whether those decisions are right or wrong, is often secondary to the ability to make them in the first place. Besides, "right" and "wrong" are highly subjective.

I shouldn't be here; I know I'm right about that. Loitering outside the house my ex-wife grew up in might be frowned upon — even though I have my reasons — but there are some people we never really let go of in life. Or death. Even when we pretend to. They are always still there, lurking in our loneliest thoughts, haunting our memories with dreams that can no longer come true.

I'm no Casanova; more of a serial monogamist . . . until Rachel came along. I can count the number of women I've slept with on one hand. But, regardless of how many women I have known, I only truly loved one.

137

I left London because it was the right thing to do for Anna. People don't know what real love is until they lose it. Most never find it in the first place, but when you do, you'll do *anything* for that person.

I know, because I did.

It was what was best for her, but it might turn out to be the worst mistake I've ever made.

Regardless of whether I should or shouldn't be here now, I *am,* and I'm certain I just heard someone scream. I wouldn't be much of a man *or* a detective if I didn't do something about it.

I use my phone to take a picture of the parking ticket showing yesterday's date in Anna's car, then head toward her mother's house. I lift the broken gate and check over my shoulder to see whether anyone is watching me. I conclude that they aren't and carry on along the uneven, weed-stained path. I ignore the front door, choosing instead to walk down the side of the house, toward the back, where I expect they will be.

I stop when I hear voices inside.

I can't quite make out what is being said, but also don't want to risk being seen. I wait for a minute, leaning against the wall, concluding it might be best to just turn around. The sensible thing to do would be to get in my car, head back to HQ, and do my job. But then I hear it again, what sounds like another scream.

It scares the hesitation out of me long enough to look through the kitchen window. I see Anna and her mother, who I notice is taking the kettle of the hob, and realize that must be what I heard. I had forgotten that boiling water that way is one of my former mother-in-law's many old-fashioned and odd habits. My ex-wife has more in common with her than she would like to believe.

In my experience, there are two kinds of women: those who spend a lifetime trying not to turn into their mothers, and those who literally seem to want nothing more. I often find both varieties get the complete opposite of what they hoped for — one set become carbon copies of the women they didn't want to be, while the others never live up to their own expectations of who they think they should have become.

I head back to the car, not wanting to be seen.

I have been made a fool of on more than one occasion by the women inside this house. Anna has always been clear that she doesn't want or need saving. Confusing the sound of a kettle with some kind of cry for help was probably just wishful thinking on my part. You can't help someone find their way if they won't admit they're lost.

HER

Tuesday 10:18

I think my mother might have lost it, but keep my thoughts to myself. The kettle starts to scream and she takes it off the hob. Out of the corner of my eye, I think I see something move outside the kitchen window. But I must have imagined it, because when I go to check there is nothing there. I turn back and take in the state of the place again. Knowing her the way I do, I don't know how she can stand it. When I was a teenager, I sometimes felt embarrassed that my mother cleaned other people's houses. Now I feel ashamed of myself for caring what they thought. She did what she did for me.

Jack has e-mailed a few times over the last few months, to say that Mum was much worse than before. I thought it was just an excuse to get in touch; I didn't believe him. When I look at the state of her now, I hate

141

myself for it. Sometimes the roles of parents and children get reversed, and I have not played my part well. I didn't just forget my lines — I never learned them in the first place.

Mum was constantly cleaning our home when I still lived here, almost obsessively — a habit I confess I inherited — and I have never seen the house, or her, look like this. Presentation was always *very* important to my mother. We never had a lot of spare cash, but she always dressed nicely — often finding the prettiest clothes in charity shops for us both to wear — and she always, *always* did her hair and makeup. I rarely remember seeing her without it. She really was rather beautiful, but now she appears, and smells, as though she hasn't washed for days.

"How have you been, Mum?"

"Me? Oh, I'm fine."

She starts to open and close the kitchen cupboards, and I can see that they are almost all completely empty. Jack mentioned that she had been forgetting to eat and had lost some weight. He said she had been forgetting a lot of things.

"I'm sure I had some biscuits around here somewhere —"

"It's okay, Mum. I'm not hungry."

"All right then, I'll just make us the tea."

I watch as she opens two different tins —
she likes to blend it herself — then takes
down the old teapot that stirs up a thousand
memories of us doing this before. I do need
a drink right now, but not tea. I should have
come home sooner, I should have taken care
of her, the way she used to take care of me.
I had my reasons for staying away. Self-
preservation is just one of them. I feel an
urge to leave again now while I still can, but
Mum grabs my arm.

"Here, have this."

I look down at the crystal tumbler of
whiskey, then back at her. She smiles, and it
brings a strange sense of comfort to know
that my mother knows me — even the worst
version — and still seems to love me anyway.

My mum started drinking when my dad
left, and despite her numerous claims over
the years, I know that she never really
stopped. I've always blamed her occasional
memory loss on her desire to obliterate
them all with alcohol. She was never a
sociable woman. Her two best friends were
wine and whiskey, and they were always
there when she needed them. Nobody else
knew about how much she drank. She hid
her habit well, and I learned that the best
way to keep a secret is never to tell. Like
mother, like daughter.

143

Jack brought up the subject of dementia a few times over the years, but I always dismissed it, certain that I knew my mother better than he did. Even when he described her worsening symptoms, I still thought it was manageable.

Perhaps I was wrong.

I can remember her forgetting small stuff, like the milk, or where she'd left her keys, or occasionally turning up to clean the wrong houses at the wrong times. But it was easy enough to explain away; the kind of forgetfulness that happens to us all. She forgot my birthday a couple of times, but it didn't seem like a big deal, just one of those things. Besides, my birthday tends to be a day I would rather forget too.

Jack said she forgot where she lived a few months ago.

I thought he must be exaggerating, but now I don't know what to believe. If dementia is taking my mother's memories away, then I guess sometimes it gives them back. Despite appearances, she does at least seem coherent today. I drain my glass and wonder how bad it would be to pour another.

"What are these?" I ask, noticing a row of prescription pills lined up on the windowsill.

The look on her face is hard to translate; an unfamiliar mix of fear and shame.

"Nothing for you to worry about," she says, opening an empty drawer and hiding the little brown bottles inside.

My mother never takes drugs, not even painkillers. She always thought that pharmaceutical companies would be responsible for the end of mankind. It was one of her more melodramatic theories on the world, but one she absolutely believed in.

"Mum, you can tell me. Whatever it is."

She stares at me for a long time, as though weighing up her options and concluding that the truth might be a little too heavy.

"I'm fine, promise."

I look around the filthy kitchen and say the words as gently as I can.

"I think we both know that's not true."

"I'm sorry about the mess, love. Nobody's visited for so long. If I'd known you were coming . . . it's just that I've been so busy trying to pack everything into boxes — there is a lifetime hidden away inside this house — and the pills make me *so* tired . . ."

"What are the pills for?"

She stares down at the floor before answering.

"People say I've been forgetting things."

A ray of light from the kitchen window casts a pattern on her face, and she appears to feel the warmth of it. Her cheeks blush

145

and her mouth cracks into an embarrassed smile.

"What people?" I ask.

A cloud must have covered the sun, because the light leaves the room and the smile slides off my mother's face at the same time. She shakes her head.

"Jack. I forgot to pay for my shopping at the supermarket a few weeks ago. I was so embarrassed. I don't even know what I was doing there — you know how much I hate shops — but they showed me the security footage afterward, and I watched myself walk straight past the cash registers and to the parking lot, with a cart full of things I didn't even need to buy; books by authors I don't like, sirloin steaks — having not eaten meat for decades — and a pack of diapers!"

I look away and she hesitates while choosing her next words, as though regretting sharing the last ones.

"What happened?" I ask, still not quite able to look her in the eye.

"Oh, they were very nice about it. But they did insist on calling the police. I had Jack's number written inside my bracelet. They called him and he told them that he *was* the police, as well as my son, so they let him come and pick me up."

I stare down at the silver SOS Talisman

bracelet on her wrist. A gift from me last year to ease my own guilt — she was involved in a minor car accident and nobody at the hospital knew who to call — but for some reason she now has *his* name, and *his* number written inside instead of mine.

"You do know that Jack isn't your son, don't you? He used to be your son-in-law, but we got divorced, so he isn't that either anymore. Do you remember?"

"I know. I might be a bit forgetful, but I'm not senile! I still think it's a shame; you were good for each other and he's been good to me. He made me go and see a doctor."

"And?"

"I don't want you to worry, love. There are lots of things that can slow down dementia now; sadly they seem to slow me down too. I'm so tired. That's why the place is a little disorganized. Jack thinks it might be time for me to move on, get a bit more help, and I think he might be right. Most days I feel fine, but then sometimes . . . I don't really know how to describe it. I just seem to disappear. There's a residential care village not too far from here; it really is quite something. I'll still have my own place, just with a few gadgets and gizmos to call for help if I need it. People to keep an eye on

147

me when I lose myself."

Part of me knows I should feel gratitude, but all I feel is a growing anger inside me.

"Jack should have told me. Why didn't *you* tell me what was going on? I could have helped."

"He was *here,* my darling. That's all." She doesn't need to add that I wasn't. "Anyway, while *you're* here, why don't you pop up to your old bedroom and see if there is anything you'd like to keep. I was hoping you might pay a visit before I needed to start on it. Go on, you go up and I'll finish making the tea. I'll add a splash of fresh honey the way you used to like it."

"There's no need, Mum."

"Let me do that for you. I can't do much else."

I reluctantly head up to my old room. Even the narrow staircase is littered with clutter; mostly dusty books and old shoes. She was never good at throwing anything she had once loved away. I also spot a few Christmas presents I have given her over the years, things that she's never used that are still in the boxes they came in, including a mobile phone I suspect she never even opened, an electric blanket, and an electric kettle. I should have known. The landing is the same: a cardboard obstacle course obstructing my path to the bedroom at the back of the house. The one that was always mine.

I don't know what to expect, and reach for the door with a certain amount of dread, but when I open it, I see that my room is exactly the same as it was when I moved out. I was sixteen when I left and it's as though time has stood still in here. I take in the sight of the dark wooden furniture, the homemade floral curtains and matching cushions, the shelves of books, and the desk in the corner where I used to do my homework. There is a folded-up piece of cardboard still wedged under one leg to keep it steady.

Unlike the rest of the house, which appears to be covered in a thick layer of dust, everything in here is perfectly clean. The bed linen smells recently washed — even though I haven't been to visit in such a long time — and the furniture isn't just spotless, it's been recently polished. A faint whiff of Mr. Sheen still in the air. On the dressing table I see a familiar perfume that I was fond of as a teenager — Coty L'Aimant — and spray a little on my wrist. The scent brings it all back, and I almost drop the bottle, before wiping away the residue of a memory I'd rather forget.

I notice movement outside again, and peer out of the little back window that overlooks my mother's beloved garden. For as long as I can remember, it has been divided into four sections: the reading lawn (as she always called it, despite being a rectangle of grass no bigger than a bed), the orchard (which consisted of just one apple tree), the vegetable patch (which is a little unsightly), and the potting shed. The front yard may be pretty, but the one at the back of the house has always been practical.

My mother takes organic to the extreme, and started to grow almost all of her own food after my father disappeared. She's a big believer in foraging, and would often disappear into the woods, always knowing exactly where to find edible mushrooms, berries, seeds, and nettles for us to eat. She also makes honey.

I watch as she shuffles her way to the far corner of the garden, before lifting the lid off the old beehive. She doesn't wear a mask or gloves, never has done, instead she just reaches inside with her bare hand. It used to scare me as a child, but then she taught me that if you trust the bees, they will trust you back. I don't know whether that's true, but she never got stung. She looks up at me looking down at her and waves. She seems

150

okay to me. Maybe she doesn't need what-ever pills some doctor has prescribed and my ex-husband has encouraged her to take. Maybe the pills are the problem.

She disappears back inside the house, and I return my attention to my old room. Not all of the memories it reawakens are wel-come. I'm drawn to the wooden jewelry box that was a gift from my father, the last one he ever gave me. It is engraved with my name on top and was a souvenir from one of his many work trips.

I feel the four symmetrical letters spelling out the name he gave me, and push down hard on the wooden shapes, until they leave an imprint on my fingertips. Then, when some form of morbid curiosity prevents me from resisting any longer, I open the box. There is a single red-and-white friendship bracelet inside, along with a picture of five fifteen-year-old girls, one of whom used to be me. I put the photo in my pocket and the bracelet on my wrist, then leave every-thing else exactly as it was.

A thought occurs to me then which stings, so much so I wish I could unthink it: Mum always kept my room nice like this in case I might come home. She's still waiting, and it breaks my heart a little to know how much my distance must have hurt her.

Something about the old Victorian fireplace catches my eye. Our house was always so cold growing up — my mother refused to turn on the central heating unless the temperature was below freezing — so open fires were often the only way to keep warm. I remember the last time I used mine, but it wasn't for heat. I burned a letter that nobody should ever read.

The bedroom door bursts open, making me jump, and my mother appears, wearing her warmest smile and carrying two cups of honeyed tea. Her face changes as soon as she sees me, and she drops them both, pieces of china and a pool of steaming liquid forming a murky puddle on the wooden floor. She stares at the fireplace, then at the friendship bracelet on my wrist, then she takes a step back and looks genuinely afraid. I barely hear the words she whispers.

"What are you doing?" she asks.

"Nothing, Mum. I was just looking at my old room, like you said I should —"

"I'm not your mum! Who are you?"

I take a step forward, but she takes another step back.

"It's me, Mum. It's Anna. We were just talking downstairs, do you remember?"

Her fear morphs into anger.

"Don't be bloody daft! Anna is fifteen

years old! How dare you set foot in my home pretending to be her! Who are you?"

This is the sort of behavior Jack had described but I didn't believe it. Her face is twisted into fear and hate and a mother I no longer recognize.

"Mum, it's me, Anna. Everything is okay —"

I reach for her hand, but she pulls it away and lifts it above her head, as though preparing to strike me.

"Don't you touch me! Get out of my house right now or I'll call the police! Don't think that I won't."

I'm crying. I can't help it. This version of the woman I used to know is destroying my memories of the real her.

"Mum, please."

"Get out of my house!"

She screams the words over and over.

"Get out, get out, get out!"

HIM

I get in my car and wait, unsure exactly what for, already knowing it won't be good. I have mixed memories of my former mother-in-law's home, and being here always makes me feel bad. Anna never liked to visit. I used to wonder if it had something to do with her father. Losing a parent leaves a huge hole in a person's life, but losing a child leaves an even bigger one. This house was the last place where we saw our little girl alive. Not that we could have known that at the time; dropping a child off to spend a night with their grandmother should have been a safe thing to do.

I think you reach an age — and it is different for everyone — where you finally realize that all the things you thought mattered, don't. It often happens when you lose the one thing that really did, but by then it's too late. Our little girl was only three months and three days old when she died. I sometimes think she was just too precious and perfect to exist in such an imperfect world.

My phone buzzes, and when I read the words in the message, I feel a rush of nausea mixed with an excitement I am ashamed of. Then a fist bangs on my rather dirty car window, and I only just manage to swallow what I'm sure would have been a very manly scream. I wish I'd taken another cigarette from Priya to keep for later. By later I mean now. Today is turning out to be a very bad day indeed.

I wind the window down by hand — that's how old my car is — and get a clearer view of my angry-looking ex-wife.

"Are you following me?" she asks.

Her face is blotchy and I can see that she has been crying. She's carrying her coat, despite the fact it's freezing outside, as though she might have left in too much of a hurry to put it on.

"Would you believe me if I said no?"

"How dare you interfere with my mother's health and living arrangements!"

"Now, hang on. I don't know what she told you, or what kind of state she was in just now, but she's been getting progressively worse over the past six months. You would know that if you ever paid her a visit."

"She is *my* mother and this is none of *your* business."

"Wrong again. I have power of attorney."

"What?"

Anna takes a tiny step back from the car.

"There was an incident a while ago. I tried to tell you, but you kept ignoring my calls. She asked for my help; it was her idea."

Anna's face reddens as though it has been verbally slapped.

"What's this really about? Are you trying to sell my mother's house out from under her? Is that it? Trick her into giving you money, because you've realized that life is a bit harder on one salary?"

The low blow she delivers in self-defense stings.

"You know it isn't like that," I say.

"Isn't it?"

"Regardless of whether or not we are together, I still care about your mother. She was good to me and to us. What happened to Charlotte was not her fault."

"No, it was yours."

It feels like she just punched me in the chest.

Anna looks as though she might regret saying the words as much as I regret hearing them. But that doesn't make them less true. I take a breath and carry on.

"Look, your mum isn't well, and someone needs to do what's best for her."

"And that's you, is it?"

"In the absence of anyone else, yes. She's been seen wandering around the town, lost, wearing just her nightdress in the middle of the night, for God's sake."

"What? I don't believe you."

"Fine, I'm making it up. I suppose you weren't in Blackdown yesterday either?"

I didn't mean to blurt the accusation out like that, but the look on her face tells me a lot more than I expect her response will.

"Have you finally lost what was left of your tiny mind? No, I wasn't here yesterday," she says.

"Then why is there a pay-and-display ticket in your car that says you were?"

She hesitates for just a second, but it's a second long enough for me to see, and she knows it.

"I don't know what you're talking about, and I suggest that from now on, you stay away from me, my car, and my mother. Do you understand? Maybe just stick to looking after your own family, and doing your job, given what has happened."

I see her then, my daughter in Anna's face, her eyes. People always say that children

157

resemble their parents, but sometimes it's the other way around. It brings it all back and I can't hurt her any more than I already have.

"That's good advice," I say.

"This is some form of harassment. You shouldn't be here."

"No, I shouldn't."

She pauses, as though I have started speaking a foreign language she is not fluent in.

"Are you agreeing with me?" she asks.

"Yes. It would appear I am."

I study the face I have loved for so long now, and enjoy the unfamiliar shape it makes when surprised. Anna is rarely that. Even though it goes against everything I know about what not to do, I want to see how she reacts to what I shouldn't say.

"The dead woman was Rachel Hopkins."

I feel physically lighter once I've said her name out loud.

Anna's face doesn't change at all, as though she didn't hear me.

"You do remember Rachel?" I ask.

"Of course I do. Why are you telling me this?"

I shrug. "I just thought you should know."

I wait for some kind of emotional reaction, and can't yet decide how to interpret the lack of one.

Anna and Rachel used to be friends, but that was a very long time ago. Perhaps her lack of emotion is normal, to be expected. People our age are rarely still in touch with the friends they went to school with. There was no social media or e-mail back then; we didn't even have the Internet or mobile phones. Hard to imagine a life like that now — it must have been so much quieter. We're both from a generation that was better at moving on, rather than holding on to friendships that had run their course.

I regret telling her almost instantly.

I've gained nothing from doing so, and it was unprofessional. Next of kin haven't even been informed yet. Besides, it isn't as though I need Anna to confess to how much she hated Rachel Hopkins. I already know that.

My phone buzzes again, interrupting the silence that had parked itself between us.

"We're going to have to pause this little reunion. I need to go," I say, already rolling up my window.

"Why? Worried the whole town might find out that you're stalking your ex-wife?"

I consider not telling her any more, but she's going to find out soon enough.

"They've found something that might help

identify the killer," I say, starting the engine and driving away without looking back.

HER

I watch Jack drive away, and wonder what my face did when he told me that the dead woman was Rachel Hopkins. I hope I didn't react at all, but it's hard to tell, and Jack knows me a lot better than anyone else. He has always been able to see straight through me when I'm trying to hide something.

I saw his crappy car parked on the street as soon as I stepped outside Mum's house. It's a secondhand rust bucket, probably all he can afford, now that he's living with a woman who is allergic to working for a living. Since leaving me, Jack has found himself a new home, along with a new mortgage to pay, and a new child to support. All on just the one salary. We were together for over fifteen years, and for a long time I couldn't imagine my life without him in it. I think I understand now. It's as though I've lived lots of different lives in one lifetime, and

161

the one I shared with him was never meant to last forever. Sometimes we hold on too tight to the wrong people, until it hurts so much we have to let go.

I wait until his car has completely disappeared from view before taking the photo out of my pocket. Finding it inside the jewelry box in my old bedroom gave me goose bumps, and what Jack just told me made them return. It might have been a very long time since we were all at school together, but I still recognize every one of the faces in the picture. And I remember the night it was taken. When we all dressed up trying to look older than we were, getting ready to do something that we shouldn't. An evening not all of us would live to regret.

I peer down at the face of Rachel Hopkins, a younger version of the dead woman in the woods staring back at me. We are standing next to each other in the photo. Her arm is wrapped around my bare shoulder, as though we were friends, but we were not. She's smiling — I am too, but I can see mine isn't real. If only I'd been more honest then, I might not have to hide behind a lifetime of lies now. I wish I'd never had to move to that awful school. We would never have met and it would never have happened.

■ ■ ■ ■

I found out something was wrong during a double English lesson, a few months after my father had disappeared. The school secretary, with her unnaturally pale face and contrasting colorful clothes, knocked once then stuck her too-small head around the classroom door.

"Anna Andrews?"

I didn't answer. I didn't need to. The whole class turned to stare at me.

"The headmistress would like to see you."

It made very little sense at the time; I'd never been in trouble before. I followed the secretary in obedient silence, then sat outside the office with no clue as to what I had done, or why I was there. The head-mistress didn't keep me waiting long, and as she beckoned me inside the warm room — which I remember smelled like jam — I saw all the books on her shelves and felt a little better. It looked like a library, and I thought nothing too terrible could ever happen inside one of those. I was wrong.

"Do you know why I've asked to see you?" she said.

The woman had short gray hair, styled in a way that made it look as though she was wearing rollers and had forgotten to take them out. She always wore twinsets, pearls, and pink lipstick, and had a large brown mole on her cheek that I struggled not to stare at. I thought she was prehistoric at the time, but she was probably no older than I am now. People my age seemed ancient back then.

I could think of no reason why I had been summoned to her office, so I shook my head. I can still picture the twisted expression resembling a smile on her face. I couldn't make up my mind whether it was the kind or cruel variety.

"Is everything all right at home?" she asked.

I knew enough to know that meant she suspected it wasn't.

My father never came back after the night he hurt my mother. I had heard them argue before, and I knew he had hit her on several occasions. I'm ashamed to say that back then — having seen them behave like that my whole life — I thought it was normal. People will go to extraordinary lengths to hurt those they love; far more than they ever do for those they hate.

From the day he disappeared onward, my mother was either selling her jewelry at the pawnbroker's, planting things in her new and expanding vegetable patch — because we could no longer afford to shop at the supermarket — or drinking what little money we had left, pouring it into wineglasses. At all other times she was asleep in front of the fire in the living room, as though guarding the front door. She didn't like to sleep upstairs anymore, in the bed she had shared with him, and we couldn't afford a new one. Anything belonging to my dad that she couldn't sell, she burned to keep us warm. So, the answer to the headmistress's question was most definitely no.

"Yes, everything is fine at home," I said.

"Nothing that you might want to talk about?"

"No. Thank you."

"It's just that your school fees weren't paid last term and, despite writing several letters to your parents, and calling, we haven't managed to speak to either of them about it. I'd hoped that your mother or father might have come along to parents' evening last week. Do you know why neither of them was able to attend?"

Because my mother was too drunk, and my father was too busy not being my father anymore.

I shook my head.

"I see. And you're sure everything is okay

at home?"

I waited a while before answering. Not because I had any intention of telling her the truth. I just hadn't had enough time to come up with the right lies, to fill the gaps her questions kept making.

Everyone stared at me again when I got back to class, and I felt like they all knew things about me that they couldn't, didn't, and mustn't ever know. I've hated people staring at me ever since. It might make my choice of career — presenting the news every day to millions of people — seem a little odd. But it's just me and a robotic camera in the studio. If I can't see them looking at me, it's okay. Like a child who thinks nobody can see them if they cover their own eyes with their hands.

I slip the photo back in my pocket, and notice the red-and-white friendship bracelet I'm wearing. I remember making it all those years ago, along with four identical others. It seemed like a good idea at the time, one that has often come back to haunt me. I pull the end until it tightens around my wrist. I deserve the pain, so I feel bad when I start to enjoy it.

A noisy bird catches my eye and I look up at my mother's house. It feels like I need to get away from this place; it's bad for me in more ways than one. I get back in the Mini and rest my hands on the steering wheel. Then I look down at the bracelet again, pulled so tight that it hurts. I loosen it a little, and see the angry red groove it has cut into my skin.

We pretend not to see the scars we give one another, especially those we love. Self-harm is always harder to ignore, but not impossible. I rub the line, as though trying to erase it with my fingertips, to undo the hurt I've caused myself. The mark on my wrist will fade, but the scar on my conscience because of what happened the first time I wore this bracelet will be there forever.

HIM

Anna's face did nothing when I told her the dead woman was Rachel Hopkins. I'm not sure what I was expecting, but a *normal* person would have given some kind of reaction. Then again, normal was something my ex-wife never aspired to be. That was one of the things I loved most about her.

I stop at the gas station to buy cigarettes on my way to meet Priya. From what she said in her text I know I'm going to need them. The roads are empty, so it doesn't take long to get where I am going, and I decide to have a quick smoke before getting out of the car. Something to stop my hands from shaking.

Visiting a mortuary is something I've done a hundred times before — a regular part of my job when I was in London — but it's been a while and this feels very different. I can't stop thinking about last night and how

168

I left Rachel the way I did. What happened wasn't my fault, but I doubt other people would see it that way if they knew the truth.

I force myself to step inside the building, trying not to gag at the smell, which is so much worse in my head than it is inside my nostrils. When I see Rachel's body on the metal table, I have to cover my nose and mouth. If there weren't other people in the room I'd close my eyes too, but Priya is staring at me in her customary intense way. She sees me as her boss and sometimes I think that's all it is, but there are other times, like now, when I can't help wondering if there is more to it than that. Not that I'd ever do anything about it. She isn't unattractive or anything, but mixing business and pleasure has never worked out well for me.

I ignore Priya's stare and return my attention to Rachel. Somehow it wasn't as bad in the woods, when she was still fully clothed and lying among the leaves, like a modern-day Sleeping Beauty. Seeing her like this — naked on a silver slab and cut open like an animal — is all a bit too much. I would not have chosen to remember her this way, but I expect it is the version I will not be able to forget. Along with the smell. Her eyes are closed now at least.

"Will you be needing a bucket?" asks a

man I've never met.

I think it's reasonable to assume he is the forensic pathologist, given where I am and what he looks like. But always best to be sure who it is you are talking to, I find.

"DCI Jack Harper," I say, "and thanks for the offer, but I'm fine."

He stares at my outstretched hand but does not shake it. I think he is being rude, until I notice that the gloves he is wearing are covered in blood.

He is a wire coat hanger of a man, thin and twisted as though a little bent out of shape, while at the same time looking like he may have sharp edges if handled the wrong way. His messy gray eyebrows make an exaggerated effort to stretch across his heavily lined forehead, like long-lost friends who only fight when they finally meet in the middle. And the hair on his head is still black, as though it has forgotten to age at the same time as the hair on his face. He smiles with his eyes, not his mouth, and the man looks a little too thrilled to have something to do, in my opinion. I can see spots of her blood on his apron and have to look away.

"Dr. Jim Levell, pleased to meet you," he says, without sounding it. "It was the stab wounds that killed her."

If that's the best he can come up with, I fear I've had a wasted journey.

His casual tone seems a little unprofessional — even to me — but then this is the first murder I've had to deal with since I came back to this quiet corner of the countryside, so perhaps he is out of practice. Regardless, I have already decided not to like him. From the look on his face, I conclude that he isn't an instant fan of mine either.

"Any thoughts on the weapon?" I ask.

"Relatively short blade actually, kitchen knife, perhaps? She might not have died as a result of one or two, but there were over forty wounds of almost identical depth — all over her chest — so . . ."

"So she didn't die straightaway?" I finish the sentence he seemed unable to.

"No, I doubt that very much. It wasn't the wounds that killed her, it was the blood loss. It will have been rather . . . slow."

Priya stares at the floor, but he doesn't seem to notice or care and carries on with his findings.

"It's my belief that the killer cut the victim's fingernails at the scene, and probably took them with him. A souvenir, perhaps. Or, if she managed to scratch him, perhaps he was worried about what we might find beneath them. I've taken swabs, but I suspect he wore gloves. I have no doubt this was planned."

I picture the Tic Tac box that I found in my car earlier, full of nail clippings.

I need to get rid of it.

"You keep referring to the killer as male —" I start to say.

"We found semen."

Of course he did, and of course it is mine.

"Any update on the victim's car?" I ask, turning to Priya.

I need time out from the pathologist.

"No, sir," she replies.

I know that Rachel's Audi TT was in the parking lot outside the woods last night; she parked right next to me. But nobody else is aware of that and her car certainly isn't there now. I continue to stare at Priya.

"Did we get any usable tire tracks in the end?"

"No, sir. The rain washed almost everything away. Anything we did get turned out to be a car or van belonging to either the press or . . . us."

"Meaning?"

"The tracks of your car, for example."

"I told you that failing to cordon off the parking lot was a mistake. Don't beat yourself up about it. Nobody knows it all, and those who pretend they do know even less than the rest of us."

She looks less abashed than I would have expected.

"The footprint found right next to the body might lead to something though. The lab used a casting compound, and say it was a size ten Timberland boot," she says.

"That's very specific of them."

"The size and make are on the sole, sir. The trees sheltered the footprint from the rain, and none of the team were wearing anything that matched that description, so it seems quite likely it was made by whoever killed her."

The pathologist clears his throat, as though to remind us that he is still here. I stare down at my own size tens, glad I chose to wear shoes instead of boots today.

"I went with the family liaison officer to inform the next of kin before coming here," Priya adds.

"That must have been difficult. I'm guessing her parents were quite elderly?" I say, knowing full well that they are. Rachel sometimes mentioned them.

Priya frowns.

"It was her husband that we went to see, sir."

I have a strange sensation in my chest, as

though my heart just skipped a beat.

"I thought she was divorced."

Priya frowns again, combines it with a shake of the head this time.

"No, sir. But he was practically old enough to be her father. So that might be why you were confused. Rumor has it she married him for his money, then spent it."

"Right," I say. Rachel definitely told me that she was divorced. Even showed me the indentation on her finger where her wedding ring used to be. I look at her body now, and see the band of gold on her left hand, shining beneath the fluorescent lights as though it is winking at me. I wonder what else she lied about. "Where was the husband at the time of death? Does he have an alibi? We should probably —"

"It wasn't him, sir," Priya interrupts.

"I wouldn't have expected you to be guilty of ageism, Priya. Someone being over sixty doesn't disqualify them from being a suspect. You know as well as I do that it's almost always the husband."

"He's eighty-two, bedbound, and has twenty-four-hour live-in care. He can't use the bathroom without assistance, so chasing a woman through the woods seemed like a bit of a stretch. Sir."

The pathologist clears his throat a second

time, and I turn my attention back to him.

"I was told that you found something?"

"Inside her mouth, yes," he says quickly, as if we have already taken up too much of his time. "I thought you might like to see it before I run some tests."

His apron makes a *shh* noise as he walks to the side of the room. He removes his dirty gloves with an unpleasant *thwack,* washes his hands for an uncomfortably long time, dries them on a towel, then slips on a new pair, before flexing his fingers repeatedly. To say the man is strange would be an understatement. He picks up a small rectangular metal tray, and comes to stand on my side of the table, like a ghoulish waiter serving an unpleasant appetizer.

I stare down at the red-and-white object.

"What is it?" I ask.

The question is a lie because I already know the answer.

"It's a friendship bracelet," Priya says, coming a little closer to get a better view. "Girls make them for each other out of different-colored thread."

"And this was inside the victim's mouth?" I ask, ignoring her now, and looking at him.

The pathologist smiles, and I see that his teeth are unnaturally white and a little too big for his face. Once again, he looks as

175

though he is enjoying his job more than he should.

"It wasn't just in her mouth," he says.

"What do you mean?"

"The friendship bracelet was tied around the victim's tongue."

Her

Tuesday 11:30

I wrap my coat around my shoulders, feeling the cold now, before turning on the
engine. I'm about to drive away when I see
a white van pull up behind me. A small, thin
woman gets out, wearing a baseball cap and
dressed in black clothes that are too large
for her tiny frame. She's young, but a worried expression is pulled across her face and
casts a series of premature lines.

I watch as she carries a large box to my
mother's front door, before dumping it on
the porch. She doesn't knock, or even try to
close the gate behind her when she leaves.

I lower my window as she passes me by.

"Hello, I —"

The words slip out of my mouth as though
by accident, and the woman gives me an
odd look and a slightly wide berth instead
of a reply. She's gone before I get to ask
what was inside the box. It reminds me of

another time when I arrived home to find people I did not recognize coming in and out of our front gate.

I left school at lunchtime the day the headmistress said that my fees hadn't been paid. I just walked out without a word. It felt like the whole school was staring at me, and I couldn't take it any longer. We weren't rich — far from it, living in our little old house with its damp-infused rooms, drafty windows, and homemade *everything* — but my parents believed that education could overcome *anything.* I had attended private school from the age of eleven, and the year when I was due to sit my GCSEs was not a great time to stop. So, I hurried home, hoping that my mother had a secret stash of cash somewhere.

She didn't.

When I got there, far earlier than I should have, strange men were coming out of our house, carrying boxes. I stood on the lawn in the garden allowing them to pass me on the path, and only started to panic when two men came out of the front door with our TV. Unlike a lot of homes those days, we still only had the one. I rushed inside to find my mother standing in an empty room.

"Why are you home?" she said. "Are you sick?"

"Why are they taking all our stuff?"

I was always good at answering questions with questions. It was one of the many skills I learned during childhood that has come in handy as a journalist.

"Things have been a little difficult, moneywise, since your father . . . left us. A lot of our things were bought on credit cards and I can't pay for them on my own."

"Because you're a cleaner?"

I hated myself for the way I said it, not just the words themselves.

"Well, yes. My job doesn't pay as much as your father's used to."

I knew she had only started cleaning other people's houses because we needed the money. She wasn't really qualified to do anything else — that's why she wanted me to finish school, because she hadn't.

"Can't we just call Dad and ask him to send us some money?"

"No."

"Why?"

"You know why."

"I only know that you said he was gone and was never coming back, and now we can't afford to have a TV."

"We'll get a new one once I've managed

179

to save up, I promise. Word is starting to spread and I'm getting more and more work. It won't take long."

"And what about my school? They pulled me out of class today, said that my fees hadn't been paid. Everyone stared at me."

She looked like she might cry and that wasn't what I wanted to see. I wanted her to tell me that everything was going to be all right, but I didn't get to hear that either.

"I'm so sorry," she whispered, and took a step toward me. I took a step back. "I've tried everything that I can think of, but we're going to have to find you a new school."

"But that's where all my friends are . . . ."

She didn't reply, perhaps because she knew I didn't really have any.

"What about my exams?" I persisted; she couldn't deny those.

"I'm sorry, but we'll find somewhere good."

"Sorry, sorry, sorry! That's all you ever say!"

I stormed past her and ran upstairs to my bedroom. I noticed that it was the only room in the house where nothing had been taken, but I didn't say anything about that. Instead I yelled loud enough for her to hear before slamming my door.

"You are ruining my life."

It was only years later that I understood how wrong I was — she had been trying to save it.

I stare at the box delivered to my mother's porch just now, then use my phone to Google the name written on the side. It's a cheap and nasty meals on wheels company. The idea of my mother — a woman who for years would only eat organic food or things she grew herself — eating ready meals makes me want to cry. But I don't.

Holding my phone in my hand has sparked something in me, the beginning of an idea that I already know isn't good, but sometimes bad ideas turn out to be the best. I'm aware that Jack didn't tell me that the victim was Rachel Hopkins so I could broadcast it, but if I'm going to save my career I need to get back on-air. I call the newsroom. Then I dial my cameraman's number and Richard answers immediately, almost as though he had been watching and waiting for my call.

A couple of hours later, I'm hooked up and about to do a live two-way on the program I used to present. Rachel's social media accounts were public and also, un-surprisingly, full of photos of herself. I

181

selected a few and sent them to the producer back at base to build a graphic. Richard filmed a couple of shots outside her home, and then we gathered some short interviews with local residents — none of whom really knew her, but were more than happy to speak as though they did.

I've always been good at getting people to talk to me. My methods are very simple, but they work:

Rule Number One: Everyone likes to feel flattered.

Two: Establish trust. Always be friendly, regardless of how you really feel.

Three: Start a conversation that suggests you have plenty in common with the subject.

Four: Get them to say what you want fast, before they have time to overthink it, or you.

Works every time.

Finally, we recorded a piece to camera in the woods where Rachel died, as close as the cordon would allow, with the police tape fluttering in the background. It was very atmospheric. After popping in a brief clip of Jack speaking at the press conference earlier, we had a two-minute package for me to talk around. Not too shabby for a morning's work.

The sat truck arrived just in time, and now

I'm standing at the closest and best position we could find at the edge of the woods. We need a clear view of the sky in order to see one of the satellites and broadcast live. Trees and tall buildings can be problematic in this business. So can ex-husbands.

I'm wired up and ready to go when I see Jack's 4 × 4 pull into the parking lot. He's too late. I stare down the barrel of the camera when I hear the director in my ear, then Cat Jones — sitting in the chair that used to be mine — reads the intro for the story.

"The body of a young woman has been discovered in woods owned by the National Trust in Surrey this morning. Police have now named the victim as Rachel Hopkins, founder of the homeless charity . . ."

Jack steps into my eyeline. If looks could kill, I'd have flatlined.

". . . Our correspondent, Anna Andrews, joins us now with the latest."

I top and tail my package with twenty seconds of memorized words, doing my best to ignore Jack's persistent glares and arm waving. By the time I throw back to the studio, he is standing so close to the camera that he could easily have turned it off or knocked it over. Luckily Richard was in the way. I wait for the all clear, then remove my earpiece.

"Is this thing off?" Jack asks.

"It is now," Richard replies, lifting the camera off the tripod and joining the engineers in the truck.

He didn't need to be asked to leave us alone.

"What the hell do you think you're doing?" Jack says.

"My job."

"What if we hadn't already informed the next of kin?"

"You told me the name of the victim, I reported it."

"You're fully aware that isn't why I told you."

"Why *did* you tell me?" I ask, but he doesn't answer.

He looks over his shoulder at the sat truck, then leans in a little closer, his voice barely more than a whisper.

"Why were you here yesterday?"

"What are you talking about?"

"The parking lot ticket with yesterday's date on. You still haven't explained —"

"Wow, that again. You think *I* had something to do with this?"

"Did you?"

Jack accused me of a few bad things when we were married, and a few more when we

184

weren't, but never murder. It makes me wonder whether he always had a negative view of me, even when we were together. Perhaps he was just better at hiding it then.

"I was presenting a network bulletin to millions of people yesterday, so I have a few alibis who can confirm I wasn't here if you need to check."

"Then how *do* you explain it?"

"I don't know, maybe the machine is broken?"

"Sure. Why not. That's a plausible explanation."

Jack marches over to the pay-and-display machine, then reaches inside his pocket for a coin. I don't realize I'm holding my breath until his hand comes out empty. He looks over his shoulder at me, as though I might offer to give him some spare change. When I don't, he turns his attention back to the meter. I watch the familiar way he strokes the stubble on his chin, a habit that never bothered me when we first got together, but caused unfathomable irritation by the time we parted.

I'm expecting him to walk away without another word, but he stands perfectly still, staring at the ground as though in deep thought. All of a sudden he bends down, brushes some dead leaves away, then picks up a silver-colored coin from the forest floor. He holds it in my direction before putting it in the slot. I can feel my heart thudding in my chest as he stabs the green button with his finger. I have a crazy urge to run but stay exactly where I am.

He snatches the ticket the machine spits out, and stares at it.

Time seems to slow down as I wait for him to turn around or say something, but he doesn't. I don't know what this means.

"Well?" I ask eventually.

"It's yesterday's date; the machine is broken."

"Is that your idea of an apology?"

He turns to face me.

"No. Unlike you, I don't have anything to apologize for. You shouldn't be here. I realized a long time ago that your career means more to you than people do. More than your mother, more than me, more than —"

"Fuck you."

The tears come fast, bursting over the banks of my eyelids. I feel ridiculous for thinking it, given how much I hate him right now, but I want him to hold me. I just wish that *someone* would hold me and tell me that everything is going to be okay. It doesn't have to be true. I'd just like to remember what that feels like.

"You're too close to this. I'm not sure it's right for you to be reporting on this murder."

"I'm not sure it's right for you to be trying to solve it," I reply, wiping my tears away with the back of my hand.

"Why don't you just do us both a favor, and go back to London? Sit in that studio, like you always dreamed of?"

"I lost my job presenting the program."

I don't know why I tell him; I didn't plan to. Perhaps I just needed to tell one person the truth about what has happened, but I regret it immediately. The brave face I have been wearing slips, and I hate the way he is looking at me now. I prefer wonder to pity. People who get to know the real me are the ones I need to learn to hide from the most.

"I'm sorry to hear that. I know how much the job meant to you," he says, and his words sound genuine.

"How's Zoe?" I ask, unable to hide my resentment.

His face resets itself. The woman my ex-husband now lives with was also an old school friend of mine, just like Rachel Hopkins. I've seen pictures of Zoe and Jack playing happy families on social media, although I wish I hadn't. She posts them, not him. The little girl posing between them a constant reminder of who we used to be, and who we could have been if life had unfolded differently.

"I hope you're all very happy together."

My words sound insincere, even though I meant them.

"Why do you always do that? You talk about Zoe as though she's some woman I left you for. She's my sister, Anna."

"She's a selfish, lazy, manipulative bitch, who caused nothing but problems before, during, and after our marriage."

I'm as surprised by my outburst as he looks.

"You haven't changed at all, despite everything, have you?" he says. "You can't keep blaming everyone else for what happened to *us*. Maybe if you'd ever worried about *us,* as much as you worry about what other people think, your work and all *this,* things wouldn't have turned out the way they did —"

I lift my hands, as though to cover my ears before he can say our daughter's name, but he grabs my wrist and stares at it.

"What is that?"

I look at the twisted plait of red and white. I've been so busy I forgot I was wearing the friendship bracelet I found earlier. I try to shrug him off but he tightens his grip.

"Where did you get this from?" he asks, his voice no longer hushed.

"What is it to you?"

He lets go and takes a small step back before asking his next question.

"When did you last see Rachel?"

"Why? Am I a suspect again?"

He doesn't answer and I dislike the way he is looking at me now even more than before.

"I haven't seen Rachel Hopkins since I left school," I tell him.

But it's a lie. I saw her much more recently than that. I watched her get off a train less than twenty-four hours ago.

HIM

I know that Anna is lying.

The drive back to the station is a blur, trying to piece together the parts of the puzzle that don't fit. I still haven't eaten anything today. The fingernails inside the Tic Tac box, along with the visit to the mortuary, have successfully put me off food for the foreseeable future. I'm already halfway through my packet of cigarettes, and while they help calm my nerves, they do nothing to ease my guilt.

I can't stop thinking about the friendship bracelet on Anna's wrist, the look on her face when I asked her about it, or the way she refused to explain where it had come from. It was exactly the same as the one tied around Rachel's tongue.

Anna is lying about something, I can tell. But then so am I.

Her cameraman resurfaced before we had

190

a proper chance to talk. I can't put my finger on it, but there's something a tad off about him, too. I don't like the way he looks at her, not that I've got any right to feel that way anymore. It's easy to recognize people with bad intentions when you know what it is like to be one.

My afternoon mostly consists of dealing with media inquiries and false leads, instead of being allowed to get on with my job. The press has been harassing almost every member of the team. It reminds me of being back in London, and the first time Anna shoved a microphone in my face. That's how we met: she was covering a case that I was working on. It was hate at first sight but that changed. She didn't remember me from her school days, but I always remembered her.

I work until late and feel mildly irritated, if not at all surprised, when Priya decides to stay too, even though I told her not to. When the rest of the team have left the office, she orders us a pizza. I listen to her on the phone as she chooses *my* favorite toppings and sides, wondering how she knows what they are. Whenever she looks in my direction I stare at my computer screen. The rest of the time, I watch her.

I notice that she has taken off her jacket,

and appears to have undone the top three buttons of her shirt; her collarbone and a hint of her breasts are now visible. Not that I care. Her hair is down, released from what I thought was a permanent ponytail. She looks quite different like this. Less . . . irritating.

We eat in silence. Priya barely touches the pizza, and I can't help thinking she only ordered it for me. She fetches us both a drink from the watercooler — without asking if I want one — then stands a little too close to my desk when she puts it down. I can smell her unfamiliar perfume as she rests her little hand on my shoulder.

"Are you okay, Jack?" she asks, dropping her usual "sir" or "boss."

If her body language means what I think it might then I'm flattered, but am not remotely interested in a junior colleague with daddy issues or whatever this is. Besides, all I can seem to think about right now is Anna, and how good our life together used to be before it got broken. I don't want to stay here. I don't particularly want to go home either, to face all the questions I know I won't want to answer. But, as it is approaching midnight, I figure this is probably a good time to leave work.

"I'm tired, you must be too," I say, standing rather awkwardly.

I never had much luck with the opposite sex as a boy or as a young man. It's only in the last few years that women seem to find me attractive. I'm middle-aged with gray hair and more baggage than Heathrow Airport; I don't understand it. Although I do like the idea — who wouldn't — when I think a woman is flirting with me, I still revert to being an awkward teenage version of myself. The one who doesn't know how to talk to girls.

"I'm going to head off. So should you. Separately," I add, to avoid any confusion.

Priya frowns. Her cheeks flush a little and she returns to her desk.

"I'm going to stay a bit longer. Goodnight, sir," she says with a polite smile, while staring at her screen.

In trying to defuse the situation I fear I may have made it worse.

Sometimes I think people change their expressions just to give their faces something to do. A smile doesn't mean someone is happy, just like tears don't always mean someone is sad. Our faces lie just as often as our words do.

On the way home, I see that there is a light on in St. Hilary's. It's the school that Rachel and Anna went to when they were teenagers. It was where they met. It's late, nobody should be there at this time of night, but someone clearly is.

I drive into the parking lot, but decide to have another cigarette before going inside the school. Just half should sort me out, so I snap it in two. I flick my lighter a couple of times but it doesn't work. I shake it and try once more, but it still refuses to ignite. I scan the various nooks and crannies in the car. I don't really want to look in the glove compartment again; I haven't forgotten what's in there.

I find relief in the shape of an old match-book inside the armrest instead. I light up and take a long drag, enjoying the instant head rush. Then I flip the matches over, and see that they are from the hotel where I first spent the night with Rachel. It was months ago now, but I still remember every detail: the smell of her hair, the look on her face, the shape of her neck. The way she took pleasure from pretending to be powerless, and letting me think I was in control. I wasn't. There are two words written on the back of the matches: *Call me.* Along with her number.

The sight of her handwriting seems to push me over the edge I've been teetering on all day. I chain-smoke for a while, simultaneously longing for a drink. I don't even care about whoever is in the school anymore. When I've smoked my third full-length cigarette in a row, right down to the butt, I look back up at the building and it is in complete darkness. Maybe I imagined seeing the lights on and the shadow of someone standing in the window.

The matchbook with Rachel's handwriting scrawled across it catches my eye again. The idea of hearing her voice, one last time, brings a strange sense of comfort. So, I dial her number. I hear a phone start to ring, but it isn't on the other end of the line, it's in my car.

I turn so fast, I'm amazed I don't get whiplash, but the backseat is completely empty. I get out, still holding the phone to my ear, and walk to the back of the 4 × 4. Then I stare down at the trunk where the ringing appears to be coming from.

I look around, but the school parking lot is unsurprisingly empty at this time of night, so I open the trunk. My eyes find the phone immediately. Its ghoulish glow in the dark illuminates two other unexpected objects. When I lean in a little closer, I can see that they are Rachel's missing shoes: expensive designer heels caked in mud.

I don't understand what I'm seeing.

I feel dizzy and strange and sick.

I think I might throw up, but then the phone clicks to voicemail and I hear her voice:

"Hi, this is Rachel. No one answers phone calls anymore, so send me a text."

I hang up and slam the trunk closed.

My hands start to shake a little when I remember all the missed calls from her last night, and the messages she left on my mobile that I have since deleted. I have to make sure nobody finds out. If they do it will be impossible to deny being with her, or what happened. I genuinely have no idea what Rachel's phone or shoes are doing in my car, but I know I didn't put them there. Surely I'd remember if I had.

I remember to keep an eye on the main cast of the drama I have created. It's informative, educational, and entertaining, which I'm sure used to be the remit of the BBC before those in charge forgot . . . I made it a habit not to forget anything or anyone, especially people who have wronged me. What I lack in forgiveness I make up for in patience. And I pay attention to the little things, because they are often the biggest clues to who a person really is. People rarely see themselves the way others do; we all carry broken mirrors.

There are several characters in this story, each with their own perspective of what has happened. I can only give you my own and guess at the others. Like all stories, it will come to an end. I have a plan now, one which I intend to stick to, and so far I think it is going rather well. Nobody knows it was me. Even if they did suspect something, I'm reasonably confident they could never prove it.

I had an imaginary friend when I was a child, just like a lot of lonely children. He was called Harry and I would pretend to have conversations with him. I even did a funny voice for his replies. My family thought it was hilarious, but in my mind, Harry was real. It was as though I was him and he was me. Whenever I did something wrong, I blamed Harry instead. Sometimes I insisted that he was guilty for so long, even I believed it.

I've almost tricked myself into believing I didn't kill Rachel a few times now, pretended that it was someone else, or that I imagined it. But I did kill her and I'm glad. There was nothing good about that woman, nothing real anyway. She was a serpent in sheep's clothing and I should have known better; people who charm snakes often get bitten.

It wasn't that she didn't know the difference between right and wrong, Rachel simply redefined them to suit her own needs. Doing something wrong was often the only thing that made her feel right.

Not all broken moral compasses are beyond repair. Some can start to work again with an ethical shake from another person. We all travel alone inside our own heads, but it is possible to navigate someone's intentions north of bad and south of wrong. People can change, they just tend to choose not to.

I've read that some killers want to get caught, but not me. There would be no more fun if the game were over, and although I've lost a lot, I still have too much to lose. All I want is for people to get what's coming to them. I don't even think of myself as a killer really; I'm just a person who has decided to do a public service for the benefit of others. The official power of the police can be rather limited and disappointing, and it was better to take this matter into my own hands.

It's taken me a long time, but I understand now where and why and when things went wrong for me. It all leads back to here, to this place, and to the people who did something they shouldn't have. It is time for me to move on now, and finish what I started.

HER

Tuesday 22:30

I don't think I've ever really moved on since Jack left.

For me, the benefits of being alone outweigh the pain of it. Plus, I think it's what I deserve. The sting of loneliness is only ever temporary, like that of a nettle. If you don't scratch at the solitude, it starts to feel normal again soon enough. But I still think about him, and us, and her. Some memories refuse to be forgotten.

I think about Jack all afternoon and all night, despite the steady stream of live interviews for various BBC outlets: the News Channel, Radio 4, Five Live, the Six, everything from BBC London to BBC World. By the time I wrap up my final two-way on the *Ten O'Clock News,* we are no longer the only ones broadcasting from the woods. Sky, ITN, and CNN are here too, each with their own team and satellite

200

trucks. They might all have the story now, but I was the one who broke it. I knew the identity of the victim before anyone else, even if nobody knows how.

Given it's so late, and the ridiculously early time they want us to start doing lives on *BBC Breakfast* tomorrow morning, the overnight news editor offers to pay for a hotel for Richard and me. The engineers will head back to London, to be replaced by the early team tomorrow, but I think it makes sense for us to stay down here, rather than drive back to the city only to have to return a few hours later. We'll get more sleep this way, and be close by should there be any further developments. Richard agrees.

I didn't need to ask what hotel we had been booked into; there is only one, and I know it well. The White Hart is more of a pub really, with some rooms upstairs. The only other accommodation in the village are a couple of cute B&Bs, or my old bedroom at my mother's house. That isn't somewhere I want to go.

We're too late for food — the restaurant is long closed — but Richard suggests getting a drink in the bar before last orders. Against my better judgment, I say yes. A bottle of Malbec and two packets of salt-and-vinegar chips later, I can feel myself start to relax, and I'm glad. Sometimes colleagues are like old friends, the kind you can not see for a few months and then pick up right where you left off.

"Fancy another?" I ask, taking out my purse.

Richard smiles. His jokes and easy conversation have made me feel young again tonight, as though I might still be someone fun to hang out with. It's a shame he dresses in retro clothes and refuses to cut his hair. I think there is a man hiding inside the boy he pretends to be.

"Tempting," he says. "But we have a very early start, *and* the bar is closed now."

I look behind me and see that he's right. Most of the lights have been dimmed already, and it would appear that the staff have left us to it.

"Shame," I say, sliding my hand across the table until it is almost touching his. "Could always check out the minibar in my room?"

He moves his hand away and holds it up, pointing at the ring on his finger.

"Married, remember?"

The rejection smarts a little, and I say something I already know I'm going to regret.

"It never bothered you before."

His face stretches into a polite and apologetic smile, which only makes me feel worse. "That was different. We have the kids now, it changes things. It changed us," he says.

Being patronized stings far more than being rejected, and he's telling me something I already know. Having a child changed things for me too, until I lost her. I never talk about what happened with people at work, or anyone else really.

I was on attachment to the Arts and Entertainment unit when I was pregnant — a department that lives on the top floor of the BBC — so most people in the newsroom rarely saw me. And if they did, I honestly think they just thought I had put on weight. There were complications that meant I was at home, confined to weeks of bed rest for the final few months. So a lot of people didn't know I was pregnant in the first place. Or that my daughter died three months after she was born.

I wonder if Richard knows. I conclude that he doesn't when he picks up his phone and starts scrolling through endless pictures of two pretty little blond girls. He seems eager to share what he thinks I'm missing out on.

"They're beautiful," I say, and mean it.

His smile widens. "They take after their mother in the looks department."

I feel winded again. I can't remember Richard ever mentioning his wife before, not that I didn't know he was married. And not that there is anything wrong with a man loving his wife and children. I suppose having a family does push some couples closer together, instead of pulling them apart. Right now, this all just feels like another reminder of what I don't have.

"Well, goodnight," I say, standing to leave. "For the record, a drink was all that was on offer."

I manage a smile and he does too. Never good to leave things feeling awkward with a colleague, especially someone who gets to decide whether you look good or bad on-screen to an audience of millions.

I raid the excuse of a minibar alone when I get back to my room. It doesn't have the biggest or best selection of nightcaps, but it will have to do. Then I sit on the bed, eating overpriced chocolate bars and drinking miniatures while wondering how I got here. Forty-eight hours ago, I was a BBC News anchor. My private life may have been in tatters but at least I still had my career. Now, I'm literally back where I started, in the village I grew up in, reporting on the murder of a girl I knew at school. A girl who hurt me, and who turned into a woman

204

who tried to hurt me again, years after the night that ended our fragile friendship for good.

Rachel called me out of the blue quite recently; I still don't even understand how she got my number. She said that her charity was in trouble, and asked if I would host an event to help. When I said no — suspecting that if the charity *was* in trouble, it was most likely the result of her being in charge — she turned up at the BBC. She sat in main reception waiting for me, then hinted that she had something that would damage my career if people ever saw it.

I still said no.

I go to get myself another drink, but the minibar is already empty, so I decide to get ready for bed. I need to be on-air again in a few hours; best to get some sleep if I can.

I take a shower. Sometimes, on stories like these, it can feel as though the stench of death gets on your skin and in your hair. I need to wash it all way, with water so hot, it burns. I don't know how long I am in the bathroom, but when I come out, the empty bottles and chocolate bar wrappers have been put in the bin, and the bed covers have been pulled back, ready for me to get into.

It's strange, because I genuinely don't remember doing it, and this isn't the kind of hotel to have a turn-down service.

I must be more drunk than I thought.

I climb beneath the sheets and turn off the lights, blacking out almost as soon as my head hits the pillow.

Him

The house is in complete darkness when I pull into the drive and I'm glad; the last thing I need after a day like today is to have to face an interrogation when I get home. I open the front door as quietly as I can, careful not to wake anyone, but it soon becomes apparent that I needn't have bothered. The lights might be off, but the TV is on, and when I walk into the living room I find Zoe watching my ex-wife on the news. I drove past the woods on the way home, and the media had all packed up and left for the night, so I know it isn't live. It's just a rerun of her earlier package, but it still feels strange seeing Anna in my home.

"What the fuck is happening?" Zoe asks, without looking up.

She's been texting and calling all day, but I didn't have the time or inclination to get back to her.

"If you've been watching that, then I expect you already know," I say, unable to stop myself from sighing.

"One of my *best* friends gets murdered, and you didn't think to tell me about it?"

"You haven't been friends with Rachel Hopkins since you left school. It must be twenty years since you even spoke to her." Zoe's face twists into a rather ugly pattern of fury and hurt, but I'm not in the mood for one of her tantrums tonight. "Not everything is about you, Zoe. I've had a really long day, and you know I can't talk about my job, so please don't ask."

I've never wanted to pollute her world with my problems.

"You're wrong about that. Rachel and I spoke quite recently," she says, turning off the TV. Then she looks me up and down, as though making a formal assessment and reaching a negative conclusion. "Why is your ex-wife *here*, reporting on the murder of your latest girlfriend?"

I'm too shocked to find a suitable response, because I had no idea that she knew I was sleeping with Rachel. I thought *nobody* knew. I consider the possibility that she might not know for sure.

"I don't know what you mean —"

"Cut the crap, Jack. I know you've been

banging her for the last couple of months, though god knows why, of all the people! Were you with her last night?"

I don't answer.

"Well, were you?"

"You're not my wife, Zoe. And you're not my mother."

"No, I'm your sister, and I'm asking you if you were with Rachel last night?"

"Are you asking me if I had something to do with this?"

She shakes her head and starts to re-arrange the fake fur cushions on the sofa, something she always does when she is most upset. She makes them herself — the cushion covers — and sells them online. It's a far cry from the fashion design job she dreamed of when we were young.

I notice that she's dyed her hair bright red again, probably one those DIY box kits she likes so much. She's missed a bit of blond hair at the back; last month's chosen shade. Her pink pajamas would look more appropriate on my two-year-old niece upstairs than her thirty-six-year-old mother, but I keep my opinions to myself.

"When I said you could move in with us for a while after the divorce, I meant for a couple of weeks, not a couple of years . . ." she says, without looking up.

"And then how would you have paid the mortgage?"

I moved in with my sister when I moved out of the London apartment I shared with Anna. This used to be our parents' house before they died, and I feel like I have as much right to be here as Zoe. Firstly, she didn't have a clue about inheritance tax, which meant re-mortgaging the house in order to keep it. Secondly, our parents died rather unexpectedly. To my dismay, and Zoe's surprise, there was no will. Although our parents were highly organized in life, their death was not planned for at all. At least not by them.

The only reason I went along with my sister treating the house as though it were hers was because she had a daughter. They needed a place to call home more than I did, and besides, I never had any real desire to come back to this town then. Like my ex, I would rather leave the past where it belongs.

Zoe barges by me and storms out of the room. She doesn't look, or smell, like she washed or dressed today. Again. My sister doesn't have a real job. She says she can't find one, but that might be because she hasn't bothered looking for ten years. She relies on cushion covers, benefits, and selling our dead parents' belongings on eBay — which she thinks I don't know about — and insists that being a parent is a full-time job, even though she acts like a part-time mother.

I follow her into the kitchen. Then I watch while she takes longer than could ever be necessary to wash up a single cup in the sink. I notice that everything is spotlessly clean — something Zoe rarely does whether she is upset or not — and put away in its proper place, except for one knife from the stainless-steel block on the counter. I noticed it was missing this morning too.

"How did you know about Rachel?" I ask.

Zoe still has her back to me, rinsing her wineglass now, as though her life depended on it. I take a clean one from the cupboard, and pour myself a drink from the open bottle of red on the counter. Sadly, my sister has the same taste in wine as she does in men; too cheap, too young, and headache-inducing.

"How did I know that she was dead? Or how did I know that you were sleeping with her?" she asks, finally turning to face me.

I can't look her in the eye, but I manage to nod as I take a sip.

"I'm your sister. I know you. You kept saying you were working late, but Blackdown isn't exactly crime central. Or at least, it wasn't. Then I saw her in the supermarket one day last week, and she started a conversation. Like you said, she hasn't said hello to me for almost twenty years so . . ."

"So, you automatically thought she must be screwing your brother?"

She raises a penciled-in eyebrow. Zoe always wears full makeup, regardless of whether she gets washed or dressed or leaves the house.

"Not at first, but she wore a very distinctive perfume, and you came home smelling of it that night, after 'working late,' so . . ."

She makes air quotes with her hands, something she has been doing since we were children. It has only grown more irritating over time.

"Why didn't you say something?" I ask.

"Because it was none of my business. I don't tell you who *I'm* sleeping with."

She doesn't need to; this house has thin walls.

"*You're* sleeping with someone?" I say, but she ignores me.

The question was meant to be ironic. Zoe is always sleeping with someone, and has a rather casual attitude to sex. She's never told me who her daughter's father is, I suspect because she doesn't know.

"I thought you'd probably tell me yourself when you were ready. Besides, I wasn't sure until last night," she says.

"Why last night?"

"Because she called here."

The wineglass almost slips through my fingers.

"What did you just say?"

"Rachel Hopkins called here last night."

It suddenly gets very loud inside my head, even louder than before. I didn't know that Rachel even had this number, but then I guess it has never changed. It's the same one she used to call my sister on when they were school friends. I'm terrified of the answer, but I have to ask the question.

"Did you speak to her?"

"No. I didn't even hear the phone. She left a message around midnight; I only listened to it this morning when I saw the machine flashing."

She walks to the other side of the kitchen, to the ancient answering machine that used to belong to our mum and dad. So many of their things are still here — the things that Zoe hasn't sold, yet — that I honestly sometimes forget that they're dead. Then I remember, and the grief hits me all over again. I wonder if that is normal.

Time became a bit nonlinear inside my

head after they died. Bad things just kept on happening. Not just the death of my daughter and the divorce; it was as though any future I had once imagined for myself had decided to unravel. Now it's happening again.

Zoe seems to move in slow motion. I want to tell her to stop, to not press Play on the machine. I don't know if I want to hear Rachel's voice again anymore. Maybe it would be better to remember her the way she was rather than . . .

Zoe presses Play.

"Jack, it's me. Sorry to call the landline, but you're not answering your mobile. Are you on your way? It's getting late and I'm so tired. I know I should be able to change a tire myself; I don't know how it happened, it's almost as though someone slashed it. Hang on, I think I see your headlights coming into the parking lot now. My knight in shining armor!"

Rachel laughs and hangs up.

I stare at the machine as though it were a ghost.

My sister stares at me as if I were a stranger.

"What's that scratch?" she asks.

I feel for the little red scar on my cheek without meaning to. I saw Priya looking at it several times today but, unlike my sister, she was too polite to mention it.

"I cut myself shaving."

Zoe frowns, and I remember the mask of stubble currently hiding my face.

"Was it you?" she asks eventually, in a voice so quiet, I barely hear the question.

I wish I hadn't.

An unexpected montage of us as children silently plays inside my head. From me as a toddler pushing my baby sister on a swing, to birthday parties with our friends, to all the shared Christmases with our family. Only last week I was pushing her daughter, my niece, on the same swing hanging from the weeping willow in the back garden. There used to be a lot of love in this house. I'm not sure when or where it went.

"How can you ask me that?"

I stare at her, but Zoe's eyes refuse to meet mine. I feel my heart thudding inside my chest; irregular palpitations caused by hurt, not anger. I always thought my sister would stand by me through *anything*. The idea that I was wrong about that isn't like a slap in the face, it's more like being repeatedly run over by a truck.

"I have a child sleeping upstairs, I had to ask," she whispers.

"No, you didn't."

We stare at each other for a long time, having the kind of silent conversation that only close siblings can have. I know I need to say something out loud, but it takes a while to arrange the words in the right order.

"I did see Rachel last night."

"In the woods?"

"Yes." Zoe pulls a face I choose to ignore. "But then I left. I didn't know there was anything wrong until I saw the missed calls on my phone when I got home. I drove back to help, but her car was gone and so was she. I called her mobile, but she didn't answer, so I just presumed she'd managed to fix it."

"Does anyone else know that you were there?"

"No."

"You didn't tell your police colleagues."

I shake my head. "No."

She stares at me for a long time, before asking her next question.

"Why didn't you tell them?"

"Because they would look at me the way you are now."

"I'm sorry," she says eventually. "I had to ask, but I do believe you."

"Okay," I say, even though it isn't and I'm not.

"I know we don't ever say it, but I do love you."

"I love you too," I reply.

When she leaves the room, I cry for the first time since my daughter died.

Losing someone you truly love always feels like losing a part of yourself. Not Rachel — that was lust — I mean my sister. We might not have always been close — she never approved of my choice of wife, and I never approved of her choice of, well, anything — but I always thought she'd be the one to unplug the fan if the shit ever hit. I guess I was wrong, because it feels like something got broken between Zoe and me tonight. Something that can't be fixed.

I sit alone in the semi-dark for a while, finishing the wine she probably left here deliberately, knowing that I would need it. When the bottle is empty and the house is silent again, I walk back over to the answering machine. Then I delete the message.

Sometimes it feels like I don't know who I am anymore.

HER

I wake up covered in sweat and not knowing where or when I am.

The first thing that comes to the surface is her, my little girl. It is always the same.

Then I remember the hotel, and the drinks — before and after my embarrassing encounter with Richard — and I squeeze my eyes shut. As though if I keep them closed for long enough, it might be possible to delete all of my memories.

I was having a nightmare before I woke up.

I was running through the woods, and I was scared of something or someone that was chasing me. I fell, and as I was lying in the dirt, someone came into view then stood towering over my body, holding a knife. I was screaming for help in the dream, and now my throat hurts, as though I might have been screaming in real life.

218

I'm probably just dehydrated. I'd give anything for a soft drink right about now. I turn on the lights and am surprised to see a bottle of still mineral water by the bed. I don't remember putting it there, but I silently thank my past self for being so thoughtful. I twist off the cap and gulp down the chilled liquid, so cold it is as though it has just been taken out of the fridge.

I check my phone and see that it was a text from Jack that woke me. For some reason it makes me feel better to know that he is having trouble sleeping too. It's not sweet, but it is short, just four of his favorite words arranged in a familiar order:

We need to talk.

Not at four in the morning we don't.

I climb out of the bed and creep over to the minibar, in search of a little something to help me get back to sleep. I fear I might have emptied it completely before I passed out, but gasp when I see that it is actually fully stocked. I look in the bin, but it is empty. I was sure I had sat on the bed eating snacks and drinking alone last night, but that must also have been a dream.

I open a miniature bottle of scotch and knock it back, then I notice the photo on the desk, the one that I found in the jewelry box at my mother's house yesterday. We're all there. Five young teenage friends the night before it happened, some of us with no knowledge of what was to come. I've spent so many years trying to forget these girls and now, once again, they are all that I can think about. I remember when we first met.

The grammar school was my mother's idea. I used to be cleverer back then — before all the alcohol drowned my brain cells — too clever for my own good, she used to say. Without my father, there was simply no way to pay private school fees. I had to finish my education somewhere, and she thought that St. Hilary's would be the next best fit.

It wasn't.

The all-girls school was a twenty-minute walk from our house, but Mum insisted on driving me there on my first day — probably to make sure I went in — and pulled up right outside the gates. She'd bought an old white van, and had her brand-new company name stenciled on the side: *Busy Bees Professional Cleaning Services.* It was like a tin can on wheels.

I could see people staring at us, and it, as though it were an ancient relic that belonged in a museum, not on the road. I didn't want to get out of the van, or go into St. Hilary's, but I didn't want to let my mother down either. I knew she had sweet-talked my way into the school mid-term.

Mum was the headmistress's cleaner — she seemed to be cleaning for half the village by then — and I think she persuaded the woman to take pity on me and us. I was getting used to her calling in little favors here and there. Cleaning for influential people and local businesses had its benefits, including free bread from the bakers, and just-past-their-prime flowers from the florist. She always did whatever she needed to do, to pay the bills and keep a roof over our heads. I tried to look happy and grateful about it as I stared up at the imposing brick building, but my first impressions were that the school looked like a Victorian asylum, with its ancient-looking sign above the main door, its name carved into the stone:

ST. HILARY'S HIGH SCHOOL FOR GIRLS

When I didn't get out of the van, my mother tried a few words of encouragement.

"It's never easy being the new girl, no matter how old you are. Just be yourself."

This seemed like terrible advice to me then, just as it is now. I want people to like me, so being *myself* is never an option.

I still didn't open the van door. I remember looking up at that school, as though it were a prison I might never be allowed to leave. I wasn't far wrong. There are some self-inflicted life sentences. We all carry prisons of regret inside our heads, unable to break free of the guilt and pain they cause us.

There was a knock, followed by a smiling face peering inside the van window. My mother leaned across me to wind it down. The girl was dressed in the same uniform I was wearing, except that hers looked new. Like the rest of my clothes, mine was secondhand. My shoes were new, but they were also a size too big. Mum always bought them like that, so I could grow into them, and stuffed cotton wool in the ends to stop my toes from slipping around.

The girl standing outside the car was slim and very pretty. We were the same age, but she looked considerably older than fifteen. She had highlights in her hair; long golden strands of it shone in the morning sunlight. Her dimpled smile made you want to be as happy and kind as she looked. That was the first thing that I thought about Rachel Hopkins: that she looked like a nice person.

"Hello, Rachel. How lovely to see you," said my mother.

I was starting to think that there was

nobody left in the village that she didn't know.

"Hello, Mrs. Andrews. You must be Anna?" said the beautiful stranger.

I nodded.

"First day today, right?"

I nodded again, as though I had forgotten how to speak.

"I think we're in the same class. Want to come with me? I can show you around and introduce you to everyone?"

I remember that I did want to do that, very much. She seemed so nice that I think I might have followed her anywhere. My mother leaned over to kiss me, but I got out of the van before she could — I have never been comfortable with public displays of affection — and she drove away before either of us had a chance to say a proper good-bye. I didn't have to ask how Rachel knew my mother; I had guessed already that Mum probably cleaned her house too.

Rachel talked. A lot. Mostly about herself, but I didn't mind. I was just grateful not to have to walk into that building on my own. She led me to a classroom that was already full and loud with teenagers. A hush fell over them when we stepped inside, and I wasn't sure whether that was for her or for me, but the chatter soon resumed and I

223

tried not to feel too self-conscious.

Rachel marched over to a group of girls, with a swagger only the most popular people know how to perform. They were sitting by the antique-looking radiators — that school was always cold in more ways than one — and she didn't hesitate to interrupt her classmates in order to introduce me.

"Anna, this is everyone you need to know. My name is Rachel Hopkins and I am your new best friend. This is Helen Wang, she is the clever one and edits the school newspaper, and this is Zoe Harper, she is the funny one, who likes to make her own clothes and get random parts of her body pierced to annoy her parents."

Zoe tucked her strawberry blond hair — which did not look natural — behind her pierced ears. Then she raised her shirt high enough to display a pierced belly button, as though that were her idea of a greeting. I soon discovered just how good Zoe was with a sewing machine; half the school had paid her to take up the hems of their skirts.

Helen, "the clever one," had Cleopatra-style black hair, and cheekbones so defined they looked like they hurt her face. She quickly lost interest in me, and went back to what she had been doing — stapling sheets of pink A4 paper, to make them into what I would later learn was the school newspaper. She was using her full weight to push down on the stapler, and the sound of it repeatedly firing seemed to rattle my remaining nerves. It made me think of a gun.

Rachel reached inside her bag and produced a Kodak disposable camera. I'd never seen one before, but soon discovered that it required film and patience. There were no such things as digital cameras in those days — we didn't even have mobile phones. The whole camera had to be sent off to be developed, which could take days, in order to see a single picture taken on it.

I always remember the sound it made when Rachel took a photo of me.

Clickety-click. Clickety-click. Clickety-click.

She had to wind the film on afterward, every time, and the little gray plastic wheel would make a sound, as well as leave a mark on the skin of her thumb.

"Take a picture of me and the new girl on her first day," Rachel said, smiling that pretty smile before giving the camera to Helen, who looked a little cross about having to pause her stapling.

Rachel posed with her arm around me. I blinked when the flash went off, so two pictures were taken in case I ruined the first.

"This way we'll have a before and after," Rachel said, snatching the camera from Helen and putting it back inside her bag. I didn't think to ask before or after what. "The rest of them are all losers, especially *her,*" Rachel added, glancing around at the rest of the class. I turned to see a girl sitting alone at her desk reading a book. "That's Catherine Kelly, odd as you like and best avoided. Stick with us and you'll be okay, kid."

I stared at the lonely-looking girl, with hair and eyebrows so blond, they were almost white. Her skin was also unusually pale, making her look like an apprentice albino. I couldn't help but notice the ugly braces on her teeth, as she chomped away on a chocolate bar for breakfast. Her clothes were creased and covered in stains. Like the girl wearing them, they looked in need of a wash. As soon as she finished eating one chocolate bar, she opened the lid of her desk and took out another, tearing the wrapping as though she were famished. She was a skinny little thing, despite the snacks. Her big eyes reminded me of Bambi, munching on fresh grass, completely clueless that the hunters were watching. Deciding to stay away from her was not a problem. It was deciding *not* to that would result in disaster, but I didn't know that at the time.

All I wanted to do for so long was to leave Blackdown and never return. Looking around the hotel bedroom now, I don't understand how I have ended up back here. I take one last look at the photo of five girls, whose lives were changed forever not long after it was taken, then I flip it upside down and put it back on the desk. I don't want to look at their faces anymore.

I go to the bathroom, wash my hands as though the memories have made them feel dirty, then splash some cold water on my face. When I come back out into the bedroom, the photo catches my eye again. It is faceup, even though I could have sworn I turned it over. And that isn't all. Someone has used a pen to mark a black cross over Rachel's face.

HIM

The race to sleep is beaten by the sound of my phone ringing, rather than the alarm.

It's Priya, again, and I have to tell her to slow down. My head hurts from the cheap red wine, and she's speaking too fast for my brain to process what she is saying. I've slept in my clothes, lying on top of the bed in the room that was mine as a boy. I am so cold my hands struggle to hold the phone to my ear. I don't understand at first, but then I can see that the window is open where I had a cigarette late last night. If Zoe finds out I smoked in the house — with my niece sleeping in the room next door — she'll kill me.

I remember how good it felt at the time, not just the rush from the nicotine, but the natural high from doing something wrong and thinking I'd gotten away with it. I also remember that feeling disappearing when I

228

sensed I was being watched from the street below. It was so dark outside that someone could easily have been staring right up at me from the shadows, and I'd never have known. I try to forget about last night, but when I sit up my head hurts even more, and I know I need coffee.

I make Priya repeat her final words, just to be sure I've understood them, and she says it again.

"A second body has been found in Blackdown."

I try to formulate a response, but nothing comes.

"Did you hear me, boss?" she asks, and I realize I still haven't said anything.

"Where was the body found?"

My voice sounds strange when I finally remember how to use it.

"St. Hilary's. The girls' grammar school," she says.

I take a moment to think. I want to smoke, but I only have one cigarette left after last night, and it feels like I should probably save it.

"Did you say the girls' school?"

"Yes, sir."

My mind races my reactions. Two murders within two days, *here,* suggests we might be dealing with a serial killer. The bosses will be all over it once they know, like flies on fresh shit.

"I'm on my way."

I shower quickly and quietly then head downstairs, trying not to wake anyone. I needn't have bothered. Zoe is already up, fully dressed for a change, and in the kitchen. She's watching the *BBC Breakfast* program.

"Want some?" she asks, sliding a pot of coffee in my direction, without looking away from the screen.

"No, I've got to go."

"Random question before you do, have you seen the nail clippers? They seem to have disappeared from the bathroom and I need them," she says.

My mind flashes to the Tic Tac box, and I stare at Zoe for a long time without answering.

"What?" she asks.

"Nothing. No, I haven't seen them. Speaking of missing things, have you seen my Timberland boots?"

"Yes. They were by the back door yesterday, covered in mud."

My blood seems to chill in my veins.

"Well they're not there now," I reply.

"And I'm not your mother; find them yourself. Why the rush to leave so early?"

"Work stuff."

"Because they've found another body?"

I stare at Zoe again, taking in the fact that she is fully dressed, the way her cheeks look rosy — like they do when she has been for a rare run — and how her car keys are on the kitchen table, as if she has just come back from somewhere. It's six in the morning, and I can't think of anywhere in Blackdown that is open at this time of day.

"How do you know they found another body?" I ask.

"Because I'm the murderer."

She doesn't smile and neither do I. Zoe has always had a warped sense of humor, but a tiny part of me wonders if that's all this is. I've never known the real reason she fell out with Rachel Hopkins or the other girls she went to school with.

Finally, a corner of her mouth turns upward, and she nods in the direction of the TV.

"Your ex-wife told me."

This answer isn't much better than her first, and makes just as little sense, until I see Anna appear on the screen. She's standing outside the school, and reporting on the second victim, before I've even managed to get to the scene of the crime. There haven't been any press statements yet; the only

231

people who should know anything about a second murder at this stage could be counted on one hand.

"I've got to go," I say again, before heading for the hall and grabbing my jacket from the banister where I always leave it. Something else I do that irritates my little sister. I reach for my Harry Potter scarf, but then decide to do without it.

"Jack, wait up." Zoe follows me. "Be careful today, okay? I know you used to be married, but you shouldn't trust Anna."

"What does that mean?"

"She's more of a journalist than she was ever a wife, so watch what you say. And don't . . . lose your temper with anyone."

"Why would I?"

She shrugs and I open the front door.

"One more thing," she says, and I turn to face her, unable to hide my impatience.

"What?"

"Please don't smoke in the house."

I get in my car, feeling like a chastised child who has been caught out in more ways than one. I drive to the school I was parked outside only last night and, once again, it would appear that the entire Surrey police force has arrived before me.

There is only one TV truck here for now — Anna's — but no sign of her or the BBC team, just an empty van. They must be taking a break. I looked up her cameraman on the system last night. It was unprofessional, but I was right to be suspicious. He's got a record and a past I expect she knows nothing about.

Priya is waiting to meet me in the school reception, and hands me a coffee and a croissant. Her hair is tied up in a ponytail again, but her face looks different.

"I'm not wearing my glasses," she says, as though reading my thoughts.

"If you didn't want to see another dead body so soon, you just had to say."

"I can see fine, thanks, sir. I thought I'd try contact lenses."

Seems like an odd time to experiment, but women have always been a mystery to me.

"Looks good," I say, and she smiles. I instantly worry that I shouldn't have said it — concerned that perhaps paying a female colleague a simple compliment somehow constitutes sexual harassment nowadays — so I take it back. "I meant the coffee," I add, and take a sip.

Priya's smile vanishes and I feel like an asshole. I try to steer us toward a less personal subject.

"Where did you find something that tastes this good, at this time, around here?" I ask, holding up the cup.

"It's from Colombia."

My response skips a beat.

"That's a long way to go."

Her smile returns.

"I made it for you at home before I left this morning; I thought you might need coffee. I have a whole thermos in the car, but I know how you like it in a paper cup — even though that is a little strange *and* bad for the environment — so I ordered some online. Paper cups, I mean. I just poured it when I saw you pulling in, so that it would be hot."

I knew it. She's in love with me. I might be middle-aged, but I've still got it. Not that anything can or will happen. I'll let her down gently when the time is right. I take a bite of the croissant and it's good. I decide not to ask where that came from; she probably baked it herself or had it flown in from France.

My phone rings, revealing my boss's name, and I take longer than I should to answer it.

"Good morning, sir."

Kissing arse always leaves an unpleasant taste on my lips.

I listen while the weasel of a man tells me everything he thinks I've done wrong with the investigation, and bite my tongue so often I'm surprised it doesn't have a hole. He'd never say it to my face. Firstly, I doubt he could find his way out of his office to do so, plus it's hard for him to look down on me in person; I'm considerably taller. The man suffers from stunted growth as well as intellect, but I wait until he has said everything he wants to say, then tell him what he wants to hear. I find this is the fastest approach to get management off my back.

"Yes, sir. Of course," I say, promising to keep him in the loop before hanging up.

Priya looks disappointed.

"What?" I ask.

She shrugs but doesn't answer. Her eyes judge me even if her words don't. I think she overheard what the chief said:

"This is a major fuckup by the Major Crime Team on *your* watch."

Myself and the entire MCT unit all worked eighteen-hour shifts yesterday. They've hardly slept, but something about what he said still stings. For some reason, on some level, it does feel as though all of this might be my fault.

"Shall we?" I ask Priya.

"Yes, sir," she says, returning to her normal, efficient self. A version I'm much more comfortable with.

Priya leads the way through a warren of corridors. I ignore all the colorful posters on the walls, and focus instead on her lace-up shoes as they squeak along the polished floor. The black brogues — which oddly enough resemble school shoes to me — are considerably cleaner than yesterday in the muddy woods, so much so that I can't help wondering whether they are a brand-new pair. Her ponytail swings from side to side as it always does, a hair-shaped pendulum, counting down as we get closer to victim number two. I am in no doubt that the murders are linked.

I keep a couple of steps behind Priya all the way, pretending to follow, but this is a building I am already surprisingly familiar with. I used to get dragged here by my parents all the time, to see my sister perform in school plays. Zoe was never top of her class academically — too much competition for that at a school like this — but she was a terrific actress. Still is. Perhaps it runs in the family. I can no longer pretend to myself that I wasn't here last night, or that I didn't see the light in the window of the office we are headed toward. If I had behaved differently then, this wouldn't be happening now.

When we step into the room, the sight that greets us cannot fail to shock. It's still pitch-black outside, but not in here. The bright police lights make the room seem like a film set, with the victim center stage.

"Can we cover up these windows, please, before the press start posting pictures online?" I say, and several heads turn to stare in my direction.

There are a couple of uniformed officers I know, as well as some I don't, and I'm pleased to see that Forensics have already arrived. It's more or less the same target response team as yesterday, and they all seem a little shell-shocked. Looking at the crime scene, I don't blame them.

"I thought it was best to wait for you, sir," Priya says.

"Fine, well I'm here now."

The school office is more like a miniature library. Bookshelves line the back wall, and there is a huge framed map of the world on another. I see a glass cabinet full of trophies, and a large mahogany desk in the middle of the room. The headmistress is still sitting in her chair behind it, but her throat has been cut and her mouth is stretched into a scream.

Even from the doorway, I can see the foreign object inside her mouth. Just like with Rachel, there is a red-and-white friend-ship bracelet tied around the victim's tongue. Her head has fallen to one side, her black Cleopatra-style bob revealing gray hinges. Her hair hides half her face, but I still know who she is. I expect everyone here does. The head of the girls' grammar school is both well respected and a little feared in the local community.

Helen Wang used to attend St. Hilary's herself as a pupil, and was in the same year as Zoe, Anna, and Rachel. She went from being head girl as a teenager to being headmistress before she was thirty. A high-flying academic with an oversized IQ, and very little patience for people who didn't share her view of the world. I know that she and Rachel were still friends, and it's possible that Helen might have known about our affair. If she did, at least she can't tell anyone about it now.

I don't need a pathologist to tell me that a knife was used to slit her throat, that much is obvious, but those aren't the only visible injuries on the body. The victim's blouse has been undone all the way down to her waist, and the word LIAR has been written across her chest, just above her bra. The letters appear to have been made using a staple gun. There must be over a hundred tiny slivers of silver stuck in her white flesh, spelling the word like metal stitches.

I already feel out of my depth, but nobody else on this team can swim any better. One murder in Blackdown would have been unusual, but two is unprecedented. Even in London, I only worked on an active serial killer case once before. I look around the room, and get the impression that we're all just trying to tread water, waiting for someone to rescue us. But they won't. This is it.

I take a step closer and see the white powder on the tip of the victim's nose.

"Are we really supposed to believe that the headmistress was a cokehead?" I say.

"The substance is being tested," Priya replies.

When my initial examination of the scene is complete, I step outside, walk back along the corridor, and find the exit that leads to the school playing fields. My hands shake a little as I search inside my coat pocket to find my final cigarette. I think I deserve it now.

I was here when it happened.

I must have been.

I feel almost drunk with tiredness, and everything about the last couple of days seems unreal to me, as though it might be nothing more than a bad dream I can't wake up from. When I'm done smoking, I head back inside, and walk straight into Priya.

It's as though she must have been standing there, behind the glass door, watching me. I want to know why, but the sound of a school bell drowns out my question before I can ask it.

"What is that noise?" I say when it stops.

"It's a bell, sir."

"Yes, I'm aware of that. Why is it ringing?" She stares at me as though I might be dangerously stupid, and I feel a shot of bile climb up my throat. "The school *is* closed, isn't it?"

"I think so, sir. I expect people will know by now not to come in, having seen it on the news."

"You *think* so? Are you telling me parents haven't been told not to bring their children here today? What did I tell you, only yesterday, about securing crime scenes?"

She looks down at the floor. I know how badly she wants to impress me, and how upset she feels whenever she gets something wrong, but I can't always let things go.

"It's okay. Just go to the school secretary's office now, and make sure they tell parents and all staff to stay away until further notice — not everybody watches the news — and put a couple of uniforms on the front gates, just in case. Also, if you see that BBC team, ask them to leave the parking lot. They

240

shouldn't be on school property without our say-so. I don't know how they got here so fast, but they can bloody well report from the street like everyone else."

"Sir, I should probably —"

"Can you please just do as I've asked?"

She nods and retreats down the corridor. I step back outside for a moment, I need some more air before I can face going back into that room. Everyone expects me to know what to do, but this is new even for me. Things can get a little dark when the blind lead the blind.

I stare at the school playing fields, which slope down to the woods below. As the crow flies, we are probably less than a mile from the spot where Rachel was killed. When I hear footsteps approaching on the path behind me, I presume it is Priya again.

"Did you get it done?" I ask.

"What do you mean?"

I turn and see Anna. "What are you doing here?"

"Your sidekick sent me around this way to find you."

"Priya? Why would she do that? And how did you get here so fast? There have been no statements to the press as far as I know, and *I* would know because it would be *me* making them."

241

Anna doesn't answer. I glance over my shoulder to check that we are alone and can't be overheard.

"Why were you wearing that cotton bracelet yesterday?" I whisper.

She looks as though she might laugh.

"Why do you keep asking me about that?"

"Where did it come from?"

"It's none of your —"

"I'm telling you this because I still . . ." *love you.* That's what I was about to say. While I know it's true, I also know I can't tell her that. Sometimes love is keeping your feelings to yourself. "I still worry about you" is what I settle on. She smiles, but my irritation levels have already exceeded the recommended daily limit. "I'm serious, Anna."

"You're always serious; it's one of your many flaws."

"I mean it. If you repeat what I'm about to tell you to *anyone* else, or dare to report it —"

"Okay, calm down, I'm listening."

"Good, I hope you are. Both dead women were found with friendship bracelets, just like the one you were wearing, but inside their mouths. Tied around their tongues."

She turns visibly pale, and I'm glad the information has caused some kind of emotional response. I would have been deeply troubled if it hadn't. I don't like feeling as though I didn't really know the woman I was married to for all those years.

"So why do you have one?" I ask, hoping to get an answer this time.

"I don't, I've lost it." It sounds like a lie, but she looks like she is telling the truth. "You sent me a text in the middle of the night saying you wanted to talk, was that why —"

I'd forgotten I had drunk-texted her.

"It was early this morning, hardly the middle of the night, and this really doesn't seem like the time or place. You haven't answered my questions. Any of them —"

"Why did you text me, Jack?"

She looks toward the doors leading inside the school — still thinking about the story first, I see — and I steer her away.

"I really don't have time for this right now, in case you can't tell. I just wanted to say that I wouldn't get too close to your colleague if I were you."

She stares at me, her mouth forming a perfect little *O*.

"Just so I understand this, you're dealing with a double murder, but what you're really worried about is me sleeping with my cameraman?"

"I don't care who you sleep with, but he has a criminal record and I thought you should know —"

"You had no right to look Richard up. It's completely unethical. And if I *were* sleeping with him, which I'm not, then I really wouldn't care if he had an unpaid speeding ticket, or whatever other trivial nonsense you've managed to dig up —"

"It wasn't trivial. He was arrested and charged with GBH."

"Grievous bodily harm? Richard assaulted someone?"

"Yes. Now, I have work to do, and you need to go back the way you came and remove yourself, and your team, from school property."

Priya walks through the doors toward us then, blocking my escape route.

"The school is officially closed," she says.

"Great, and you thought it would be a good idea to let a member of the press back here because?"

Priya looks from me to Anna then back again, confusion drawn all over her face in a series of lines that don't belong there.

"Well, I thought you'd want to see her."

"Why would you think that?"

"Because Ms. Andrews was the one who found the body."

Like most things in life, the more you do something, the easier it gets. The same rules apply to killing people, and the second murder was far less tricky than the first. All I had to do was be patient, and that's something I'm rather good at.

Helen Wang loved power more than people, and that was her downfall. She was a smart cookie, but a lonely one too, often working late at the school when the rest of the teachers had long since departed for the day. I slipped into her office when she popped out, hid behind the curtains, and waited. My feet were sticking out underneath, but she didn't notice. Some people use a filter on life as well as photos, which allows them to only see what they want to. When Helen walked back in, she sat down at her desk, and stared at her screen as though looking at a lover.

I presumed she was working on school matters, but was amused to see over her shoulder that she was trying to write a novel. After I slit her throat, I read the opening chapter while stroking her hair — sadly the words were less satisfying. Helen's writing was disappointingly mediocre, so I deleted the whole thing and replaced it with some lines of my own:

Helen should not tell lies.

Helen should not tell lies.

Helen should not tell lies.

I used an antibacterial wipe from her desk to clean the keyboard when I was done. Then I put the drugs up her nose as well as in her drawer, to be sure nobody would miss them. I wanted everyone to know that the good headmistress was really a bad role model for young girls. Addicted to power, illegal substances, and secrets.

Her tailored suit looked expensive, so it was a little disappointing to unwrap her, and find a cheap tatty supermarket bra hidden beneath her blouse. The stapler was not part of the plan, but I'd seen it on her desk, and it looked too tempting not to have a go. The letters made of staples on her skin were not as symmetrical as I might have liked, but it was easy enough to see that they spelled the word *LIAR.*

I tied the friendship bracelet around her tongue before standing back to admire my own work; it was rather impressive. Then I borrowed a pen from the pot on the desk, to write a note on the back of my hand. A reminder to myself that I needed to make a quick call.

HER

Wednesday 06:55

"Put the phone down," says the female detective.

She stares at me as though I just committed a hideous crime. Patel, I think he called her, and she's not being nearly as nice to me as she was the first time we met. It was pretty easy to win her over in the woods yesterday. I didn't really care about the shoe covers I asked to borrow, I just needed an excuse to talk to her. It's amazing how much information I was able to extract. I may have repeated some of it; I suspect that's why she is cross.

I swear she saw me reaching for the landline on the desk long before she said anything. I wouldn't have picked it up in the first place if she'd told me not to, but I put the phone back down without further argument. I was never good at disobeying people in authority, even small ones. The ftwo of us are cocooned inside the school secretary's office, for reasons that make very little sense to me.

"I'm due on-air in ten minutes. Your boss has taken my mobile, and I need to make a phone call to let someone know where I am," I say.

"DCI Harper took your mobile because you said that someone called you on it, tipping you off about the latest murder. I'm sure you can understand the reasons why we need to check out that call and who made it."

I regret giving Jack my phone, but didn't want to come across as being unhelpful.

"Fine, but I need to tell my news desk where I am."

"It's been taken care of."

"What does *that* mean?"

"Your cameraman is aware that you've been delayed."

"Delayed or detained? Am I under arrest?"

"No. As I have already explained to you, you're free to go at any time. You have been asked to stay here for your own protection, and to assist with our investigation."

I stare at her and she doesn't look away. She might be small and young, but she is surprisingly confident. No wonder Jack likes her. I can feel myself falling in hate. It's a lot like falling in love, but tends to happen harder and faster and often lasts a lot longer, too.

She steps outside the room, leaving the door open. I can hear her talking to someone a little further down the corridor, so I reach inside my bag, open a miniature brandy, and down it. Then I find my little tin of mints and pop one in my mouth. When I look up, the detective is standing in the doorway staring at me. I don't know how long she has been there, or what she has seen.

"Mint?" I ask, rattling the tin in her direction.

"No, thank you."

"You do know I'm Jack's ex-wife, don't you?"

Her smile looks out of practice.

"Yes, Ms. Andrews. I know who you are."

I'm not sure what makes me more uncomfortable, her words or the strange expression on her face. I told them both how scared I was when I got the call this morning, but it's as though neither of them believe me. The fact that I contacted the newsroom before I notified the police didn't go down particularly well either. I'm a journalist, so of course I followed up the tip-off and drove to the school. In hindsight, I can see how it might look a little foolish, dangerous even, but some stories are as addictive as success. Individual murders don't make or save careers, but a story about a serial killer could keep me on-air for weeks.

I'll never forget seeing Helen's lifeless body for the first time though. The girl I went to school with had grown into a woman I barely recognized, but of course I had known who she was. Same hair, same cheekbones; for all I knew it might even have been the same stapler she used on the school newspaper sitting on her desk. It's the kind of mental image you can never erase, and the sight of all that blood first thing in the morning would make anyone want a drink.

The young detective continues to stare at me, as though her big brown eyes have forgotten how to blink. I look away first, and feign interest in the pictures on the office walls. Staring at them brings back memories of being summoned to this room as a teenager. I was never in trouble at my first school, but when I moved to St. Hilary's everything changed. Not that it was my fault. It was almost always down to Rachel Hopkins or Helen Wang, both of whom are now dead.

■ ■ ■ ■

Rachel took me under her wing when I first arrived at the school, and I was so grateful. She was the most popular girl in our class, which made sense, because she was beautiful, clever, *and* kind. Or so I thought. She was always doing things for charity, even then — sponsored runs, bake sales, collections for Children in Need. I didn't think it at first, but after a few weeks, I soon started to wonder if she just saw me as another one of her little projects.

She had invited me to her home, let me borrow some of her clothes, and taught me how to do my makeup. I'd never bothered wearing any before. She liked to paint my nails when we hung out together, a different color every time we met. Sometimes she would draw letters with varnish, one on each nail to spell out a word on my fingers: CUTE or SWEET or NICE were her favorites. She was always calling me *nice.* It's still the word people use most often to describe me now. I've grown to detest it. The sound those four letters make translates from a compliment into an insult inside my ears. As though being *nice* is a weakness. Perhaps it is. Perhaps I am.

Rachel also bought me little presents all the time — lip gloss, scrunchies for my hair, sometimes tops and skirts that were a tad too tight, to encourage me to lose weight — and she even took me to her hairdresser's one weekend, to get my hair highlighted the same way as hers. She knew I couldn't afford it, and insisted on paying for everything. I did wonder where the money came from, but never asked. Rachel also let me sit next to her and her friends at lunchtimes, and I was glad about that too. There were some people who sat alone and I didn't want to be like them.

Catherine Kelly seemed nice enough to me. She was always eating chocolate or chips, and she looked a little strange — with her white-blond hair, braces, and scruffy uniform — but she didn't do or say anything to upset anyone. She didn't say much at all really, just sat quietly reading her books. Mostly horror, I noticed. I'd heard that her family lived in a strange place in the woods, at the edge of town. Some people said it was a haunted house, but I didn't believe in ghosts. I thought it was a shame that she didn't seem to have any friends at all, and I felt sorry for her.

"Should we invite Catherine to sit with us?" I asked one day, slowly eating the lunch ladies' interpretation of lasagna and fries.

The other girls stared as though I had said something offensive.

"No," said Rachel, who was sitting directly opposite me.

"Are you actually going to eat all of that?" said Helen, staring at my plate. I had noticed that she always skipped lunch. "Do you know how many calories are in that processed crap?" she continued when I didn't answer.

I didn't know; it wasn't the sort of thing I thought about much.

"I like lasagna," I replied.

She shook her head and put a small bottle of pills on the table.

"Here, have these. Call them an early birthday present."

"What are they?" I asked, staring at the unexpected "gift."

"Diet pills. We all take them. It means you can be slim without feeling hungry. Put them in your bag; we don't want the whole school knowing all our little secrets."

"Why do you want to invite *Smelly Catherine Kelly* to join our gang?" Rachel asked, changing the subject.

The others laughed.

"I just know how happy it makes me to eat lunch with all of you, and I thought she looked lonely —"

"And you wanted to be *nice,* right?" Rachel interrupted. I shrugged. "You know, being too *nice* is a sign of weakness."

Rachel stood abruptly, her chair scraping the floor. Then she picked up her can of Coke and left the cafeteria. Nobody spoke, and when I tried to make eye contact, they all stared at the uneaten salads on their plates.

Rachel returned a few minutes later, her smile reattached to her face. She put the can back down on the table, and picked up her cutlery to continue barely eating. The other girls did the same. They always took their lead from her.

"Well, go on then," she said between mouthfuls. "Invite her over."

I hesitated for a moment but then dismissed the uneasy feeling in my stomach, choosing to believe that Rachel was being as kind as I knew she could be. It seems naïve looking back, but sometimes we believe what we want to about the people we like the most.

I weaved my way through an obstacle course of chairs, tables, and schoolgirls to reach the sad little corner of the cafeteria where Catherine Kelly always ate alone. Her long blond hair looked like it hadn't seen a

255

brush for a while. She tucked it behind her sticky-out ears, and blushed when the other kids called her Dumbo. Despite all the snacks she liked so much — chips, chocolate bars, endless fizzy drinks — she was a skinny girl. Her shirt was a little loose around her neck where a button was missing, and there were stains on her tie. I noticed that her navy blue blazer was covered in chalk, as though she had rubbed up against a blackboard. Close up, I could also see that her eyebrows were almost completely bald, where she was always plucking the hairs with her fingertips. I'd watched her doing it in class, making tiny piles of herself on the desk, before blowing them away like wishes.

She pulled a face as though she thought I was joking when I invited her to join us. She stared at the girls on my table — who were all giggling at something Rachel had whispered to them after I had left — but when they saw her looking, they smiled and waved and beckoned her over. I felt very pleased with myself indeed when she carried her tray to our table, and sat down next to us all.

Until I read the scrap of paper that had been tucked beneath my plate.

Rachel made a little speech before I could

say or do anything about it.

"I just wanted to say sorry if I've ever hurt your feelings, Catherine. Friends?" she said, reaching across the table to shake her hand.

The quiet girl obliged, holding out her own. I could see how badly bitten her nails were, the skin around them red and raw. I noticed a bit of lasagna had gotten stuck between the braces on her teeth, too.

Catherine's cheeks flushed red as she shook Rachel's hand, and her can of Coke got knocked over. Helen — ever the clever and practical one — immediately produced some napkins to soak up the mess, as though she had known it was going to happen.

"I'm so sorry," said Rachel. "I am such a klutz. Here, have my Coke instead. It's still full and I haven't touched it."

"I'm fine, I'm not even really thirsty," Catherine replied, even redder than before so that her face and the can appeared to match.

"No really, I insist."

Rachel slid the drink across the table, and the conversation seemed to move along with it.

I kept staring at the slip of paper, reading the words and wondering what was the right thing to do:

I pissed in the Coke can. If you tell her before she drinks it, then you'll be the one sitting alone at lunch tomorrow.

Of course, I already knew the right thing to do, but I didn't do it. I just sat there, looking at the plate of food I no longer wanted to eat.

Five excruciating minutes after she sat down with us all, Catherine picked up the drink. Rachel managed to keep a straight face, but Helen looked delighted, and Zoe was already giggling. I wish I could say that she just took a sip, but the girl tilted her head right back, and took several gulps before realizing that something was wrong.

"You just drank my piss!" said Rachel, an enormous smile on her face once more.

Everyone laughed, and news of what had happened soon spread from our table to the next, until the whole school seemed to be pointing and laughing at Catherine Kelly.

She didn't say a word.

She just stared at me.

Then she got up and left the cafeteria, without clearing her tray or looking back.

HIM

"I need you to come back with me."

Anna and Priya both turn to look in my direction, but it's my ex-wife that I'm talking to.

"Please say she hasn't touched anything in here?" I say to Priya, who looks strangely sheepish.

"Only the phone."

I close my eyes. I think I knew she was going to say the words before she said them. It was my idea to ask Anna to wait in the secretary's office, so I can't really blame anyone else. I turn to face her, anxious to see her reaction.

"The call to your mobile — the alleged tip-off about the latest murder — was made from the landline in *this* room."

Anna stares at the old-fashioned phone.

"Well, you can still dust it for fingerprints, can't you? Or whatever it is that you do?"

259

"I expect the only prints we'll find now are yours, and there is no way of knowing whether they were there before this morning."

"Of course my fingerprints weren't on that phone before now; how could they be?"

Priya steps forward.

"Sir, I'm so sorry. I —"

"Are you suggesting I called *myself* with the tip-off?" Anna interrupts.

"I'm not suggesting anything yet. Still gathering evidence. Can you come with me, please? Priya, I want you to stay here and wait for the team. Make sure they check every nook and cranny of this office. Whoever killed Helen Wang was in here."

I hold the door open for Anna — gentleman that I am — and she offers me one of her unimpressed looks in return as she passes. I got quite used to those in the last few months of our marriage. We walk along the school corridors in silence at first, but she doesn't need to say anything for me to know that she is fuming. Husbands and wives develop a silent and private language. They don't forget how to speak it — even if they separate — still fluent in each other's expressions, gestures, and unspoken words.

"Where are we going now?" she asks eventually.

"I'm escorting you off the premises."

"I'm still going to cover the story."

"That's up to you."

"You think I shouldn't?"

"Since when do you care what I think?"

She stops and I don't want to do this anymore. I'm so tired of fighting about everything except the thing that broke us, the thing we should have but never did properly talk about.

"You do believe me, don't you?" she asks.

The thirty-six-year-old woman standing in front of me morphs into the shy and scared teenager I knew twenty years ago. The quiet girl that my sister and Rachel Hopkins befriended, for reasons I never knew or understood. She was nothing like them. Girls were even more of a mystery to me then than women are to me now.

"You say that you got the call at five A.M. on the dot this morning."

"Yes."

"That you didn't recognize the voice, and that you couldn't even tell whether the caller was a man or a woman?"

"That's right. I think they used a voice distorter."

I can't stop myself from raising an eyebrow.

"Interesting. So, why do *you* think that

someone would have tipped *you* off about this murder?" I ask, and she shrugs.

"Because they saw me covering the first one on the news?"

"You're not worried it might be more personal than that?"

She looks as though she wants to tell me something, but then seems to think better of it. I don't have time to play games, so I carry on.

We reach the parking lot, and I see that the TV truck has gone. The place is pretty deserted actually, not unlike when I was here last night. I haven't mentioned that fact to anyone, because just like being at the scene of the crime in the woods on Monday evening, I know it does not look good. The police vehicles, and the rest of the press, are parked at the front of the school, which is where I plan to take Anna now.

"Where is your team?" I ask.

"They didn't know how long I was going to be *detained,* so I expect they went to get some breakfast."

"I'll walk you to your car then," I say, clocking the red Mini I can't stand in the distance.

"Gosh, you really *do* want me to leave."

She waits for a response but I don't give

262

one. We carry on, each step a little heavy, weighed down with our own bespoke awkward silence. She doesn't appear to see the broken glass until I point it out.

Someone has smashed her car window.

"Well, that's just perfect," she says, stepping a little closer, trying to peer inside.

"Don't touch anything."

I call Priya and tell her to send someone out, keeping an eye on Anna the whole time.

"Something missing?" I ask, as soon as I've hung up.

"Yes, my overnight bag. It was on the backseat."

"Do you still think this has nothing to do with you? Someone, and my money is on the murderer, called to tip *you* off about the second victim. Now *your* car window has been smashed and *your* bag has been stolen. You knew both of the victims. Do you think it might be some kind of warning?"

"Do you?" she says, looking up at me.

Her face is visibly paler than before and she looks genuinely afraid. I don't know whether to hug her or hate her. There is something she's not telling me, I'm sure of it.

"I lied," she says.

My heart starts to beat so hard inside my

chest, I worry she can hear it.

"What do you mean? About what?"

"I *am* worried that this might have something to do with me, but I swear I'm not involved in any way. You must know that."

"Okay," I say.

I'll tell her whatever she needs to hear, in order for her to tell me what I want to know. It's a trick we're both familiar with.

"Last night, I felt like someone was watching me," she says, and I resist the urge to tell her that I've been feeling the same. "And, I know how silly this will sound, but I think someone might have been in my hotel room, moving things around. I thought I was being paranoid because I was tired and . . ."

I don't need her to tell me that she'd had a drink. I can guess that much. I think I can smell a little something on her breath, even now.

"Was your cameraman staying at the same hotel?"

"It wasn't Richard."

"How do you know?"

"Because why would he? This all seems connected to Blackdown, someone who knew me from before, maybe?"

"What makes you say that?"

"How well did you know Rachel?" she

264

asks. "Had you seen her since you moved back here?"

Several times, in all sorts of places and positions.

"I think everyone *saw* her. She was the kind of woman people looked at."

Anna pulls another face when I say this, one that really doesn't suit her. I still think I handled the question as well as I could without lying. She always used to know when I did that.

"But how well did *you* know her?" she asks again.

I imagine a thin film of sweat forming on my forehead, but then my ex carries on speaking without waiting for a reply, something she's always been rather good at. "Everyone always thought she was so kind when we were kids . . . but Rachel had a dark side. She hid it well, but it was there, and maybe it still was."

"Sorry, you've lost me. What does that have to do with you?" I ask.

"She was blackmailing me."

"What?"

"Over something that happened when we were at school. She got back in touch recently, asked me to do something, and when I said no . . . What if she was trying to blackmail other people too?"

265

"What happened when you were at school?"

"It doesn't matter."

"Clearly you think it might, or you wouldn't have mentioned it."

"Being married to a person doesn't mean you know everything about them, Jack."

She looks away. My face tries to form an appropriate reaction to what she just said, but I'm not sure there is one.

"Oh my god," she whispers, staring inside the car.

"What?"

"You kept asking about the friendship bracelet I was wearing yesterday. I genuinely thought I'd lost it, or that someone might have taken it from my room last night. I swear I have never seen *that* inside my car before."

I bend down to look through the smashed window, and see a smiley-face air freshener made of bright yellow cardboard. It is hanging from the rearview mirror, spinning in the breeze, and has been tied there with a red-and-white friendship bracelet.

Her

I watch as a team of strangers start to examine my car and I feel physically sick. It's going to take forever to wipe it clean when they are done. Jack walks toward me, and there is something inside the clear plastic bag he is holding that I can't quite see.

"You have a personal breathalyzer in your glovebox?"

He says it loud enough for the whole team to hear, and they all turn to stare at me.

"It's not a crime, is it?" I reply, and he smiles.

"No, it's just . . . funny."

"Well, I'm glad to have amused you. Can I have my phone back now, please?"

Jack stares at me for a long time before reaching inside his pocket.

"Sure, but if you get any more calls or texts, I want you to tell me straightaway.

267

Not the bloody news desk, okay?"

I dislike him the most when he speaks to me as if I am a child. He often did that during our relationship, as though always believing he knew best. He didn't then, and he doesn't now. Jack never learned to tell the difference between when I was telling the truth, and when I was telling him things he wanted to hear.

What *I* want now is a drink, but instead I stand at the edge of the parking lot, watching and waiting. Besides, everything alcoholic I had left was in my overnight bag; all I have on me now is a collection of empty miniature bottles.

I can't stop thinking about Jack's face when he described how the friendship bracelets had been tied around both of the victim's tongues. It felt like some kind of out-of-body experience. His expression was definitely different when he talked about Rachel. He thinks I don't know he had a thing for her, which was a foolish mistake. Wives always know.

I didn't talk to Rachel, or Helen or Zoe, for several days after the Coke can incident. I would sit on my own in class and at lunch, ignoring the sound of their laugher that seemed to fill every corner of the school. I missed Rachel terribly, but couldn't forgive her for what she did to Catherine Kelly. The poor girl was quieter than ever before, with permanently red eyes. That, combined with her wild white hair, made her look like an animal that had been experimented on. People had even started to joke that she belonged in a cage.

My mother picked up on my bad mood. She soon noticed that I was once again coming straight home from school, instead of hanging out with my new friends, and kept asking me to invite Rachel to our house. I couldn't tell her what had happened — I worried that she might think less of me if she knew — so I just kept making excuses.

Imagine my surprise a week later, when Mum came home from cleaning Rachel's house one afternoon with Rachel sitting in the van beside her. I stood in the open doorway, not knowing what to think or say as I waited for them to get out.

"I thought we'd have a sleepover; both our mums said it was okay!" Rachel said, running up the front path holding an overnight bag.

She smiled and hugged me tight, as though the incident in the school cafeteria had never happened.

As though we were friends again.

I didn't know how to feel; I was confused and happy at the same time. It was like the relief you experience when you find something you thought you had lost. Something precious and irreplaceable.

It was so strange, *her* being in *our* little home. She had never been to visit before; I always went to her house instead. My mother had barely let a soul inside since my father left us, and it was as if Rachel did not belong there. To me, she seemed like someone who should only ever be surrounded by beautiful and perfect things. Our cottage was cozy, but it was a mismatch of different secondhand furniture, and homemade curtains and cushions. Our bookshelves were crammed full of treasured stories rescued from charity shops, and although everything was spotlessly clean, it was also old and tired-looking. Rachel, on the other hand, always had a shiny new quality about her, and was as bubbly and full of life as it was possible for one human being to be. The kind of girl who always had a smile on her face.

Our conversation was not at all stilted; she was too good an actress for that. Even when I struggled with my own lines, she kept the performance going with carefree ease. My mother — who appeared to have no idea that there had been a falling-out — made a vegetable cottage pie, using nothing except ingredients grown in our own back garden. This was something she was rather proud of. "Fast food will be the end of human beings" was one of her favorite mottos, but I never shared her fear of preservatives. Takeaways were always a treat after so many years of being denied them.

I thought it was a little embarrassing that we didn't eat food from the supermarket, like normal people, but Rachel complimented my mother and praised the dinner, as though it was the best meal she had ever eaten. Once again, I marveled at her ability to charm people and make them like her. It seemed almost impossible not to, regardless of knowing what she had done.

"Would you like some chocolate ice cream for dessert as a special treat? I have some of that magic sauce somewhere, the one that goes hard when you pour it on top," Mum asked us both as she cleared the table.

We always had dessert in my house.

"No, thank you, Mrs. Andrews. I'm full," our guest replied.

"Okay, love. You'll have some, won't you, Anna?"

Rachel looked at me. I said no too, and

she smiled when my mother was gone. She had spent weeks trying to persuade me to change my dietary habits, and said that I needed to eat less and move more in order to lose weight. I'd started taking the pills Helen had given me, and according to the bathroom scales they were working. Not that I was terribly big to begin with. I remember how good it felt when Rachel looked pleased with me. Missing out on a little ice cream, and swallowing a few tablets, seemed like a reasonable sacrifice to experience the satisfaction of her approval.

There were no spare rooms in our house. All available space was very much taken, so Rachel slept in with me. In my room. In my bed. We brushed our teeth in the bathroom together, spitting out our toothpaste at the same time, taking it in turns to use the toilet.

My mother stayed downstairs watching the late TV news bulletin, as always. She'd earned enough cleaning by then to buy a new one. She once told me I was named after Anna Ford, the newsreader, and I don't think she was joking.

"It's warm tonight, isn't it?" Rachel said, starting to undress.

I watched as she unbuttoned her shirt, letting it fall to the floor, before reaching behind her back to unhook her bra. She always wore grown-up, lacy underwear. Not like me. I didn't think it was warm at all. Our house always felt freezing. But my mother had lit the fire in my bedroom for us, and it crackled and hissed in the background.

I've never been very comfortable with my body, even back then when — although I didn't know it — I had nothing to worry about. Perhaps it was the diet pills that started my paranoia. I changed into my PJs as quickly as possible, so that Rachel wouldn't see me naked. I was only half undressed when she asked to take my picture. She was standing in the middle of the room, in just her underwear, already holding the disposable camera.

"Why do you want a photo?" I asked.

It seemed like an appropriate question.

"Because you look so pretty. I want to have something to remember you this way."

It felt strange to complain about having bare legs when she was almost completely nude, so I let her take my picture. She took several, then put the camera away. Rachel didn't seem to share my body image anxiety, she removed the rest of her clothes, then walked around my room wearing nothing at all. She took her time looking at the posters on my walls, and the books on my shelf, while the light from the fire cast a dancing pattern of shadows all over her body. I lay in the bed, unable to take my eyes off her. Until she climbed in beside me, still naked, and turned off the light.

We lay there, side by side, in the silence and the dark for a while. I seemed unable to stop myself from breathing unusually fast, and I worried that she could hear me and might think that I was strange. The more I tried to control it, the worse it got, until I feared I might actually be having an asthma attack. Then Rachel slipped her hand inside my pajama bottoms, and I almost forgot how to breathe altogether.

"Shh," she said, before kissing me on the cheek.

I didn't move and I didn't say anything. I just lay there, and let her touch me in a place that I had never been touched before. When she was finished, she slid her wet fingers across my tummy and wrapped her arm around my waist. She squeezed me tight, as though I were a favorite doll, then whispered something in my ear before falling asleep. The sound of her gentle snoring created a curious lullaby.

I didn't sleep at all.

I just kept wondering what had happened and why, hearing her words constantly

repeating themselves inside my head:
"That was *nice,* wasn't it."

HIM

reassuring themselves inside, together.
"Has anyone got a sweat—"

Wednesday 08:00

It's not nice seeing Anna so upset, but I do my best to reassure her.

A phone vibrates in the inside pocket of my jacket. I know it isn't mine, because I'm holding that in my hand. I walk away from the team that has gathered around Anna's Mini, and take out Rachel's mobile. I think I've been in denial about finding it in my car trunk, but when I read the text message on the screen, it's a little harder to ignore:

Miss me, lover?

Rachel is definitely dead, and I do not believe in ghosts, so there is only one conclusion I can reach: someone, somewhere, knows something they shouldn't.

I put the phone away and look around. If whoever sent me the text is watching, waiting to see my reaction, I'm determined not to give it. I scan the parking lot and see Anna in the far corner. She's a short distance away from everybody else now, staring down at her own mobile. It's as though she feels my stare and immediately looks straight up at me, looking at her.

"I thought you might need these, sir."

Priya appears out of nowhere, and it actually makes me jump. I'm about to snap at her, when I see a brand-new packet of my favorite cigarettes in her hand.

"Why do you have these?" I ask, but she just shrugs.

The way my junior colleague is staring up at me makes me feel even more uncomfortable than the phone in my pocket receiving text messages from a dead woman. Unlikely as that may sound.

"Well, thank you," I say, taking the packet.

I open it immediately, pop a cigarette in my mouth, light it, and take a long drag.

The satisfaction is instant, only spoiled by Priya's presence.

"Look, it's very sweet of you, but you don't need to keep buying me things and being so . . . thoughtful. It's about the work, right? Solving cases. You don't need to be so *nice* all the time. Just do your job and we'll get along fine."

"You're welcome," she replies, as though she didn't hear my impromptu speech. "And I think I have an update that might cheer you up."

"Go on."

"Rachel Hopkins's phone was never found, so I told the tech team to put a trace on it."

I inhale far harder than I intended, and start to cough.

"I don't remember asking you to do that?"

I continue to smoke with one hand, while reaching inside my pocket with the other, trying to switch off Rachel's phone.

"You didn't, sir. But you did tell me to start showing some more initiative. The phone received a text a couple of minutes ago, and someone read it. Someone has Rachel's mobile, and they are somewhere near here. The guys are trying to triangulate the signal now. So long as the phone stays switched on, I think they'll get a pretty accurate location."

She stares at Anna.

"You think *Anna* has Rachel's phone? You think she might be involved?" I ask.

Priya shrugs. "Don't you?" She interprets my silence as an invitation to keep talking. I do my best to hide any signs of the panic I feel, while trying to turn off the phone inside my jacket pocket at the same time. "We know that someone called Anna's mobile from the landline in the school office at five A.M. But we have no way of knowing where *her* phone was at the time. She could have been standing right next to it and called herself."

My fingers finally find what they are looking for, and I turn off Rachel's mobile. I laugh and it sounds as false as it feels.

"You had me going for a moment there! Great work on the phone trace, and good joke about my ex-wife being the killer," I say, fully aware she wasn't joking.

Priya gives me a strange look, then heads back over to the rest of the team by the car, her ponytail in full swing. Someone sent that text deliberately just now, and I'm sure I'm being watched. When I look around to try to locate Anna, I can't see her anywhere.

It was a shame to do it, but I had to smash the window on the Mini. It isn't as though it can't be repaired, and the car will be good as new as soon as it gets mended. Not like me. But then people do tend to be trickier to fix than things. I've decided that succeeding in my plan is highly dependent on misdirection, so damaging the car was a necessary act of vandalism. Not that anyone would have suspected me of doing it. That sort of behavior goes against the idea that others have of me, but I am not who they think I am. Like most people, there is more to me than my job.

Watching things unfold and people unravel afterward was delicious. Better than anything I've read or seen on TV, because it was real. And I was the author of it all. I made use of that opportunity — seeing the fruits of my labor with my own eyes, enjoying the reactions of my handpicked cast. It left a bittersweet feeling.

I think I've always been very resourceful, perhaps because I had to be. Good at finding a use for things. Take the voice changer, for example, left to gather dust in a box of confiscated items in the school office. It was surprisingly simple and fun to use, so much so that I kept it. One man's trash is another man's treasure, as my mum used to say.

I also took the school's drama trophy from the headmistress's office, and used that to smash the car window. It seemed appropriate somehow. Nobody saw me; the parking lot was empty and it didn't take long. Afterward, when I experienced the pure rush of adrenaline that always accompanies the feeling of getting away with something, I felt invincible and invisible all at once. I kept the trophy too. My acting skills deserve some kind of award.

I have spent a lifetime trying on new skins like new clothes, seeing which version of myself suited me best, shedding the ones that didn't. Not everyone seems to know that personalities can be altered, until a person finds the perfect fit. I didn't know who I was when I was younger or, if I did, I pretended not to. People often see what they want, rather than what is really there.

I only took the bag because of how I needed things to look.

We all try to buy a little more time, but it's

priceless. We get what we're given, not what we can afford. Time is a trapdoor we all tumble down at some point in our lives, often completely unaware of how far we have fallen. Captivated by an audience of our own worst fears, that demand an encore whenever we dare to stop feeling afraid.

The emotional walls we build are there to keep the real us inside, as well as to keep others out. I'm making mine stronger, one brick of revenge at a time.

We all hide behind the version of ourselves we let the rest of the world see.

HER

Wednesday 08:15

I can see it even if he can't.

The pretty junior detective clearly has some sort of crush on Jack, and although we are no longer married, it still feels very strange to watch. Uncomfortable and mildly distressing, to be honest. I'm not naïve. I'm fully aware that he must have moved on with his life in more ways than one since we stopped living together, but seeing another woman looking at him like that still makes me want to scratch her eyes out. While nobody is watching, I slip away into the woods. I head toward the exact same spot where Rachel and I would sometimes skip lessons to hang out.

I was aware that the other girls in our little gang — Helen Wang and Zoe Harper — were becoming increasingly jealous of the amount of time Rachel and I were spending

283

together. They didn't do a very good job of hiding it; not that I cared. I'd never even been kissed by a boy let alone a girl before, and for the first time in my life, I felt pretty.

After a couple of months, I was already falling behind with my studies. We'd been spending too many nights staying at each other's houses, or going shopping — for clothes only Rachel could afford to buy — or hiding in the woods at the back of the school together, when we should have been in class. I was willing to do whatever I could to make her like me, always afraid she might stop. Then my mother found out that I'd got an F in English, because of failing to hand in an essay on time.

I'd always been a straight-A student before that. Mum was more upset than I had ever seen her and grounded me for two weeks. She had promised I could have a party for my sixteenth birthday — just a few of the girls round to our house — and this meant I would have to cancel. I did not take the news well.

Rachel insisted that she could fix things and that Helen would help. She marched right up to her the following morning before registration.

"We need you to write our English essays for Monday, as well as your own. You always get A grades and we both need one, otherwise Anna won't be allowed to have her birthday party next weekend."

She brushed a stray wisp of Helen's shiny black hair behind her ear as she said it, and I felt strangely jealous.

"Can't. I'm busy," Helen replied, looking back down at her math textbook, cramming for our upcoming test.

Rachel folded her arms and tilted her head to one side, the way she always did on the rare occasions when she didn't get her own way. Then she closed Helen's book for her.

"So, change your plans."

"I said no."

Helen had become increasingly cranky since I started at St. Hilary's. She spent more time studying or writing for the school newspaper than ever before, and had lost a dramatic amount of weight. I guessed the diet pills really did work, plus I hardly ever saw her eat.

"Why don't you have a think about it?" Rachel said, wearing one of her best smiles.

To my surprise, on Monday morning Helen gave us two essays that were bound to have been better than anything we could have come up with ourselves. They were written in two different sets of handwriting, each of which looked remarkably like our own.

"Are you sure this is okay?" I asked Helen.

"I'm sure you'll get the grade you deserve," she said, then walked away, disappearing down the corridor without another word.

I had always done my own homework before, and this was all new to me.

"Should we check them?" I asked Rachel, but she just smiled.

"Why bother? Helen is so good at knowing what teachers want, I expect she'll be one herself when she's older. 'Miss Wang.' I can already picture her sitting in the headmistress's chair during school assembly! Can't you?"

It was true. Helen was always exceptionally clever, but she was a liar too.

We handed in our essays to Mr. Richardson at the end of our English class. He was a bespectacled spindle of a man, short on hair and patience. The whole school knew that he had aspirations of becoming a writer of literature one day, rather than a teacher of it. He was known for collecting first editions of books, dandruff, and teenage enemies. All the girls hated him, and often flicked ink from their fountain pens onto the back of his shirt when he wrote on the blackboard. The way he looked at Rachel when she gave him her essay made me feel strange. It was like seeing an elderly lame dog drooling over a leg of lamb in a butcher's window.

The bell rang for lunch, but while everyone else headed for the dining room, Rachel dragged me in the other direction.

"Come on, I've got you a little present, but you have to open it in private."

She took me by the hand, her fingers entwining themselves with my own. It was something lots of girls did at school, but when Rachel held mine it always felt special, as though I had been chosen.

She led me to the restrooms where we walked right into Catherine Kelly. Her long white-blond hair was a turbulent mess of tangled knots. Her skin was even paler than usual, with a cluster of angry-looking red pimples on her chin. Her patchy eyebrows were almost completely bald — she was literally pulling out tiny pieces of herself and throwing them away. I could see why someone like Rachel wouldn't like her very much, they were complete opposites.

"Stand by the door, skank, and make sure nobody else comes in here. If you don't, I'll do something far worse than making you drink piss out of a Coke can."

It was the one side of Rachel's character I disliked — the way she picked on Catherine — but I had reached the conclusion that there must be a very good reason for it, even if I didn't know what that was.

Rachel dragged me into a cubicle and closed the door.

"Take your shirt off," she said.

"What?"

I was fully aware that Catherine could hear every word.

"Don't worry, Dumbo and her big ears won't listen if I tell her not to," Rachel replied. "Take it off."

"Why?"

"Because I told you to."

We had fooled around in our bedrooms and in the woods by then, but it was always dark. Although I had seen Rachel naked more times than I could remember, I still felt shy about *her* seeing *my* body. When I didn't move or answer, she smiled and started to undo the buttons of my shirt for me. I let her, just like I'd been letting her do all the things she had wanted to. Even when they hurt.

As soon as my shirt was off, she slipped her hands behind my back and unclasped my bra. I tried to cover my breasts, but she pushed my fingers away, before reaching into her bag and producing a black lacy bra for me to wear instead. I had never worn anything like it — my mother still bought all my underwear, and it was inevitably white, cotton, and purchased in Marks & Spencer — this was something a *woman* would wear.

"It's a Wonderbra! I never wear anything else now; you're going to love it," said Rachel, putting it on me like a child dressing their favorite doll.

To my horror, she took a picture on her disposable camera of my breasts in their new outfit, then opened the door and pushed me out of the cubicle. Catherine Kelly just stared at the floor, so I peered at my reflection in the mirror. It was like looking at someone else.

"Look how much bigger they are now!" Rachel said, then frowned at my face.

"What?" I asked.

"Your lips are all chapped. That's no good."

She took a tiny tin of strawberry-flavored lip balm out of her bag, and slowly applied some to my lips with her fingertip.

"Does that feel better?" she asked, and I nodded. "Let me see," she said, and kissed me.

She had her back to Catherine, but I

didn't. And I was more than a little disturbed by the way the girl stared at us the entire time Rachel's lips were on mine. I stood as still as a statue while she pushed her tongue inside my mouth, fully aware that someone was watching.

"Don't worry about her," said Rachel, glancing over her shoulder. "She won't tell anyone, will you, skank?"

Catherine shook her head, and when Rachel kissed me again, I closed my eyes and kissed her back.

HIM

"You need to come back," I say, as soon as I find Anna in the woods.

It wasn't hard. There is a place right at the basin of the valley, not far from the school, where all the naughty girls used to sneak off to after lessons, and sometimes during them. It was used for smoking, drinking, and other things. Each year, the new class of "cool" kids thought of it as their own secret outdoor den, but its existence was common knowledge — even boys like me knew — and its whereabouts were passed down from one teenage generation to the next. The small clearing is defined by three large fallen tree trunks, dragged together to form a triangular seating area. There is evidence of a recent fire in the middle, surrounded by stones.

Anna looks at me as though she has seen a ghost.

291

"How did you know where I was?" she asks.

"I remember you telling me about this place."

"Did I?"

No.

"How else would I know?" I say.

She looks so confused. Her face wears what looks like a secondhand expression inherited from her mother. I almost feel bad not confessing that it was Rachel who told me that they used to come here together, not Anna.

"You look a bit like her, you know," I tell her.

"Who?"

"Your mother."

"Thanks."

I can see her comparing herself to the forgetful old woman living in the cottage at the top of the hill, but that isn't what I meant. Everyone in the village remembers how beautiful Anna's mother *used* to be twenty years ago. I always thought of her as a suburban Audrey Hepburn. I might have had a bit of a crush on my future mother-in-law back then, when I was a teenager. The wild gray hair used to be long, dark, and shiny, and she was the best-dressed cleaner I ever saw. I think a hard life stole her looks. Funny how age can be kind to some and cruel to others when it comes to beauty.

"I mean when she was younger. It was meant to be a compliment," I say, but Anna doesn't respond. "Are you okay?" I ask, knowing it's a stupid question.

She shakes her head. "I don't know anymore."

The subject of Anna's mother is always a sensitive one; I should have known better.

"I'm sorry that you think I interfered with your mum. You're right, I should have told you that she was getting significantly worse. I did try, and I only wanted to help."

"I know. It's just that she never wanted to leave that house, and I feel like I've let her down —"

I take a step toward her.

"You haven't let anyone down. I understand why you stayed away, and what being here does to you. Maybe you should go back to London?"

Her body language instantly translates into something completely different.

"You'd like that, wouldn't you, Jack?"

"What does that mean?"

"How old *is* Detective Patel? Twenty-seven? Twenty-eight?"

293

I've never known Anna to be jealous before.

"She's actually in her thirties" — I checked her HR record myself recently — "she's good at her job, and she's not my type."

"What is your type now it's no longer me?"

I don't know whether to laugh or kiss her, and both options seem inappropriate.

"You'll always be my type," I say, and her face strains to hide a smile.

"I'll try to remember that if you ever need a blood donor."

I laugh. I think I'd forgotten my wife can be funny. Ex-wife. Mustn't forget that.

A magpie swoops down onto the path behind us, and Anna can't stop herself from saluting in its direction. Some superstitious nonsense her mother taught her.

"Come on, everything will be okay," I say, holding out my hand.

I'm surprised when she takes it. I always loved the way her fingers seemed to fit right inside my own. I find myself pulling her closer without really meaning to, and she lets me. The hug feels rusty, the kind you have with someone who hasn't had much practice. Anna starts to cry, and all at once, I am back in her mother's house again that night two years ago. Holding my wife just after we discovered that our daughter was dead. I'm sure the memory comes back to haunt her too, because she pulls away.

I take a clean hanky from my pocket, and she uses it to wipe the tears and smudges of mascara beneath her eyes.

"People will wonder where we both are," I say.

"Sorry, I just needed to be on my own for a moment."

"I know. Me too. It's okay."

We start to walk back toward the parking lot, and my eyes are drawn to the magpie that landed on the forest floor just ahead of us a few moments ago. It doesn't fly away, or even look remotely distracted from its task, and it's only when we get closer that I can see what it is doing. The living magpie is pecking at the flesh of a dead one. Despite my line of work, the sight still turns my stomach a little. Anna sees it too and I can't help wondering whether, given her superstitious beliefs, this sighting still counts as two for joy.

HER

Wednesday 09:00

I can't get the image out of my mind. The sight of one magpie eating the other. I keep thinking about Jack saying that I resemble my mother, too. I can't see it myself, but even if I do *look* like her, we are not the same. It might be true that the apple doesn't fall far from the tree, but sometimes the apple can roll down a hill, far, far away from where it landed.

Being in this corner of the woods always makes me think of Rachel.

I didn't think anything could spoil the happy feeling inside my chest after she kissed me in the school restroom. She was the champagne of friends, and I was sure no other friendship would ever be as good. We were both smiling all day, until Mr. Richardson — our disgusting English teacher — asked to see both Rachel and me

296

in his office. We were pulled out of gym class and made to go there wearing just our hockey gear.

I was called in first. I sat on the very edge of the chair opposite his desk, and when he told me that I'd been caught cheating, and that he was going to have to write to my mother about it, I started to cry. I fear my tears gave away my guilt, long before my words had a chance to defend me.

He said that Rachel and I had both handed in exactly the same essay. One of us had clearly copied the other, and unless he could determine who was in the wrong, he had no choice but to punish us both. His right hand was hidden below the desk, as though he were scratching something, and I could tell from the twisted smile on his face that he was enjoying watching me cry. I still couldn't stop — the thought of my mother finding out what I had done was killing me.

Eventually he said I could go, and told me to send Rachel in. She knew from my tearstained face that it must be bad. I wanted to warn her — so that at least she would know what to expect — and whispered in her ear as we passed each other.

"Helen tricked us. She wrote the same essay twice."

To my surprise, Rachel was still a picture

of calm.

"Try not to worry," she whispered back. "I promise everything will be okay. Go wait for me in our secret place; I'll come find you."

It was dark and cold in the woods, especially when wearing nothing except a T-shirt and hockey skirt. The long socks did little to keep me warm. It seemed like a ridiculous thing to say — Rachel telling me not to worry, when it felt like the whole world was about to end — but I reminded myself that she *did* have a habit of always getting what she wanted, regardless of the odds. Ten minutes later, she appeared in the clearing with a big smile on her face.

"Don't suppose you've got a mint or some chewing gum?" she asked.

I shook my head.

"Don't worry, I'll get some later. Need to brush my teeth too."

"Why?"

"Never mind," she said, then hugged me. "Everything is okay again, you don't need to worry. We'll both get A grades for those essays we just handed in, even though we didn't write them, and our parents won't know a thing about it. Given you just got an A, I'm hoping your mum might let you have that birthday party next weekend after all."

I tried to pull away, so I could see her face, but she held on tighter.

"I don't understand. How did you get Mr. Richardson to change his mind?"

"Doesn't matter," she whispered, then slid her free hand up my hockey skirt.

Her fingers pushed my underwear to one side, while her other arm continued to hold me close. When my knees started to shake, she let me lie down on the forest floor, and, as usual, I let her do whatever she wanted.

"Feel better?" she asked afterward.

She stood without waiting for an answer, dusted the dirt off her hands and knees, then pulled me up from the bed of dead leaves I had been lying on.

"I need to have a word with Helen before she goes home today, so we should head back to the changing rooms," Rachel said. "Do you have any chewing gum in your bag when we get there?"

"Do you want one?" says Jack, offering me a cigarette.

I am rudely torn from the memory of the day Helen Wang pissed off Rachel Hopkins and lived to regret it. Remembering the things we used to do makes me blush.

"I'll pass, thanks. Smoking is not my addiction of choice, as you know."

My drinking is something we never talked about. Jack understood why I started and why I can't stop; crutches come in all shapes and sizes. The new expression on his face looks a lot like pity. I don't want it, so I give it back.

"I'm sorry all this horror is happening on your doorstep. I'm sure this isn't what you expected when you ran away to the country."

"I didn't run away, I was pushed."

This is a road neither of us wants to go down again, so I take an alternative route.

"I'm guessing I'm not going to be able to use my car anytime soon?" I ask.

"Afraid not. Do you need a lift somewhere?"

"No, it's okay. I already texted Richard."

He shakes his head. "After everything I told you about him?"

"Whatever he did in the past, I'm sure he had his reasons."

"Call me old-fashioned, but a conviction for GBH is cause for concern in my book. You said you thought someone might have been in your room last night. Wasn't he staying at the White Hart too?"

"You know he was. It isn't like there's

more than one hotel around here, but it wasn't him."

"What made you think there was anyone there at all?"

I hesitate, still a little unsure how much I should say.

"You're going to think I'm crazy if I tell you . . ."

"I already know you're crazy. We were married for ten years, remember?"

We both smile and I decide to try to trust him, like I always used to.

"I had an old picture of me and some of the girls from school. I found it at Mum's and I was looking at it in my hotel room last night, because of what had happened to Rachel."

He stares at me for a long time, as though waiting for me to say more.

"And?"

I shake my head, still a little worried about how this is going to sound.

"It was a picture of a group of us."

"Okay . . ."

"I left the bedroom, just for a few minutes, and when I came back there was a black cross drawn over Rachel's face."

He frowns and doesn't say anything for a while.

"Can I see it?"

"No. It was in my bag, the one that got stolen from the car."

"Who else was in the photo?"

I still feel uneasy about telling him this part. I wonder if he'll think I was drunk and did it myself, then lost the picture. That explanation certainly crossed my mind. He takes a step closer. Too close.

"Anna, if other women might be in danger, I need to know about it."

"It's just a picture from twenty years ago. It might not mean anything. But it's of me, Rachel Hopkins, Helen Wang, a girl you wouldn't remember, and . . . ."

"Who?"

"Your sister."

HIM

I call Zoe as soon as Anna has gone.

I watched my ex-wife being driven away by her cameraman, with an uneasy feeling I can't explain. She looked more vulnerable just now than she has for a long time. Sometimes I forget who she really is, underneath the tough exterior. The version of herself she presents to the rest of the world isn't the same as the woman who was once my wife.

Zoe seems amused by her older brother's sudden concern for her safety and well-being. I don't explain why I'm worried, or mention the photo. Instead, I just listen to the familiar sound of her voice, as she insists for the third time that she is safe *and* that the house is completely secure. I ask her to turn on our parents' old burglar alarm — I'm fairly sure we are the only two people who know the code — then I do my best to get back to my job. I've always been a bit concerned that Zoe's past might catch up with her one day. My sister got in with the wrong crowd for a while when we were young. I know, because I did too.

It turns out to be another long and tedious morning, consisting of my second trip to the pathologist, new reports to write, lengthy briefings with an inexperienced team, more unanswered questions as well as questions to answer. Along with the worst part of my job: telling a parent that their child is dead. Age is never a factor in the pain that particular news inflicts. Everyone is somebody's child, no matter how old they are.

"Who did this?" asked Helen Wang's elderly mother, as though she thought I knew the answer.

I sat in her front room, not drinking the Earl Grey tea she insisted on making, or touching the tin of shortbread biscuits open on the table. Her gray hair was cut in the same Cleopatra style as her daughter's, and her immaculate clothes looked like something a much younger woman would wear. There was no longer a Mr. Wang, and she lived alone in an orderly but unremarkable house. She started crying as soon as we arrived, and I think she already knew something was wrong.

I spared her the majority of the details regarding how Helen was found at the school, but I won't be able to stop her from reading them in the press. She'll know about the drugs we found at her daughter's home soon too. I can already imagine the headlines: *The Headmistress with a Habit.*

I normally let junior detectives inform next of kin, just like I had to when I was working my way up. But I missed knowing about Rachel's husband, and her mobile phone, when I sent Priya last time. I don't plan to make the same mistake twice.

I'm instructed by those on higher salaries than my own to give another scripted press statement. Preparing for the performance eats into my afternoon. I choose to do it outside Surrey Police HQ this time, in an attempt to keep journalists away from the school, and although I see Anna standing there among the other reporters, she doesn't ask a single question. When I retreat back inside, someone has turned on the TV in the office — presumably to watch the press conference on BBC News — and I see my ex-wife on the screen. It's as though she is staring right at me.

I don't know what to say at first when Priya invites me for a drink after work.

"Thanks, but with Blackdown being like it is, there's nowhere we could go without the locals or the media trying to eavesdrop every word of our conversation."

"I did think of that, sir. Perhaps a drink at my place, where it would be more private?"

I don't know what face I pull, but from her reaction I'm guessing it can't be good. She starts to speak again before I can form a response, and I dread to think what she might say next.

"I'm not really inviting you over for you — although you do look like you could do with a drink — it was more for myself, really. This is all a bit . . . new for me, and I don't know anyone here. I'm living on my own at the moment, so there's nobody for me to talk to when I get home. I guess I just didn't fancy walking into the house alone, after seeing two women brutally murdered. That's all."

She stares at me, then examines her short fingernails, as though it is imperative that they are as neat and tidy as the rest of her. Women baffle me on a daily basis. That said, I do feel a smidgen of guilt. Priya *is* alone in a town where the locals aren't always friendly to new faces. It isn't as though I have anyone to rush home to either.

I weigh up my options and conclude that

my colleague needs me more than my sister. Even though a nagging voice in my head tells me I should go home and check on Zoe, a louder one tells me not to. She's always been able to take care of herself. Besides, all we ever do when we're together is argue about money, or what to watch on Netflix. It's not so different to when we fought over toys or the remote control as children. I'm sure Zoe would rather have the place to herself for the evening. Accepting Priya's invitation would just mean having a friendly drink with a colleague; a perfectly normal and innocent thing to do. The *right* thing to do.

One hour and two beers later, Priya is cooking homemade burgers and sweet potato fries. Her house is on the edge of town. It's a new build — one of those estates where the houses are on top of one another and all look the same, with red brick walls and PVC windows — but it's nice enough. Rented, of course, but decked out in stylish furniture, and painted in a series of inoffensive neutral colors.

Everything is spotlessly clean, with low lighting and zero clutter. I note the lack of family photos, or anything remotely personal. If I'd ever given any thought to Priya's home before now — which I hadn't —

I think I might have predicted Ikea or chintz, but I would have been wrong. Everything I thought I knew about her seems to have been a little off base. The only thing that looked out of place was my scruffy jacket when she hung it on the fancy-looking coatrack, and my shoes, which I took off in the hall. I was a little paranoid that she might notice they were a size ten.

"I just need to pop out for something I forgot," she says, handing me another beer. "Make yourself at home and I'll be back in a jiffy."

The expression sounds too old for her young voice, and it seems a little strange to leave me alone in her house. She turns on the small TV in the kitchen to entertain me, and I drink another beer while watching my ex on the BBC News channel. I'm unable to tell if Anna is live this time, or whether this is just a repeat of what she said earlier.

I do something stupid then. I don't know whether it's the beer, or the tiredness, or frankly whether I'm just losing my mind, but I switch on Rachel's phone. I canceled the trace on it this afternoon — being in charge does have some benefits — and I need to know how her mobile got in my car. Feeling like someone is watching me and trying to set me up is starting to take its toll.

Her passcode is her date of birth — people can be so predictable — and as soon as the phone is unlocked I regret it. There are a mind-boggling number of selfies in her photos, endless suggestive texts to numbers and names I don't recognize, and her most recent e-mail exchange was with Helen Wang. The subject of which appears to be me. I keep reading the final message Rachel wrote before we met that night.

I know Jack is a loser, but a friend in the force could have been useful. You're right though, I'll end it tonight. Maybe a good-bye shag to soften the blow?

So Rachel planned to dump me, and Helen knew.

The front door slams. I slip the phone back into my pocket, just before Priya re-appears in the kitchen. A jiffy is by no means a specific length of time, but she must have been gone over half an hour. Longer than I expected, at any rate. She doesn't appear to have bought anything either. A lifetime of living with my mother, my sister, and Anna has taught me to know when a woman doesn't want to be asked any questions. So I don't.

"This looks and smells delicious, thank

you," I say, as Priya puts a plate of food down in front of me. I'm not lying, it really does look great, and I can't remember the last time I had a home-cooked meal. "I wasn't expecting this," I add.

"Were you expecting me to cook a curry?"

"God, no, I just meant that . . ."

"What? You didn't think I could cook?"

I can see from her face that Priya is teasing me. Sarcasm is a language that I am fluent in, but one which she doesn't always seem to understand. The beer appears to have loosened her tongue, and made us both a little more relaxed in each other's company. She sits down beside me, perhaps a little too close.

"It's nothing special, just Nigella," she says.

"I think Nigella is pretty special," I reply with a grin, and she gives me one of her polite smiles in return, as though maybe I have offended her in some way.

I've always found women to be far more complicated than men, and wonder what I've done wrong now. She can't possibly be upset because of my comment about Nigella — half the nation has a crush on the woman.

It's odd, really. I've always thought of Priya as just a girl until tonight, but she seems far more grown-up in her own home environment. At ease with herself, unlike the way she behaves when we're working. Perhaps that's why I feel so comfortable in her company this evening. More relaxed. Possibly too relaxed.

"Where did you go earlier?" I ask, unable to stop myself.

Her eyes widen and she looks as though I just accused her of something terrible.

"I'm so sorry . . ." she says.

"What for?"

"I forgot, then I remembered, then I forgot again."

She stands up from the table, abandoning her half-eaten food, and leaves the room without another word. I'll admit I'm feeling a tad uneasy, but then she reappears in the doorway holding a bottle of ketchup.

"I know how much you like this stuff with your fries, sir. You *always* practically drown them in it, but I didn't have any. I went out to get some — I wanted you to enjoy the food — but then I forgot and . . ."

She looks like she might cry, and I conclude that women are in fact a different species.

"Priya, the food is delicious. You really didn't need to go to all that trouble."

"I wanted everything to be perfect."

311

I smile at her.

"It already is."

I relax a little more now that I know where she went — it was sweet of her, really. She seems to unwind too. She clears our plates away and gets us both another beer from the fridge, without asking if I want one. I can't decide whether she is just being a good host — my bottle *was* empty — or whether I'm right to be worried about the direction things are traveling in. Her hair is down again. I notice that she's unbuttoned the top of her shirt, and I swear she sprayed herself with perfume the last time she left the room. I take a large swig of my beer, and decide to face this head on, like the man I suspect she thinks I am.

"Priya, look, this has all been lovely, but I don't want you to get the wrong impression."

She looks appalled.

"Did I do something wrong, sir?"

"No and, once again, there really is no need to call me sir, especially when I am in your home, eating your food and drinking your beer. Christ, I should have brought something. That's so rude of me —"

"It's fine. Really. Jack."

The sound of her using my actual name feels wrong too. I realize I've probably had more than I should have to drink, especially as I was planning on driving home. This was all a big mistake, and I need to set things straight before I see her again tomorrow.

"Look, Priya. I . . . like working with you." She beams and it makes this even harder. I remind myself that I'm significantly older than her, and that I need to take charge of the situation before things get out of hand. "But . . ." Her face falters, and I conclude this speech would be much easier to deliver if I just stare at the laminated wooden floor. "We work together. I'm a lot older than you, and while I think you're terrific and a very attractive young woman . . ."

Fuck, I think that last sentence could be construed as sexual harassment.

". . . I don't think of you or see you in *that* way."

There. Nailed it.

"You think I'm ugly?"

"Christ, no. Shit, is that what I said?"

She smiles and I have no understanding of the current situation. I wonder if perhaps the rejection has caused her to lose it.

"Sir, it's fine. Honestly. I'm sorry if I gave *you* the wrong impression," she says. "I was making you food all the time at work because, well, I like to cook for other people, and at the moment I don't have anyone to

313

do that for. I bought you cigarettes because I thought you might need them. And if I sometimes hang off your every word, it's because I think you're great at your job, and I want to learn from you. But that's it."

I'm confused, but women do tend to have that effect on me. I can't quite interpret the look on her face, but I fear it might be pity. I feel foolish and old and delusional all of a sudden, and perhaps I am: Why *would* someone so young, intelligent, and attractive be interested in a man like *me*?

Priya gets up and for the first time I notice what pretty little feet she has, with soft-looking brown skin, and red-painted toenails. She crosses the room, grabs two glasses and a bottle of whiskey — one I used to drink with Anna — then sits back down next to me. A bit closer than before.

"I would like to propose a toast," she says, pouring two rather large measures. "Here's to a long and happy *strictly professional and platonic* relationship. Cheers."

"Cheers," I reply, clinking my glass with hers.

She downs her drink — bit of a waste really, it's good-quality stuff — but I drain my glass too.

And then I kiss her.

HER

Christ, I need a drink. I can't remember the last time I went this long without one.

After a nonstop day of broadcasting — seemingly endless two-ways outside the school, then at the police station, as well as filming and packaging for various outlets — I am longing for my bed. I call to find out what time early bulletins want us on-air tomorrow, then scribble the requests down with a black felt-tip pen I found in my handbag. I don't remember where I got it from, but it's come in handy more than once today.

I'm cold, and my feet are killing me from standing for so long. I think I've gotten a little too used to presenting the lunchtime bulletin, sitting behind a desk in a nice warm studio. I don't really understand where the day has gone — one hour rolling into the next, like a series of mini reruns

315

stitched together. Life sometimes seems like a hamster wheel we can only step off if we know to stop running.

Time has changed too, and turned into something I can no longer tell. It started the night my daughter died. As soon as I left Charlotte — asleep in her travel crib at my mother's house — it felt as though I had been separated from her for hours, not minutes. I didn't want to leave her there at all, but Jack insisted we should go out for my birthday. He didn't understand that after what happened on my sixteenth, celebrating a birthday was something I'd never really wanted to do again.

He kept insisting that I needed to get out of the house, something I hadn't been doing too often since Charlotte was born. Motherhood doesn't come with a manual, and it was a shock when we first brought our daughter home from the hospital. I'd read all the books they tell you to read, been to all the classes, but the reality of being responsible for another human being was a heavy burden, and something I wasn't prepared for. The person I thought I was disappeared overnight, and I became this new woman I didn't recognize. One who rarely slept, never looked in the mirror, and who worried constantly about her child. My life became only about hers. I was terrified that something bad would happen if I ever left her alone, even for a minute. I was right.

Since she died, time stretches and contracts in ways I can't fathom. It feels like I have less of it somehow, as though the world is spinning too fast, the days falling into one another in an exhausting blur. I was not a natural mother, but I tried to be the best I could. *Really* tried. My own mum said that the first few months were always the hardest with a baby, but those were all I had.

People use the expression "heartbroken" so often it has lost its meaning. For me, it was as though my heart actually broke into a thousand pieces when I lost my daughter, and I haven't been able to feel or really care about anything else ever since. It didn't just break my heart, it broke me, and I am no longer the same person. I'm someone else now. I don't know how to feel anything anymore, or how to return affection. It is far easier to borrow love than it is to pay it back.

Richard has had to drive me everywhere today, as a result of the police holding on to my car. Although it's completely normal for a correspondent and cameraman to spend this much time together, I don't like it.

Something feels strange between us. A little off. I don't know whether it is because Jack told me about his criminal record, or something else.

I had some free time in the afternoon, when the engineers insisted on having yet another proper meal break — there was talk of the union as soon as I raised an eyebrow — but the truth was, I didn't mind skipping a slot. There had been no new developments in the story since early that morning. I knew that the news channel could easily rerun my live from the previous hour, giving me almost two to myself.

I was secretly glad when the rest of the team drove off in search of food. We had been doing lives from the woods for hours, and I needed some time by myself. I told them that I wanted to go for a walk. Richard offered to go with me, but I didn't want to be alone with him in a secluded corner of the forest, or anywhere else for that matter. Eventually he got the hint and went with the others.

Once they were gone, I took a familiar footpath through the trees toward the high street. All the other roads and footpaths in Blackdown spread out through the woods from there, like the veins of a twisted leaf, with the high street for a stem. The whole town seems to exist beneath a canopy of leaves and unspoken lies, as though the oaks and pines that make up the forest clawed or climbed or crawled out from under its boundaries at night, stalking the people that live here, and setting down roots outside each and every home in order to keep watch over them.

I found myself standing behind the house where Jack now lives with Zoe. I never saw eye-to-eye with my sister-in-law, and my husband never knew the real reasons why. He doesn't know her the way I do. Families often paint their own portraits in a different light, using colors the rest of us can't quite see. Zoe was dark and dangerous as a teenager, and probably still is. She was born with the safety off.

When Jack and I met as adults in London, I was a junior reporter, trying to get on-air with a story about a murder he was investigating. I didn't remember him at first, but he knew me instantly, and he threatened to make a formal complaint to the BBC about my conduct if I didn't have a drink with him. I didn't know whether to be insulted or flattered by his flirtatious blackmail at first. I found him attractive — as did all the other female reporters — but men came second to my career, and I had little interest in relationships.

In the end, I agreed to one date — thinking I might get some insider information — but instead I woke up with a huge hangover and a detective in my bed. Knowing who his sister was, and what she was capable of, almost put me off seeing him again. But what I thought might be a one-night stand led to another date, which led to a weekend in Paris. I sometimes forget that Jack used to be spontaneous and romantic. Being with him made me happy, and loving him made me dislike myself less.

Zoe did a bad job of hiding her feelings about our relationship. She'd avoid eye contact with me at all family gatherings, and was the last to congratulate us when we got engaged. She didn't come to our wedding either. She sent Jack a text saying she had norovirus the day before, then posted pictures of herself in Ibiza the day after. When our daughter was born Zoe sent us lilies, a well-known symbol of death. Jack said it was an innocent mistake, but there is nothing innocent about his sister.

I stared up at Jack and Zoe's house, filled with loathing and disgust for the woman inside it. Then I noticed that the kitchen door was slightly ajar.

A little later, back on track but having lost

some time, I walk past all the familiar shops and quirky old buildings which make Blackdown so unique. I hurry along what is often described as one of the UK's prettiest high streets, knowing that I'm running out of time to get the things I need. I make a quick pit stop at the cheap and cheerful clothing store that has been here since before I was born. Thanks to my missing overnight bag, I need something to wear tomorrow. I grab an inoffensive white shirt and some very unfashionable underwear, then pay without trying anything on. Clean clothes aren't the only thing I've run out of, and I need a drink even more badly than before, after my visit to Zoe's house.

The supermarket doors slide open — as though the place has been expecting me, just waiting to swallow me inside — and the air-conditioned aisles aren't the only thing to make me shiver. It feels like I'm walking down old familiar lanes, and the alcohol section looks exactly as it always did. There are no miniatures, sadly, but they do sell mini bottles of wine and whiskey, which I hold up against my handbag, trying to decide how many I can fit inside and still close the zipper.

I add a small box of mints to my basket at the checkout, and when I look up, to my slight horror, it becomes clear that the cashier recognizes me. Her face expresses a judgment I cannot afford.

People get preoccupied with the fiction of truth.

The lives we lead need to be gold-plated nowadays, a series of varnished truths for the sake of how we appear on the outside. Strangers who view us through a screen — whether on TV or social media — think they know who we are. Nobody is interested in reality anymore; that's something they don't want to "like" or "share" or "follow." I can understand that, but living a make-believe life can be dangerous. What we won't see can hurt us. In the future, I expect people will long for fifteen minutes of privacy, rather than fifteen minutes of fame.

"A little gift for my cameraman and engineers after working so hard today," I say to the cashier, before slipping my purchases straight into my bag as soon as she has scanned them.

She is a little older than me. A potato-shaped woman, with well-worn skin and argumentative eyes, the kind that let you know with just one look how much they dislike you. Her blotchy face attempts a smile, and I see that she has a gap between her front teeth, big enough to slot a pound coin in.

"Have you seen your mother lately?" she asks, and I try to suppress a sigh. Everyone knows everything about everyone else in this town. Or thinks they do. It's one of the many things I can't stand about the place. The woman doesn't wait for a reply. "She's been found wandering the streets late at night a few times now, your mother. Lost in the dark, crying, not knowing where or who she is, wearing nothing but a nightdress. You're lucky that husband of yours stepped in. She needs *someone* to look after her. Should be in a home if you ask me."

"Thanks, but I didn't," I reply, handing her my credit card.

I've always been more sensitive about my failings as a daughter than my weakness for a drink. I look over my shoulder, to see if anyone else in the shop heard what she said, relieved to see that they all seem content to mind their own business. If only that were true of everyone. I still remember the first time I bought alcohol in this supermarket, all those years ago.

Rachel said I couldn't have a birthday party without drinks. I was surprised that she still thought I should invite Helen — given how much trouble our clever friend had almost gotten us into — but it also made me happy. I thought that Rachel's decision to forgive her was another example of her kindness. I think that's what made me invite someone else along; it was meant to be *my* party after all, and I wanted to be kind too. It was also why I made friendship bracelets for everyone who was coming.

Rachel laughed when she saw them.

"Did you make them yourself?"

I nodded and she laughed again.

"Well, that's very *sweet,* but we're *sixteen,* not ten." She put her hand on my shoulder, and shoved the bracelets in her pocket as though they were trash. It had taken me ages to make the gifts I couldn't afford to buy. It was impossible to hide how much her words hurt, and she noticed. "I'm sorry. I like them, I really do, we'll all wear them later, but first we need to buy some booze, and for that we are going to need some money. You can't steal a bit from your mum, can you?" she asked.

Rachel could see that I was shocked by the suggestion, and seemed to think better of it. We'd stopped at her house on the way to mine, and I watched as she flung open her enormous wardrobe doors, before rummaging around inside. She turned, looking triumphant, rattling her yellow Children in Need bucket in my direction. It was the one she used to collect donations at school. She tipped it upside down onto her bed, before counting the coins that fell out.

"Forty-two pounds, eighty-eight pence," she said.

"But that's charity money."

"And you're a charity case, so what's the problem? How did you think I was paying for all those little presents I gave you?"

I didn't answer. I was too upset that she was admitting to stealing money from children who needed it far more than we did.

"Come on," she said, taking my hand in hers.

I remember it was the first time I didn't like holding it.

"Stop sulking; you're less pretty when you frown," she whispered, then kissed me on the cheek. "We'll swing by the supermarket for booze on the way to your house, a drink or three will cheer you up."

We walked there in silence.

I watched as Rachel put bottles of Diet 7 Up, tequila, and cheap white wine into her shopping basket, and wondered how we were going to buy it when we were both so clearly underage. I had a pain in my tummy as we approached the checkout; just the thought of my mother finding out was enough to make me feel physically sick. It felt like I kept letting her down.

But then I spotted Helen Wang. She had already turned sixteen, and had a job at the supermarket on Saturdays. She scanned the alcohol without calling for a manager, and Rachel hid it straight in her bag. No ID required. I was so glad that we were all still friends, despite the incident with the essays.

"What happened to your face?" I asked Helen, noticing what looked like a black eye poorly disguised with makeup.

She looked at Rachel before turning back to me.

"I slipped up."

I had seen enough of my mother's bruises when my father was still around to know that Helen was lying. But I also knew better than to ask any more questions. Just like when Mum used to insist she had walked into a door, I knew Helen wouldn't tell me the truth. I thought she might have a secret boyfriend. A bad one.

"We'll see you later. Come straight to Anna's after work," Rachel said to Helen, dragging me toward the exit.

My mother had reluctantly agreed to go out for the evening, but was still there when we arrived. I didn't need to say anything for her to know I was furious.

"I'm going, I'm going," she said as we put our bags down in the kitchen, the alcohol hidden inside. "I got you a little birthday surprise, and I wanted to show you before I left."

"What is it?" I asked, dreading the answer, hoping it wasn't something childish that would embarrass me in front of Rachel.

"It's in the sunroom, go take a look," said Mum.

I walked to the back of the house, worried about what I might find there, then saw a small gray ball of fur sitting on my mother's favorite chair.

"It's a kitten!" squealed Rachel, rushing forward, far more excited than I was.

"One of the ladies I clean for has the most beautiful cat — it's a Russian Blue — and when I saw the latest litter I just couldn't resist bringing this little one home," Mum said. "Go on, pick her up, she's yours."

I had wanted a cat for a long time, but she said we couldn't afford it. Plus, cats always seemed to be disappearing in Blackdown. Every week a new Missing poster would appear in shop windows and on lampposts around the town. There were endless black-and-white photos of lost pets, along with their descriptions, and sometimes rewards. It was the sort of heartbreak my mother worried I couldn't handle, but I still longed for one of my own. I carefully picked up the kitten, afraid I might break her.

"You'll have to choose a name," my mother said.

"Kit Kat," I whispered.

I'd already imagined what I would call my cat if I ever had one.

Rachel giggled. "Like the chocolate bar?"

"I think it's perfect," said Mum. "Play with her for a bit tonight if you want, but then pop her back in the cat carrier in the corner. The vet said it might help settle her in the first few nights. I'll leave you girls to have fun now, but I know you'll be drinking alcohol —"

"Mum!"

I felt my cheeks turn bright red.

". . . so I've left some snacks in the fridge. There are chips in the cupboard too, so help yourselves and line your stomachs. Have fun and take care of one another, and Kit Kat. Okay?"

"We will, don't worry," said Rachel. "You're so cool, Mrs. Andrews. I wish my mum was like you."

She smiled at my mother, in that clever way that seemed to make all adults adore her. My mother smiled back, before kissing me good-bye.

"Let's get this party started!" Rachel said as soon as she was gone.

She had stayed at my house so often by then that she knew where to find everything she wanted. She immediately raided my mother's old vinyl collection — Rachel was obsessed with seventies music — carefully slipping a Carpenters record out of its sleeve and putting it on. "Rainy Days and Mondays" was her favorite song. She sang along as she returned to the kitchen, then took two glasses down from the cupboard. I held on to the kitten and we both watched Rachel with fascination as she found the salt, took a lemon from the fruit bowl, and slid a sharp knife out of the block on the counter.

I had never seen or heard of a tequila slammer before, but I liked them. By the time the others arrived, I was already feeling pretty drunk.

"Did you bring the party treats?" Rachel asked Helen as soon as she walked in the door.

"What are they?" I wanted to know.

Rachel smiled. "A nice surprise."

Zoe was next to arrive. She looked miserable when I opened the door, and rolled her eyes in the direction of the older boy standing next to her on my doorstep.

"What's that?" she asked, staring at the kitten in my hands.

"She's called Kit Kat, a birthday present from my mum."

"I hate cats," Zoe said, pulling a face.

"I'm Jack, by the way," said the boy. He seemed amused by something. "My mother wanted me to drop off Zoe and check everything was okay, after what happened last time."

I didn't know what that meant. It was still only a few months since I'd joined the school and met them all.

Jack was just a few years older than us, but at that age a couple of years can make someone seem infinitely grown-up. He popped his head inside the door, holding his car keys in his hand. I had no idea what he was looking for, and I don't know whether it was his floppy hair or the cheeky grin, but I liked him instantly. I wasn't the only one.

"Hi, Jack! Why don't you come in for a drink?" said Rachel, appearing beside me.

"No, thanks. I'm driving."

"Just one?" she insisted.

I remember hating the way they looked at each other.

"Maybe just a Coke or something," he

330

said, giving in to her charm.

It was strange seeing all these people crammed into our little kitchen. My mother rarely let anyone in after my father left, and the house felt too full with them all there. Everyone looked a little surprised when the doorbell rang again, even me. I'd already had enough to drink to forget about the other person I had decided to invite.

They all came with me to the door, and they all look appalled when they saw Catherine Kelly standing behind it.

"Happy Birthday, Anna," she said, without smiling.

Everyone just stared.

Then Rachel stepped forward and put her glass in Catherine's hand.

"How lovely to see you, Catherine. Have a drink. I promise there is nothing nasty in this one, and you need to catch up," she said, pulling the girl inside.

I was so happy that she was being kind. Catherine Kelly was a little strange, but I'd wanted to invite her to my party anyway. Something terrible had happened to Catherine the week before. Baby rats were found inside her school desk. Everyone blamed it on all the chips and chocolate she kept in there, but I still couldn't understand how they had gotten inside. I felt sorry for her. I knew what it was like to be the odd one out at my old school, and didn't want anyone else to feel that way. I thought I could help make her happy.

"Well, as fun as this looks, I'm off," said Jack. "Mum says home by midnight or else, Zoe. Unless you want to get grounded again."

Zoe rolled her eyes. She did it so often I worried they might get stuck that way.

"Wait!" Rachel rushed over to her bag and took out a new disposable Kodak camera. It was still in its box, and she tore at the cardboard packaging to open it. "Can you take a picture of us all together before you go?"

"Sure," Jack said, holding out his hand.

I saw that their fingers touched as she gave him the camera, and felt a stab of irrational jealousy.

"And I almost forgot . . ." Rachel said.

She reached inside her pocket, before arranging us all in a line against the floral wallpaper in my mother's living room.

". . . lovely Anna made us all friendship bracelets, and I think we should wear them."

So we put them on, because people always did what Rachel said to do.

We posed against that wall with our arms wrapped around each other, wearing our red-and-white cotton bracelets, and looking like the best of friends. Even Catherine Kelly, who Rachel positioned right in the middle, was smiling in the photo, her ugly braces, crazy curly white hair, and horrible clothes on display for the whole world to see.

It was the same photo I found yesterday with Rachel's face crossed out.

Him

I cross the road and realize I've taken a wrong turn. I'm drunk. Too drunk to drive home from Priya's house, so I decided to walk. I know I shouldn't have kissed her, but that's all it was, a drunken kiss. No need to turn it into a drama, or blow it out of proportion. I was thinking about Anna when I did it, perhaps because of the taste of whiskey inside her mouth and mine. I don't regret it. I will in the morning, but for now I'm going to enjoy the way tonight made me feel: to know that a beautiful, intelligent young woman finds me attractive.

I choose not to linger on the question of why.

Spending time with someone younger than myself made me feel less old tonight. Listening to Priya talk about her future made me realize my own might not be set in stone. Youth fools us into thinking there

334

are infinite paths to choose from in life; maturity tricks us into thinking there is only one. Priya opened up about her past, and her honesty was contagious. She told me her mother died of cancer last year and she's still grieving. The woman raised her alone, in a community that frowned upon that sort of thing, and Priya was quite open about how much she missed having a father figure growing up.

I expect that's what made me think about my daughter. The truth is, I think about her all the time. If I don't talk about Charlotte it's only because I feel like I can't. It was my idea — to take Anna out for a birthday meal, just the two of us — so maybe that's why I still think what happened was my fault.

Anna had barely left the house at all for months. She'd been on strict bed rest before the birth, and then afterward when we brought Charlotte home, she turned into someone I didn't recognize. It wasn't right, and neither was she. Her whole life was suddenly only about our daughter, and nobody could make her see that it was all too much, that she needed to take a step back. If I mentioned getting help, it only made things worse.

I'd arranged for her mother to babysit for

one night, just *one* night for god's sake; it was meant to be a kind thing to do. For both of them. But when we went to collect Charlotte the following morning, I knew that something was wrong as soon as Anna's mother opened the door. She had promised not to drink while looking after the baby, but we could both smell the alcohol on her breath. She didn't say a word, but looked as though she had been crying. Anna pushed her mother aside, and ran into the house. I was only a few steps behind. The travel crib was exactly where we had left it, Charlotte was still inside, and I remember the relief I felt when I saw her. It was only when Anna lifted her up that I could tell our little girl was dead.

There is no such thing as unconditional love. I didn't really blame Anna's mother. She'd only started drinking after discovering Charlotte had stopped breathing in the middle of the night. She'd panicked. For some reason she didn't call an ambulance, I think perhaps because she already knew the child was dead. The coroner confirmed it was a cot death, and could have happened anytime, anyplace. But I blamed myself. So did Anna. Over and over again, screaming the silent words at me through her never-ending tears.

I loved our little girl just as much as she did, but it felt like Anna was the only one allowed to grieve. Now, two years later, I seem to be teetering on the edge at all times, a domino on the verge of falling over and taking those closest down with me. For a long while after what happened nothing about my life felt real or had any meaning. It's the reason I left London and came back here. To make some sort of family with what I had left: a sister and a niece. And to give Anna the space she said she needed.

We buried Charlotte in Blackdown — Anna was in no fit state to make a decision at the time, so I made it — and I think it's something else she still hates me for.

It's a half-hour walk, along pitch-black footpaths and deserted country lanes, from Priya's end of town to mine, but walking is the only option. There are no cabs in the countryside. No signs of life at all in Blackdown at this time of night. A black cat runs in front of me, crossing my path and contradicting my last thought. It's the sort of thing that would have worried my ex-wife, but I don't buy into all that superstitious nonsense. Besides, I've already had more than my fair share of bad luck.

It's bitterly cold, the variety that bites if you dare to stand still in it for too long. So

I shove my hands a little deeper, down inside my pockets, and keep them there rather than smoke. Strangely, I don't even feel the need for a cigarette now, after spending an evening talking to another human being instead of staring at a screen.

Rachel and I didn't really talk, we just shared polite conversation accompanied by impolite sex. It never felt like we had much to say to each other, at least not things that either of us would have wanted to hear. I keep thinking about the words that were painted on her fingernails: TWO FACED. Anna and I used to talk before Charlotte came along, but it was as though we forgot how. Tonight, with Priya, I felt like a real person again.

I decide to send her a text, and reach inside my pocket for my phone.

I find Rachel's phone instead, and there is an unread message:

You should have gone straight home tonight, Jack.

I stop walking and stare at the words for a few seconds. Then turn a full three-sixty, peering into the darkness, trying to see whether someone is following me now. *Someone* clearly has been. I wasn't imagining it. But who? And why? I shove the phone back into my pocket and walk a little faster.

I can see that my house is in complete darkness when I turn onto the street. Nothing unusual about that; it's late, and I don't expect my little sister to wait for me to come home. We've never been the kind of siblings to check up on each other. I presume Zoe has had a couple of glasses of cheap wine and gone to bed, just like she does most nights.

I start searching for my keys as soon as I get through the gate, struggling to find them in the gloom. The porch light comes on by the time I am halfway down the garden path, but despite it shedding a little light inside my jacket pocket where my keys should be, I can see they aren't there.

I hate the idea of having to wake the whole house in order to get Zoe to let me in — it can be hard to get my niece to go back to sleep — but when I step up to the front door, I see that won't be necessary. It's already open.

There is always a heartbeat-length moment when you know that something very bad is about to happen, and you are too late to do anything about it. It lasts less than a second and more than a lifetime all at once, while you are frozen in space and time, reluctant to look ahead, but knowing it's too late to look back. This is one of those moments. I have experienced only a few like it in my life.

I sober up fast.

The police part of my brain tells me to call someone, but I don't. What is left of my family is inside this house and I can't wait for backup. I hurry through the front door, switching on the lights in all of the downstairs rooms, finding each one as empty as the last. The rest of the doors and windows appear to be closed and locked. I check the alarm system, but it looks as though someone has turned it off. The only way to do that is by knowing the code.

There is no sign of forced entry, no sign of a struggle; if anything the whole place looks a lot cleaner and tidier than when I left this morning. Toddlers are experts at creating mess, but all the clutter and chaos I've grown used to has been tidied away and put back in its place. Everything feels wrong, and I've learned over the years to trust my gut about things like this.

That's when I see it.

One of the smaller knives is missing from the block on the counter. I remember that it wasn't there this morning either, or the night before. My house keys are here too, even though I'm sure they were in my pocket earlier tonight, before I went to Pri-

340

ya's home. Maybe I did leave them here — the last few days are a sleep-deprived blur. Then I see the photo. It's just like the one Anna said was stolen from her car, and it's a picture that *I* remember taking twenty years ago.

The five girls are lined up and smiling at the camera: Rachel Hopkins, Helen Wang, Anna, Zoe, and a strange-looking girl I vaguely recognize, but whose name I can't remember. They are wearing matching grins on their faces, and matching friendship bracelets on their wrists. But that isn't all. Three of the five girls in the photo have a black cross drawn over their face now: Rachel, Helen . . . and Zoe.

I drop the picture — realizing too late that I should never have touched it — and run up the stairs two at a time. I reach my niece's room first, bursting through the door to see that Olivia is safe and sound, tucked up asleep in bed. Her pillow, along with everything else in the room, is covered in a pattern of unicorns. She looks so peaceful that for a moment I think maybe everything is okay. But then I realize that the noise I just made would normally have woken her. Olivia is breathing, but she's completely out of it.

I hurry along the landing to my sister's

room, but she isn't there. All the bedroom doors are ajar, and I soon discover that each one is empty. The bathroom door is closed. When I try to turn the handle, it doesn't open.

We haven't locked this door for years due to an incident when we were children, and I don't know where the key could be. I can't remember ever seeing one. The rule in our house was always that if the door is closed, you don't go in. I knock gently and whisper her name.

"Zoe?"

It's so quiet that everything I say and do sounds loud.

I try to peer through the keyhole, but see nothing but black.

"Zoe?"

I say her name a little louder this time, before banging my fist on the wooden panels. When there is still nothing but silence, I take a step back and kick the door. It swings open, its hinges crying out as though in pain. Then I see her.

My sister is lying in the bath.

One of her eyes is open, and appears to be staring at something written on the wall; the other one has been sewn closed, a needle and thick black thread still dangling from her eyelid.

The water is red, her slit wrists visible just below the surface.

I'm sickened by the fact I already know what this is supposed to mean: turn a blind eye.

I'm sure the normal response would be to rush to the side of the bathtub and pull her out, but I can't move. My sister's head is slumped to one side at a disturbing angle, her hair is the same color as the perfectly still bloody water, and I don't need to check for a pulse to know that she is dead. Zoe's mouth is open, and I can see the friendship bracelet tied around her tongue from the doorway.

I stay in the hall, as though my feet can't cross the threshold. I feel bile rise up my throat, but swallow it down. I should call the police but I don't. I try to think of a friend I could call for help — it feels like that is what I need right now — but then I remember I don't have any left. Nobody wants to be friends with the couple whose baby died.

I surprise myself then by calling Priya.

In my drunken, shocked state, my colleague seems to be the closest I've got to having someone who cares. I don't know what I say when she answers, but it must have made some kind of sense, because she tells me she is on her way. It looks like my sister wrote a name on the tiled wall, using her finger as a pen and her own blood as ink before she died. I didn't mention that part to Priya. I couldn't say it out loud.

I slide down onto the landing floor. Time slows to a painful standstill while I wait, punctuated only by the sound of the tap dripping. It's been doing that for years, but it never bothered me until now. I watch as tiny ripples spread themselves across the surface of the red water, my eyes inevitably wandering to Zoe's. When I can't bear to look at her disfigured face anymore, I stare at the name my sister wrote in blood above the bath:

ANDREWS.

HER

Wednesday 23:30

"Anna Andrews, BBC News, Blackdown."

We film the last piece to camera of the night, then wait for a clear from the newsroom. By the time we get one, the engineers have already packed up and are ready to go. They waste no time heading back toward London when the call comes, leaving Richard and me alone in the woods. It's been relentless today, and I'm so glad I had a couple of hours to myself earlier, even if I did end up walking to Zoe and Jack's house. Seeing that place again, and knowing she was inside it, made me lose myself for a while. Some wrongs can never be made right, and it's been a very long day.

I don't really want to get in a car with Richard again — it's hard to explain, he's been acting strange all night — but I don't have a lot of choice without the Mini. I can't seem to stop myself from shivering, and when he notices, I blame the cold. There's something different about him, but it's less than five minutes to the hotel so I try to shake the feeling.

We drive in silence. I don't think either of us is going to want to share a conversation or a drink tonight. I try, but I can't think of anything I've said or done today that would have offended him, so I put the undeniable tension down to us both just being exhausted. I'm looking forward to a hot bath and getting reacquainted with the minibar.

"What do you mean you don't have a reservation?" I ask when the hotel receptionist stares blankly back at me across the desk.

She's so tall, she can't help but look down on us. Her long brown hair has been restrained in a neat French braid, the end of which rests on her young slim shoulders like a tail. She appears to have eaten half a box of chocolates single-handed so far on her night shift, and I wonder if someone gave them to her, or whether she bought them herself. She stands a little hunched over, as though she wishes she were shorter, like a flower who has been leaning the same way toward the sun for too long.

I'm certain the newsroom booked two hotel rooms for us this afternoon. I'm sure I received a confirmation e-mail, so I ask her to check again. Her body language does not inspire confidence, and she keeps us waiting for a painful amount of time. I don't think I was ever that skinny, even when I was her age, despite the diet pills Helen bullied me into taking. This girl is as thin as my patience right now.

"I'm sorry, but there is definitely no corporate booking from the BBC on the system for tonight," she replies, staring at the screen as though expecting it to verbally back her up.

I take out my purse and put down my credit card.

"Fine, I'll pay for two rooms and claim them back afterward."

She glances at her computer again, then shakes her plaited head.

"I'm afraid we're completely full. There's been a murder. Two now actually. Lots of press in town and we're the only hotel."

"You don't say. It's very late and we're very tired. I'm sure someone booked us two rooms for tonight. Can you please check again?"

Richard says nothing.

The receptionist looks weary, as though being asked to do her job exhausts her.

"Do you have a booking reference?" she says.

I feel a surge of hope. Then I find my phone and feel a rush of despair — my battery is dangerously low — only five percent left — and I remember that my charger was in the overnight bag that was stolen from the Mini earlier.

"My mobile is about to die, can you check yours?" I ask Richard.

He sighs, then reaches for his pocket. His expression changes immediately and he starts to pat himself down and search inside his bag.

"Shit, I don't have it . . ."

"Maybe you left it in the car?" I reply, and concentrate on finding the e-mail before my phone is completely out of juice.

When I do, I show the receptionist the screen with an inflated sense of triumph. She takes an extraordinary length of time to stab the reference number into her computer, using just one finger.

"A reservation was made for you this afternoon, two rooms . . ."

"Thank goodness," I say, and start to smile too soon.

". . . but it was canceled this evening."

The half-formed smile slides right off my face.

"What? No. When? By who?"

"It doesn't tell me who made the call, only

that the rooms were canceled at eighteen thirty."

Richard picks up my credit card and hands it to me.

"Come on, if she says the place is full there's no point standing here arguing about it. It's crazy late, and we've got another early start tomorrow. I know somewhere we can stay."

HIM

Wednesday 23:55

Even when I hear the familiar sound of police sirens, I stay where I am outside the bathroom. Waiting while they pull up outside before coming in through the open front door downstairs. Priya takes charge of everything, and seems remarkably sober too, given how many bottles of beer I thought we drank together earlier. I watch them all coming and going, police colleagues walking through the crime scene that used to be my home, while I seem unable to stand or think.

I only snap out of it when I hear my niece start to cry in her bedroom, woken by strangers working on the murder of her mother. Not that she knows that, or will understand it anytime soon. Doctors are checking her over now; they think she was drugged. I try to get up using the wall for support, avoiding looking inside the bathroom. They haven't moved Zoe yet. She's still lying in a pool of red water, staring up at the name on the wall.

"Take it easy," says Priya, rushing over to help me get back on my feet. "I've got this. You shouldn't be here, is there somewhere else you can go?"

There isn't.

Olivia is screaming now. I don't know how to explain what has happened to a two-year-old; I don't understand it myself. Priya carries on talking, but all I can hear is a little girl crying out for a mother she'll never see again.

"I'm guessing you'd rather avoid social services getting involved, so I've found a neighbor who says she can look after your niece; sounds like she's looked after her before. You'll need to sign something, but a family liaison officer will take care of everything, is that okay?"

I think I nod, but I don't know if it *is* okay. Maybe I should stay with her.

"Good. You can't stay here," Priya says, as though reading my thoughts.

"I need to find out who did this," I insist, my voice sounding strange inside my ears.

"I know you do. But maybe tomorrow, sir. I think it might be best if I get someone to drive you somewhere else for the night?"

"Where do you think I'm going to go? And why haven't you asked the most obvious question yet?"

Priya pulls the face she reserves for when she feels most uncomfortable.

"I don't know what you —"

"Don't treat me like a fool, Priya. You know exactly what I mean. What do your instincts tell you? Do you think *she* did it?"

"Who?"

"Anna! They never liked each other. Why else would my ex-wife's name be written on the wall in blood? She's been the first to arrive at every crime scene. I know you suspected her earlier. Maybe I could have stopped this from happening if only I'd —"

Priya stares at me with a look that lies somewhere between pity and mistrust, and it redefines her features.

"Go on, say whatever it is that you're thinking," I say when she doesn't speak.

"Well, you said yourself that the bathroom door was locked from the inside when you arrived . . ."

I don't have the patience for one of her pauses.

"Yes," I snap.

"And the key to the door was found on the side of the bath —"

"Are you suggesting it was suicide?" I

interrupt. She stares at me, the awkward silence answering the question for her. "If my sister committed suicide, then what did she use to slit her wrists? Do you see a knife or a razor?"

Priya looks back over her shoulder at the scene. I can't bear to follow her gaze, so I carry on trying to explain things the way I see them.

"There is a friendship bracelet tied around her tongue, just like the other two victims. We haven't shared that information with the press or the public. Whoever killed the others killed Zoe — or are you suggesting she sewed her own eye closed?"

"I'm not suggesting anything, sir. But she could have been working with someone else, and things went wrong. I'm just gathering the evidence, like you taught me to."

Her phone rings and I think she's grateful for the interruption until she sees who is calling.

"It's the deputy chief constable," she says.

"Well, answer it."

She does, and I watch while he talks and she listens. It feels like an eternal wait for the call to end, but in reality, it only lasts a couple of minutes.

"He wants you off the case. I'm sorry, sir, but given the circumstances I think it's probably the right call."

The short speech packs a punch and was well delivered. Either the alcohol we drank earlier has given her additional confidence, or she's been rehearsing for the moment she could justify stealing my job.

I'm distracted when someone starts to take pictures of the crime scene behind us. The flash jogs something in my tired broken mind, and I remember the photo. I push past Priya and hurry down the stairs. She follows me into the kitchen, and at first I think the picture has disappeared, that maybe I imagined it. But then I see someone walking away with an evidence bag.

"Stop," I say, snatching it from them.

"I saw the photo, if that's what you're looking for," Priya says. "I asked them to bag it up." The look she gives me is one I haven't seen before. I stare at the picture, at the faces crossed out with a black marker pen, and I start to see things the way she must. I take a step back without meaning to. It just got even louder than before inside my head.

"You *do* know that I didn't have anything to do with this, don't you?" I ask her. The respect she had for me only a few hours earlier seems to have disappeared. "I was with *you* all day, *and* all night."

354

"Technically not all night. I went out, sir. Remember? And you left my house well over an hour before you rang me. I'm not sure why it took you so long to call for help."

The room starts to twist a little, catching me off guard so that it feels like I might fall. I was sure I called her straightaway, but it must have taken me longer than I thought. Probably the shock of what I saw.

"Come on, Priya. You know me."

"No, sir. I don't, not really. We're just colleagues, like you said earlier. The team searched the trash cans outside, looking for a discarded weapon, and found a pair of muddy size-ten Timberland boots instead. Just like the footprint found next to Rachel Hopkins's body in the woods. Are they yours?"

I feel like I've fallen down a rabbit hole and landed in a parallel universe. I don't understand why Priya is behaving this way. She's been treating me like a hero for months, we kissed earlier tonight, and now she's looking at me as though I might be a suspect in my own sister's murder.

"Do you know where the knife is, sir? The one that appears to be missing from the block?"

"Please stop calling me 'sir.' Look, I think someone might be trying to set me up. The photo of the girls was here when I got home," I insist. "Somebody put it here, the same someone who killed Zoe. That's Rachel Hopkins, Helen Wang, Anna . . ." My voice falters. ". . . and my sister."

"Who is the fifth girl?" asks Priya.

"I don't remember her name."

It's obvious she doesn't believe me — I'm starting to doubt myself — but I have to try to get Priya on my side. I panic when she starts to turn away.

"Wait. Please. I don't think the other girl was very popular, and I'm surprised they were friends with her, to be honest. Three out of the five people in this picture are dead, and my sister wrote Anna's name on the wall in *blood.* Don't you think we should at least try to find her?"

"I do, but perhaps not for the same reasons as you, Jack."

I think I preferred "sir" after all.

"What is that supposed to mean?"

"As you say, three out of the five girls in this photo are dead. We only know the identity of one of the others. I think maybe Zoe was trying to write a *warning* when she spelled out Anna's name, and that your ex-wife might be in danger."

"What are you saying?" I ask the question

already knowing the answer.

"I think Anna might be next."

I've always been rather fond of the number three, and hoped it might be my best work. I waited until Zoe disappeared upstairs to put the child to bed, then emptied the crushed sleeping tablets into the glass of wine she had left behind. My GP had been prescribing them for months, so I had plenty to spare. I'd thought about swallowing the lot myself last Christmas. The pain of spending it without her almost killed me, but I changed my mind.

A lot of people grow old, but they don't all grow up. Zoe was a child trapped inside a woman's body, despite having a little girl of her own. She needed her parents far more than I ever did, always, for everything, and when they were gone she got lost. No job, no partner, no ambition, no hope. Just an inherited house she couldn't afford, and a daughter she didn't know how to love. I think it will be better for the child in the long run.

I had a sip of Zoe's drink before adding the

drugs. The wine was as cheap and unpleasant as the woman who had poured it, so I doubted she would notice any change in taste. I was right. I watched her take the glass and the rest of the bottle upstairs. Then she removed her clothes, climbed into the bath, finished her drink, and closed her eyes.

It was strange seeing her naked again. The shape of her breasts, the vertebrae of her spine, her exposed collarbones. I'd seen her without clothes when we were both a lot younger of course, but it was oddly fascinating to see the skin she wore now, the woman she had grown into. When we are young, we think we know more than we do. When we are old, we think we know less. I tend to remember people as they were in my earliest memory of them, and I will always think of Zoe as a little girl. A spoiled, selfish, evil one.

Her deciding to have a bath was a real stroke of luck; much less messy. I watched and waited until she had been still for so long, I was sure she was dead. But when I used the knife to cut into her left wrist — the proper way, not like they do in the movies — Zoe opened her eyes. She looked surprised to see that it was me.

She struggled a bit, thrashed about, spilling some water over the side of the bath. It was both a shame and unnecessary. The drugs must have drained her at least, because she was soon still again. There was no repeat performance when I slit her right wrist, but I turned my back too soon to wash my hands in the basin afterward. When I looked at my reflection in mirror, I saw her writing on the wall. She stopped breathing halfway through the *S,* so that an ugly trail of blood ran from the tiles to the tub. Some people make a mess in death as well as in life.

There were two keys for that door due to an incident when Zoe accidentally locked herself in the bathroom as a child. She was such a creative little girl; always acting or drawing or making things. Perhaps that was why I decided to get a little creative myself.

Her eyes were still open and I don't like people staring at me.

I found Zoe's sewing basket next to a pile of the ugly cushion covers she sold online, then I selected a needle, along with a nice thick black thread. Her eyelid bled a little while I was sewing it closed, so that it looked like she was crying blood. But it was no worse than the things she had done to innocent victims. Things nobody else knew about except me.

I left one key in the bathroom, before locking the door with the other. Then I crept back downstairs. I put the photo of the girls in the kitchen, and marked a black cross over Zoe's face, before letting myself out of the house. I'd turned off the security system earlier, so that wasn't a problem. I planned to take a shortcut through the woods to get where I was going, but the old shed at the end of the garden distracted me. The door was slightly open, gently banging in the breeze. When I looked inside, I saw that the scratches on the wood were still there. Twenty years after they were made. I'll never forget how Zoe locked them in that shed.

She left them in the cold, damp darkness, ignoring their cries for help.

They must have been so afraid.

She deserved to die much sooner for what she did.

I locked the shed door and tried to forget what happened there.

HER

Richard locks the car doors as we drive in the darkness.

"Why did you do that?" I ask, trying not to sound as scared as I feel.

"Don't know. Instinct? Driving through these woods late at night tends to creep me out. Doesn't it do the same to you?"

I don't answer at first.

"You said you knew somewhere we could stay —"

"Yes, I think trying to find another hotel when it is already so late is going to be impossible. My wife's parents used to own a house not that far from here; ten minutes tops. They died a couple of years ago, and it's the kind of place an estate agent would say was 'in need of modernization,' but there are beds and clean sheets and I have a spare key. Want to risk it?"

It doesn't feel like I have many options. I

don't want to take him to my mother's house, and it seems a little selfish to insist we drive all the way back to London now; by the time we got there it would almost be time to come back.

"Okay," I say, too tired to form a more elaborate response.

He switches on the seat warmers, turns on the radio and, hard as I try not to, I find my eyes closing for a little while.

I should have learned to be more careful where and when I fall asleep.

One of the last things that I remember clearly about my sixteenth birthday party was Jack taking a photo of the five of us. The rest of the night has always been a bit of a blur at best.

We drank a lot more after he left, I remember that much. Then we all did one another's hair and makeup. Zoe had brought some of her latest fashion creations that she had made on her sewing machine for us to try on: skimpy dresses, low-cut tops, and skirts so short they looked more like belts.

Rachel went to work on Catherine Kelly's face, as though it were a project in art class. She applied a thick layer of makeup, filled in Catherine's bald eyebrows with a pencil, then stuck false black lashes to the blond ones around her eyes. Zoe lent her a dress, and Helen did her hair — squirting it with the water bottle my mum used for ironing, before blow-drying her whitish-blond curls straight. She said there wasn't time to comb out all the knots, so cut them of instead. I remember random little clumps of hair discarded on the carpet.

The transformation was quite remarkable, and Catherine was almost unrecognizable when they were finished with her. Lives are like light bulbs; they're not as hard to change as people think. Catherine looked beautiful, and she knew it too, beaming at her own reflection when the girls let her look in the mirror.

"Try to smile with your mouth closed. Nobody wants to see those ugly braces," said Rachel. Catherine did as she was told. "Look at that pretty little mouth now. The boys are going to love you," Rachel added, patting her on the head as though she were a pet.

Her new smile looked uncomfortable to wear.

I didn't know what boys Rachel was talking about — we never hung around with any — but I think I must have looked jealous, because she offered to paint my nails for me then. She held my hands and wrote letters on my fingernails with red varnish, spelling the word good on one hand, and girl on the other.

I'd already drunk far more alcohol than I was used to — the room had started to spin — but Rachel, Helen, and Zoe said they were going to the kitchen to find more, leaving Catherine and me alone in the living room.

"Are you glad you came?" I asked her.

She blinked at me, her new false eyelashes exaggerating the action, and once again I marveled at how different she looked. Then she told me something I had never known about her; I'm not sure anybody did. Perhaps because they never asked. She'd clearly had too much to drink too, and her sentences were interspersed with hiccups.

"I used to have an older sister, we did makeovers like this together, but she died. My dad had a little boat and we would go with him sometimes at weekends. That's where it happened. But before then, sailing was fun and he taught us how to make lots of knots. Look, I'll show you." She pulled the laces out of her sneakers with a sudden and strange enthusiasm. "This is a square knot . . . this is a figure eight . . ." Her fingers were so fast, tying, twisting, and looping the laces together before holding them up each time. I watched with a sense of bewildered fascination. "This is a sliding knot — just like the one you've used in the friendship bracelets — and this is a bowline, which I like better because you can control how far the loop constricts . . . see?"

I stared at the final knot.

"How did she die? Your sister?"

I doubt I would have asked the question so bluntly if I hadn't been so drunk. Catherine untied the laces and started to thread them back in her shoes.

"People always presume that she drowned because it happened when we were sailing, but an asthma attack killed my sister. She forgot her inhaler. My dad blamed himself and my parents have been really sad since she died, *really* sad. He lost his job, sold the boat, and our house isn't a very nice place now. I think maybe that's why nobody talks to me or invites me to anything anymore. Until you did. Thank you."

"You're welcome," I whispered.

"Can I hold her?" she asked.

I stared down at the gray kitten asleep on my lap. Kit Kat. I was so drunk I had forgotten she was there.

"Of course," I said, lifting her up and handing her to Catherine.

She held the cat in her arms and rocked

it, as though it were a baby.

"Come on, it's time to go," said Rachel, appearing in the doorway wearing her coat. It was one I hadn't seen before, made of fur, which I guessed was fake. I looked at the clock and saw that it was almost eleven.

"Go where?" I asked.

She pointed at me, smiled, and started to sing.

"If *you* go down to the woods tonight, you're sure of a big surprise."

"I don't want to go to the woods. It's late and cold and —"

Rachel ignored me, and pointed at Catherine instead while singing the next line.

"If *you* go down to the woods tonight, you'd better go in disguise!"

Zoe and Helen appeared behind her and all three started laughing.

The woods never scared me during the day, but at night they seemed to change into something different when I was a child. Somewhere dark and dangerous, where bad things might happen. It was meant to be my birthday party, but it was clear that what I did or didn't want to do was irrelevant. Rachel took my mother's flashlight off the hook by the door in the kitchen, and led the way. There was a path from my backyard that led straight into the woods, and she knew it as well as I did by then.

I remember the sound of us all walking over a carpet of dead leaves.

I remember the cold.

And I remember seeing four men sitting on makeshift log benches, in what I thought was our secret, private place. They had lit a small fire in the middle, surrounded by white stones. It flickered and hissed and spat.

They all smiled when they saw us.

I didn't recognize the men. Even after what happened, I could never describe their faces. In my broken memory of that night they all looked the same: skinny with brown hair, four sets of small black eyes with dark shadows beneath them. They were much older than us, late twenties or early thirties maybe, and they were drinking beer. Lots of it. There was a pattern of crushed cans around their feet.

I was scared at first, but Rachel clearly knew them, as did Helen and Zoe. They went straight over and sat on the men's laps.

"This is Anna. She's new *and* she's sweet sixteen at last. Aren't you going to wish her a happy birthday?" Rachel said.

"Happy birthday, Anna," the men replied with strange smiles on their faces.

They seemed to be amused by something.

Rachel draped an arm around my shoulder, and I noticed her fur coat again. Perhaps because I was so cold in the skimpy dress she had made me wear.

"Do you like my new coat?" she asked. "Zoe made it for me."

Zoe was always making things for her friends: pencil cases, cushion covers, tiny little dresses. She bought the most interesting material she could find in markets, and borrowed her mother's sewing machine to make her creations, but I'd never seen anything as elaborate as a coat before. It looked so real. I couldn't stop staring at the fur.

"I'll let you borrow it if you come and say hello to our new friends," Rachel said. "They've been waiting to meet you."

She took me by the hand, and led me to the nearest man. Then she told me to sit down on the fallen tree trunk next to him. I didn't want to, but I didn't want to be rude either. So I sat down next to the stranger, who stank of body odor and beer. When I started to shiver, he rubbed my bare leg with his big ugly hand, saying it would help me warm up.

Catherine Kelly sat down next to me, and looked as frightened as I felt.

A bottle of vodka was passed around,

along with strange-smelling cigarettes. More logs were added to the fire, and dance music was played. Which seemed odd to me, given nobody was dancing. I thought the men must have owed Rachel some money, because they all took out their wallets and gave her a handful of notes. I thought it might have been for the pills she took out of her purse, but that wasn't all the men were paying for.

"Take one," she said, coming over to Catherine and me.

There were two little white shapes in her hand. They looked like mints, but I knew enough to know that they weren't.

"No, thank you," said Catherine, and I shook my head too.

"You *do* want to be in our gang, don't you, Catherine?" Rachel asked.

The girl stared up at her. Then she took the pill, washing it down with vodka straight from the bottle.

"And you *don't* want to be the new odd one out, do you?" Rachel asked, looking at me.

I took one too. She smiled, then kissed me in front of all the others. She stuck her tongue deep inside my mouth, and afterward I wondered whether it was just to make sure I'd swallowed the pill. The men clapped and cheered while they watched.

Rachel took off my sneakers then.

I was too drunk and cold and stupid to ask what she was doing.

She tied the laces together, then hurled them up into a tree. My shoes dangled from a branch that was too high to reach, and everyone laughed again. I didn't like how they were looking at me.

"Now you can't run away from us," Rachel whispered in my ear.

She wanted to dance, so we did, until I felt so dizzy I fell to the ground. Even when I was lying motionless on the forest floor, the woods still seemed to spin around me. I lay in the dirt and dead leaves and struggled to keep my eyes open. I was so tired all of a sudden. She pulled the top of my dress down and pushed the bottom of it up; then I remember the sound of her disposable camera.

Clickety-click. Clickety-click. Clickety-click.

The next thing I remember was her kissing and stroking me, with everyone watching. They were all smiling at us, even Catherine Kelly, and I felt strangely happy too all of a sudden. So much so that I didn't mind. When I next opened my eyes, I saw Helen on her knees in front of one of the men. He had a fistful of her shiny black hair.

Another man had his hand up Zoe's skirt, and I noticed that she was naked from the waist up. Catherine appeared to have passed out on the forest floor, and one of the men was pulling her clothes off.

Rachel put her hand on my cheek, turning my head to face her. She kissed me again, sliding her fingers between my legs. It felt so nice, but then other hands started touching me, rough ones, replacing hers. When I opened my eyes again, the man I had been sitting next to was squeezing my breast with one hand, while rubbing himself with his other. I heard someone cry. I thought it was me, but then I saw Catherine, completely naked and facedown in the dirt. One man was on top of her, another appeared to be waiting.

"Come on, don't be a cock tease, at least suck it or something," said the man who was touching me. "We've all paid good money to celebrate your birthday with you. Be a good girl like it says on your nails."

I looked down at my fingers, where Rachel had painted the words.

"Get off of me," I whispered.

"You wanted to be part of our gang, well this is what our gang does," Rachel said, trying to hold me down. "How do you think I paid for your new clothes and the highlights in your hair? Grow up, Anna. It's just sex. It will hurt the first time, but then you'll be fine, I promise. Try to relax."

I didn't want to relax. Fear flooded through my entire body as he tried to push my legs apart. Then anger. I slapped him, pushed her, and struggled to my feet.

"Get the fuck off of me," I screamed at them both.

"I want my money back," he said to Rachel.

"Just use the other one, I'll give you a discount," she replied, looking over at Catherine.

I watched as he walked over to join the other men. They were no longer forming an orderly line.

I know I should have tried to pull them off.

I know I should have helped her get away. It was all my fault that she was there in the first place — I invited her — but I was so scared of what was happening.

I don't know how many of them took their turn. I watched in horror for a little while, trying to find my clothes, while Rachel took photos of them doing it.

I'm ashamed to say that I did nothing.

As soon as I found something to cover my

naked body with, I ran all the way home in bare feet without looking back.

"We're here," says Richard.

I'm so tired, I don't know whether I was asleep or just resting my eyes. He's already turned the engine off, and as I stare out of the windows into the darkness, I see that we are surrounded by nothing but trees. It's cold in the car, as though we might have been parked here for a while, and I realize I've no idea how late it is.

"Where are we?" I ask, taking my phone out of my bag to try to check the time.

But the battery has completely died now, and the knowledge that I am in the middle of nowhere, with no way of contacting anyone, makes me panic.

He must see the look on my face.

"My wife's parents' house, remember? I promise I didn't bring you out into the woods to murder you."

He smiles at his own joke, but I don't. Given the stories we've been covering the last couple of days, it doesn't seem at all funny to me.

"Sorry, I always did have a dodgy sense of humor and, like you, I'm crazy tired. The driveway is right there, see where I'm pointing?"

"Whose car is that parked outside?" I ask, turning to face him.

"It's my wife's."

"Your *wife's*? Did you know she'd be here?"

"No, of course not. Do you think I *want* my wife to meet someone I used to cheat on her with? It's late, we have to be on-air in a few hours. I don't know what she's doing here, I thought she'd be in London, but I'm sure she will have gone to bed already. We have two young children, remember? You won't even see her."

"But why would she be here?"

"I don't know. We've been talking a lot about her coming down to sort through some of her parents' things, so we can sell this dump. Maybe with Blackdown being all over the news the last couple of days, she finally decided to do it."

"This feels a little awkward."

"It's really late. She doesn't know what happened between us. Like I said, she's probably gone up to bed already. I don't see any lights on, do you?"

He reaches to open the car door but I still don't move. I can't. It feels like I'm in danger.

"I'm sorry, Richard. I know it was years ago, ancient history and all that, but I still feel really uncomfortable about the idea of meeting your wife."

"What are you talking about? You've already met."

I have one more left to go.

Finding a way to get her here, to this old house in the woods, posed a tricky challenge at first, but in the end all it took was a phone call. The solutions to difficult problems are often surprisingly simple.

I admit I'm tired now. But like my mother used to say, if you're going to do something, you may as well do it properly. I plan to finish the job, because they all deserve to die.

Rachel Hopkins used sex to get what she wanted. When that wasn't enough, she used other people. It started with her grooming school friends, taking semi-naked pictures of them, and selling the results to men at the local pub. The photos she sold never showed any faces. Rachel saved those for a sideline in blackmail. She earned good money and a bad reputation from both ventures, and it led to other things. When the men got bored of one girl, so did she, and moved her attention and affection to another.

Her photography started to get a little more inventive and adventurous too. Teenage girls were filled with alcohol and drugs, until they were willing to take off all their clothes, and let her take pictures of them knowingly. Eyes half closed but legs wide open. I never saw a man's face in any of the photos I found, but sometimes I could see their hands. Grubby fingers touching, holding, scratching, pinching, and sticking themselves inside things they shouldn't.

Rachel kept the pictures in a shoebox in her wardrobe.

That's where I found them and I didn't like what I saw.

You have to understand that I have witnessed some terrible things during my lifetime. Human beings are capable of inflicting unspeakable misery — on themselves as well as others — and there are so many things I wish I could unsee. Police and journalists get exposed to inhumanity every day, but those horrors aren't a secret. They get reported so that the whole world knows the truth and justice can be served. The whole world doesn't need to know about what happened in Blackdown all those years ago. But the people responsible must be punished.

None of the other girls were as bad as Rachel; she turned them into the worst versions of themselves. But they let her. They could have said no. There is always a choice.

They made the wrong one.

HIM

Thursday 00:30

I think I might have got things wrong.

Perhaps because of the alcohol, or the tiredness, or the sheer horror of it all.

As soon as Priya suggests that Anna is in danger, I think she may be right.

I need to find her, but I don't know how or where, and *everyone* is watching me.

The sideways glances keep coming from my colleagues, as they traipse in and out of what used to be my home. When I take a moment to see myself through their eyes, it doesn't look good. There is no sign of forced entry. A knife is missing from my kitchen, I have a connection with every single one of the victims, and a picture of them with their faces crossed out — covered in my finger-prints — was found in my house.

I've never been honest about my relation-ship with Rachel Hopkins, or the fact that I was with her in the woods the night she died. I thought Zoe was the only one who knew, but it turns out so did Helen Wang. Now they're both dead too. It doesn't look good, no matter which way you view it. Even I am starting to doubt myself. I had an imaginary friend when I was a boy. I used to blame him when I did something wrong, but then so did a lot of children. It doesn't mean I'm pretending to be innocent now.

I did not kill my sister.

When my parents died, I blocked it from my mind for such a long time. Sometimes I still do. But I can't forget the image of Zoe lying in a bathtub of bloody water, with her wrists slit and one eye sewn closed. Whatever she did, or didn't do, nobody deserves to die like that. Whoever did this to her is a monster, and I plan to find them and deal with them my own way. But first I need to know that Anna is safe.

I dial her number for the tenth time. It goes straight to voicemail again, as though it is out of battery or switched off. Having been married to her for ten years, I know that turning off her mobile is something Anna never does.

I need to find her, but I left my car at Priya's house. I spot Zoe's keys in the dish in the hall and head for the front door.

"Going somewhere?" Priya asks, seeming to appear from nowhere.

"Just stepping outside for some fresh air."

"Okay." She nods, and stands aside to let me pass. "Don't go too far."

Even *she* seems to suspect me of something now.

I walk out to the front yard, drinking down greedy gulps of the cool night air, still trying to sober myself up. I see Priya watching me from the window as I light a cigarette. It's only when I give her a halfhearted wave that she steps back inside and lets the curtain fall. As soon as she is gone, I get in Zoe's car and reverse out of the driveway as fast as I can.

The first place I stop is the hotel. The receptionist is asleep when I knock on the glass door. I can see her head resting on her arms on the front desk, a long brown braid resembling a rope. I bang a little louder and she glares in my direction, before pulling herself upright and strutting toward me. She has a large set of keys in her skinny little hand, but seems reluctant to use them.

"We're closed and we're full."

She says the words slowly, and I wonder whether it is her inability to speak the language, or her belief that I won't understand it that causes her to do so. I hold up my badge and she lets me in.

"I need to speak to one of your guests. It's an urgent police matter."

She looks horrified at the mere suggestion of it.

"I don't know whether I'm allowed to wake people up in the middle of the night," she says, her forehead fretting into a series of ugly lines.

"You probably aren't, but I am. Her name is Anna Andrews."

"She was here earlier!"

The woman beams at me, as though she just guessed the right answer in a game show.

"Great. Which room is she in?"

"She isn't. The hotel is full."

Patience is not something I have an abundance of at the best of times. I don't mean to shout at her, but I can't help raising my voice.

"I don't understand, you just said that she was here earlier."

"She was. About an hour ago. She thought that she had a reservation, but someone had canceled it. So, they left."

"They?"

"There was a man with her. He seemed to have an idea of somewhere else to go."

The dodgy cameraman, no doubt. I *knew*

there was something not right about him.

"Thank you, you've been very helpful."

I drive around town twice, looking for any sign of the ugly blue crew car I suspect they are traveling in, knowing that Anna still doesn't have her own. I stop at the first set of red traffic lights, but not the second. Then, for lack of a better idea, I drive to her mum's house. I know how much she hates going there, but if the hotel was full, she might have decided to stay the night.

I knock on the door and wait, expecting a light to come on in the front bedroom. Anna's mum is many things, but she isn't deaf yet. When there is no answer, and no sign of life, I look beneath the flowerpot, but the key is missing. Luckily, I had a spare made a few weeks ago — I've always had a weird obsession with collecting multiple sets of keys in case I need them — and with my mother-in-law's memory deteriorating at such a rapid rate, it seemed like a responsible thing to do. It takes me a few attempts to find the right key, but then it slots into place and I'm inside.

I turn on the light and I'm surprised to see stacks of boxes everywhere.

"The only way you'll get me out of this house is in a coffin" is what she always said, whenever anyone suggested it might be time to move out. I used to think that Anna's mother was holding on to this old house for sentimental reasons — memories of her husband perhaps — but Anna always insisted that it wasn't that. Apparently, the marriage didn't end well; her dad left them and never came back. Neither Anna or her mother ever talked about him and there were no pictures. She said it was so long ago, she wasn't sure she'd even recognize her own father if she passed him on the street.

I try the light switch but it doesn't work. So I use the flashlight on my phone to navigate a path through all the clutter, toward the back of the house. I stop in the kitchen, not sure what it is that I'm looking for, but shocked by all the mess. There are dirty cups and plates everywhere. Despite the dark, I notice the back door and the glass on the floor. Someone has smashed it to get inside.

I run up the stairs and open the door to Anna's mother's room, but there is nobody there. The bed has been neatly made, but is unslept in. I close the door, wanting to leave everything as I found it. Then I backtrack along the landing to the bedroom that used to be Anna's. It is empty too.

I'm about to leave when I hear the sound

of footsteps crunching over broken glass down below. I move behind the bedroom door and stand perfectly still, then listen as someone slowly walks from the kitchen, through the dining room, and up the stairs. I feel inside my pockets and squint into the darkness, but can't find anything to defend myself with.

I hear whoever is out there open the first bedroom door — it creaks in protest — then I wait as they creep along the landing toward me. As soon as they step into the room, I slam the door in their face and throw them against the wall, my height giving me a clear advantage. They fall hard onto the floor, I switch on the light, and am completely shocked by who I see.

I wasn't expecting it to be someone I know.

HER

"What do you mean I know your wife?" I say.

"Are you serious?" Richard asks, his face full of disbelief.

"Deadly." I regret my choice of response as soon as I've said it.

He shakes his head and laughs.

"Wow. How is it that you never seem to know what's going on in other people's lives? Are you *really* that self-involved? I've known you for years, we've slept together, how can you not know anything about me?"

"I *do* know things about you. You talk about your kids nonstop, I look at your endless pictures of them. Who is your wife?"

"Cat."

"Cat who?"

"Cat Jones. The woman who presents the *One O'Clock News*, like you used to? She just came back from maternity leave. We

387

even have the same surname, although I appreciate it's a little common, bit like me."

"*You're* married to Cat Jones?"

"I know she's a little out of my league, but there's no need to say it like that."

"Why didn't you ever tell me?"

"I . . . presumed you knew. Everyone else does. It isn't a secret."

Half the newsroom is either sleeping with or married to one another, and I'm not the best at keeping up with office gossip, but this still seems a little hard to believe. It's *her* fault I'm here, not just because she has taken her presenting job back, but because it was Cat that suggested, in front of the whole team, that I should cover this story.

She insisted, if I remember rightly, as though she knew I didn't want to go to Blackdown. But she can't possibly have known my connection to the place. Nobody does. I never talk about my personal life with people at work; perhaps that's why I rarely know anything about theirs.

"You must have known about me and Cat," Richard says, shaking his head. "She had a stalker, and I found him in our backyard not long after our first little girl was born. I thought the whole newsroom knew this story. He was trespassing on our property, trying to take pictures of Cat breastfeeding, and when I punched him a couple of times, *I* got done for GBH. Can you believe that?"

I don't know if I do believe it. I don't know what to think about anything. All I know right now is that I don't want to go inside that house.

"Can I just use your phone to make a quick call, please?" I ask.

I have a strange and sudden urge to speak to Jack.

"I told you at the hotel, I can't find my mobile. I expect Cat probably called to tell me she was driving down, but I didn't get the message. I've lost my phone, or someone has stolen it. Either way, I still have my charger, so you can use it once we get in."

He gets out, walks around to the passenger side, and opens my door.

"Are you coming, or would you rather sleep in the car?"

I don't answer, but reluctantly follow him toward the house.

It's hard to see where we are going in the dark. A crescent moon does a halfhearted job of lighting our way as we crunch over dead leaves and twigs. It's impossible to find the path because it looks like nobody has swept it, or tended to this yard, for years. It's as though the place has been left abandoned for a very long time.

"That's strange," says Richard.

"What is?"

"There is another car here."

I see the sports car he is referring to but don't say anything. Everything about this situation is strange.

We carry on along the path and I get a better look at the house. It looks like something from a horror film: an old wooden building, covered in ivy, with windows shaped like eyes. It's pitch-black behind them, but then it is very late.

Richard opens the front door and we step inside. He switches on the lights and I'm relieved that they work. Then he unzips his bag and hands me his phone charger.

"Here you go. I'm just going to go and check on Cat; hopefully we haven't woken her. Make yourself at home, if that's possible in this dump, and I'll be down in a bit. I'm sure there must be something edible in the freezer, and I *know* there is something to drink — my father-in-law shunned DIY, but he was good at maintaining his wine cellar — I won't be long."

He's trying to make me feel welcome. It isn't his fault the hotel canceled our booking; I'm being ungrateful and I feel the need to apologize.

"I'm sorry, I'm just so tired —"

"It's fine. You've been a busy bee," he interrupts.

Something about the way he says it makes me shiver.

"You know, bees aren't as busy as people think. They can sleep inside flowers for up to eight hours a day, curled together in pairs, holding each other's feet," I say, trying to lighten the mood a little.

"Who told you that?" he asks.

"My mother."

As soon as I think about her I feel sad.

"Oh yes, I'd forgotten your mum keeps bees," Richard replies, before disappearing up the old wooden staircase.

It's odd because I don't remember ever telling him that. But then I suppose there must have been a few drunken conversations over the years that I've forgotten.

I stand in the hallway for a moment, unsure what to do or where to go. I see a loose-looking socket in the wall, and decide to risk electrocution by plugging in my phone. It starts to charge and I begin to feel a little better.

I head toward the first door I see, and step into an old and dusty living room. It looks like it was last decorated, and possibly cleaned, in the 1970s. There is a gothic-looking fireplace, which I can see has been used more recently; a few smoldering logs still glowing in the grate. I get a little closer for warmth, and notice the silver-framed photos on the mantelpiece.

Sure enough, there is a family portrait of Richard and Cat, with her shiny red hair cut into a razor-sharp bob. I stare at her pretty, heavily made-up face, big eyes, and perfect white smile, as she poses next to her husband, holding on tight to their two little girls. Now that I see them again, I recognize the children who came to visit the newsroom just a few days ago. They are the same faces that were in all the pictures on Richard's phone. I was a fool not to see it before.

There are lots of photos of their daughters, along with an elderly couple I don't know, presumably Cat's parents, who used to live in this house. Then I spot a framed picture of a teenage girl I *do* recognize. I observe the long, wild, curly white-blond hair, pale skin, sticky-out ears, patchy eyebrows, and ugly braces.

Fifteen-year-old Catherine Kelly stares back.

I look between this photo, and the glamorous one of Cat Jones, and feel physically sick when I realize they are the same person. The two faces are *very* different — she's clearly had some kind of work done, and not just to pin back those ears — but, without doubt, the teenage girl I used to know grew up to be the woman I know now. The eyes staring out at me from the two photos are a perfect match.

Catherine never came back to St. Hilary's after that night in the woods. Only the four of us knew what had happened to her, but all sorts of stories made the rounds at school. There were rumors that she had killed herself, and none of us saw her again, including me.

At least, I thought I hadn't.

She must have known who *I* was when she first met me in the newsroom.

I haven't changed my name, or my appearance, very much since school, unlike her.

I try to stay calm, but this is more than just a coincidence — I don't believe in those. An overwhelming sense of panic starts to take over, spreading through my body, making it difficult to move or breathe.

I need to get out of here.

I need to call Jack.

My shaking hands feel inside my bag for my mobile, but it isn't there. I remember leaving it in the hall to charge, but when I run back to get it, the phone is gone.

Someone has taken it. I spin around, expecting to see somebody waiting in the shadows, but I appear to be alone. For now.

My social safety net is filled with holes, big enough to fall through and be seen by others. I have never been good at collecting the requisite friends. That said, I can't think of anyone else I would rather call in this situation than my ex-husband. I might not have my mobile anymore, but I still know Jack's number off by heart. I remember seeing an old rotary phone in the living room, just like the one we had when I was a child. I rush back to find it, and dial his number as fast as I can, ignoring the dust on the receiver. As soon as I hold it to my ear, I realize the line is dead.

Then I hear footsteps upstairs.

Someone is walking on creaking floorboards, and they stop directly above me.

It's probably *her.*

Perhaps she can see me.

Or it might be *him.* Richard could be in on it too.

I need to get out of here. Not that I even know where I am, but if I follow the path it must lead to a road. I hurry out of the room and toward the front door, but before I get there I hear the most terrible scream.

Sometimes it can be so easy to predict how other people will react in a situation.

Too easy.

I think maybe that's because we're all the same.

There is an energy that connects us together, flowing through us like electricity. We are all just light bulbs. Some shine brighter than others, some show us the way when we are lost. Others are a little too dull to be of any real use or interest.

Some burn out.

We are the same but different, trying to shine in the darkness, but the light that connects us can sometimes grow too faint to see.

When a light bulb starts to flicker, I always think it is best to take action before it dies.

Nobody likes being left in the dark.

HIM

Thursday 01:00

I've switched on the light, but several seconds later, I still can't believe who it is I'm staring down at on the floor of my exwife's childhood bedroom.

Priya's nose is bleeding as a result of me slamming the door in her face. She's a quivering mess, slumped against the wall, but I feel suspicion rather than sympathy.

"What are you doing here?" I ask.

"I told you not to leave your sister's house. You don't seem to understand that you are now a suspect in your own murder investigation."

"I *do* understand that, which is why I have to find out who is trying to frame me. You didn't answer my question. How did you know I was here?"

"I followed you."

I *know* when I'm being followed. There was nobody else on the streets when I drove here; she's lying. My mind rushes through the last few days: the evidence planted in my car, the text messages on Rachel's phone, the constant feeling of being watched. Then I think about my sister, lying in a bath full of red water. I'm sure my missing house keys were in my jacket, the one Priya hung up on the fancy-looking coatrack in her hall.

She could have taken them, before she randomly disappeared earlier tonight.

"Does anyone else know that you're here?" I ask, and she shakes her head. "You just left without telling anyone where you were going? You're meant to be heading up the investigation now that I've had to stand aside."

"I was worried about you. I didn't know what to do. *I* trust you, but the way you took your sister's car and left the scene like that . . . well, it looks really bad. People are starting to . . . say things. I thought if I could just find you and bring you back —"

"That still doesn't explain how you knew where I'd be."

I crouch down until my face is right in front of hers.

"What are you doing?" she asks with a small voice and big eyes.

"Relax. I'm just trying to see if your nose

is broken; stay still."

A fresh trickle of blood escapes from her right nostril. Then she shakes her head, and it's as though the apology falls out of her mouth.

"Sorry, sir. I just keep getting things wrong."

I'm appalled with myself when she starts to cry. She looks like a frightened little girl, and I did this to her. I don't want Priya to be scared of me, and her tears shift my perspective, offering a different view. Maybe I'm wrong. I feel like a paranoid old fool. Her body flinches as I reach inside my pocket, but her face attempts a smile when I offer her a clean hanky.

"You *do* know I'm not involved in any of this, don't you? I wouldn't harm my sister. I wouldn't hurt *anyone*," I say. She touches her nose and winces in pain. I take her silent point. "I didn't know who was coming up the stairs. I'm sorry. I would never knowingly hurt you. I think whoever killed the others might want to kill Anna too. I came here trying to find her, but the house is empty. Someone smashed the glass in the door downstairs. Maybe Anna realized how much danger she was in, and took her mum somewhere safe."

"I take it you've tried calling her?" Priya asks.

"Several times," I say, before helping her up.

I find my mobile and try Anna again, but it goes straight to voicemail just like it did before. Either she has switched off her phone, or someone else has.

"There's something I need to tell you," Priya says, and I try not to react even though it feels like a small bomb just went off inside my head. "One of the uniformed officers recognized the unidentified girl in the picture we found at your house. Swears he knew her when they were both kids. Says she was called Catherine Kelly. Does that name mean anything to you?"

It doesn't, but then I've never been great with names.

"No."

"We know that she is married now, and we think she lives in London, but we still don't have a current address. When she lived here, it was with her parents at a property within Blackdown Woods. It used to be a gamekeeper's lodge a hundred years ago, but from what I understand it's derelict these days. Her parents died, and it has been empty since."

"Maybe it's worth checking out?" I say.

"I think so too, but like *you* said, this is my investigation now. If we go, I think we should go *together.*"

I decide it might be nice not to have to do this alone.

"Yes, boss," I reply, and she smiles.

We make our way downstairs in silence, as though both regathering our thoughts.

We're almost at the bottom step when I hear something.

There is a second door in the kitchen, which leads to a little lean-to built on the side of the house. Anna's mother used it as a garage in the past — when she was still driving — but it's more of a storage space now, I guess. Somewhere to keep all her home-grown organic vegetables. I can hear someone creeping around in there, and I know Priya hears them too.

I indicate for her to get behind me, and tiptoe to the door. I fling it open and find the light, then see a pair of startled eyes staring back at me. A large fox takes one more bite from what looks like a bag of carrots, then flees through a small hole in the wall.

Priya laughs and so do I — we need to do something to ease the tension.

"What's this?" she asks.

I smile at the old white van that Anna's

mum used to drive when she still had the cleaning business. She only retired a couple of years ago — took some persuading — but I doubt the van would even start now. There are bumblebees painted all over the side, along with a logo: *Busy Bees Professional Cleaning Services.*

"My mother-in-law used to clean for half the village," I say.

"I would never have guessed," Priya replies, staring at all the boxes and mess as we step back inside the house.

"She's not been well," I explain, meaning the dementia.

"I did notice the cancer drugs in the kitchen. They were the same ones my mother had to take, not that they helped." She reads my expression without me having to say anything. "I'm so sorry, I presumed you knew."

I didn't.

"We should get going," Priya says, and I know she's right.

We head out toward the car, and the empty street is in complete darkness. I wonder whether Anna knows about her mum, and then I worry again about where they both might be now. My mind wanders back to the cameraman and his criminal record. I have Richard's number in my phone; having thoroughly checked him out there isn't much I don't know about him. He's married to another BBC News anchor, and they have a couple of kids, but that doesn't mean anything. On the off chance that he and Anna *are* still together, or that he might know where she is, I call him.

I hear his phone ringing.

But not just on the other end of the line, it's right next to me, as though he is here in Anna's mother's garden.

It's too dark to see anything, so I hang up and fumble to find the flashlight function on my mobile again. When I turn it on, I see that Priya is holding a phone that does not belong to her.

HER

I am certain that the scream did not belong to a woman or a child; it was Richard.

There is a voice screaming inside my head too. It's my own, and it's telling me to get the hell out of this house. My fingers hover over the handle of the front door, but I can't just leave. What if he's hurt? What if I can help? Jack was right — I do always run away from my problems. Perhaps it's time to stop. I tell myself that this isn't a horror movie, and turn back toward the staircase.

I climb the first step and grip the banister, as though it might be the only thing stopping me from falling over. Facing my fears doesn't make me feel any less afraid. The stench of damp combined with something unfamiliar makes me nauseous, but I force myself to keep going.

"Richard?" I call.

But he doesn't answer.

403

When I reach the first floor, I find myself at the end of a long cobweb-covered landing. All the doors on either side of it are closed, except for the one at the very end. That door is slightly ajar, and throwing a sliver of light into the otherwise dark hall. I try the switch, but nothing happens.

"Richard?" I call his name again, but hear nothing.

I force myself to take a step closer and the elderly floorboards creak.

I can't imagine growing up somewhere like this; it's like a haunted house from a fairground, except that it's real. No wonder Catherine Kelly was a little odd at school if this was her childhood home.

The floor continues to creak beneath my weight, and I remind myself that Catherine Kelly is Cat Jones. Nothing about this scenario feels right. The voice inside my head screams at me again to turn back and get out.

But I don't.

I keep walking forward, every step heavy with hesitation, getting closer to the door at the end of the hall. I stop when I reach it, taking a few seconds to summon the courage to push it open. When I do, I can't move.

Cat Jones is swinging from a beam on the ceiling, a St. Hilary's school tie acting like a noose around her neck.

Her eyes are closed, and she's still wearing the white dress she wore to present the lunchtime news earlier today. Her bare legs and feet are sticking out underneath, as though someone took her shoes. One foot is still oddly balanced on a chair leaning against the wall, and the frayed ends of a red-and-white friendship bracelet are sticking out of her slightly open mouth.

The woman she became is so different, but I can see the child she once was hiding just below the surface. Things are always easier to see when we know what we are looking for.

I take a step toward her and almost trip over something on the floor.

It's Richard.

He is lying facedown, and there is a small pool of blood around his head. He has been hit so hard there is a concave crater on the back of his skull, and there are stab wounds all over his back.

I freeze.

I'm scared to touch him, and I can't stop my hands from shaking. I bend down and check for a pulse. The surge of relief I experience when I find one is overwhelming. He's still alive. I need to call an ambulance, but my phone has been taken and

I'm also aware that whoever did this must still be here. Not just in the house, but upstairs.

Nobody has left since Richard screamed.

An army of goose bumps line up on my skin as I realize that I would have seen whoever did this pass me *if* they had left the room. Or at the very least, heard them; the house is eerily silent now, as though my own fear has muted all sound. Everything except for the body swinging from the beam on the ceiling, like a slow, creaking pendulum. I wish I could make the noise stop.

That's when the pieces of the puzzle start to fit together, a picture forming despite the gaps. Cat Jones *must* have attacked Richard before killing herself. I can think of no other explanation for what I am seeing. Then I spot my phone on the dressing table, next to what looks like a kitchen knife.

"I'm going to get help. I'll be as quick as I can, just hold on," I say into Richard's ear.

He doesn't open his eyes, but his lips move.

"Alive," he whispers.

"I know you are, I promise I'll come back."

He tries to say something else. His lips struggle to part, and words I can't quite translate escape them. I have to hurry; he's running out of time.

I stand up and stare at my phone on the table just behind Cat. I'll have to pass her to reach it. Her lifeless body is still slowly swinging, and the sound is even worse than the sight.

Creak and squeak. Creak and squeak. Creak and squeak.

I take a step toward her, my eyes darting from her face to my phone.

Richard groans; he must be in tremendous pain.

I take another step, almost close enough to reach my mobile now. I can see that the school tie around her neck is definitely the same as the ones we wore at St. Hilary's.

Creak and squeak. Creak and squeak. Creak and squeak.

Richard moans again.

"Get. Out."

He whispers the words, but I hear them loud and clear, because the sound of swinging has stopped.

When I look up, I see that Cat's bloodshot eyes are wide open. She has pulled the chair toward her with her feet and is now balancing on it, standing on tiptoes. She starts to loosen the tie-shaped noose from around her neck. I have a mental flashback of us as schoolgirls, and remember all the sailing knots she once demonstrated using her shoelaces. My mind races, trying to process what my eyes are seeing, and reaches the conclusion that this is all some sort of sick trick. But why would she pretend to hang herself? And why would she attack her own husband?

Unless she knew about our affair?

I stand perfectly still as though frozen in fear, while Cat continues to loosen the knot. She stares at me the entire time with a look of pure hatred on her face.

HIM

Priya's eyes stare at the phone then back at me.

"Why do you have the cameraman's mobile?" I ask, hoping she has an answer and that I can believe it.

"I didn't know the phone was his. It was on the ground next to the broken glass, outside the back door."

So she does have an answer, but I don't believe her. Not anymore.

She looks scared again and I wonder whether I do too. If Priya is somehow involved in all this, then the smartest thing I could do now is play along. Hopefully she will lead me to Anna.

"Richard must have been here," I say. "Someone smashed the glass in the back door to break in, and I'm sure he's involved in this somehow. That's the only explanation. I *knew* he was no good and I should

409

have trusted my instincts —"

"We don't know anything yet."

Her interrupting *me* is a first.

"Why else would his phone be here?"

"We need to stay calm and stop jumping to conclusions, Jack."

"Jack," not "sir" or "boss" again, I notice. But then another thought pushes that one aside. Something she said earlier.

"The fifth girl in the photo, you said she was married, who to?" I ask.

Priya puts Richard's phone back in her pocket, then takes out her notepad, flicking through several pages.

"What was the cameraman's surname?" she asks, still turning them.

I doubt she has forgotten; she never forgets anything.

"Jones. Richard Jones," I reply, trying to hide the mistrust from my tone.

Priya stops turning the pages and stares at what is written on them.

"Oh my god," she whispers. Then she says something that instantly shifts all my suspicion from her to him.

"It *is* him. The fifth girl is married to Anna's cameraman, Richard Jones."

HER

Thursday 01:20

Cat Jones's eyes stay fixed on mine as she pulls the tie-shaped noose up and over her head before dropping it to the floor. She rubs the angry-looking red marks on her neck with one hand, while using the other to slowly remove the friendship bracelet that was tied around her tongue. She stares down at it, before looking at me again. I snatch my phone from the dressing table behind her, and start stepping backward toward the door. With her white dress, it's like watching a ghost come back to life.

My survival instinct finally exceeds my fear and I run.

I don't look back as I race out of the room, along the creaking hall, and down the stairs. I trip and fall before I reach the bottom, twisting my ankle and landing in a crumpled heap on the floor. I stare at the phone still in my hand. I turn it on and feel a surge of hope when it comes to life. There is enough battery to make a call now . . . but no signal.

"Anna."

I hear Cat say my name, in a strangled, haunting voice. It's animal-like.

I pick myself up and hobble to the front door, but my hands are shaking too much to open it. I can hear someone behind me. I don't want to look, but I can't stop myself from glancing over my shoulder. Cat is standing at the top of the staircase. Her head is tilted to one side at a strange angle, as though her neck might be broken. She starts to walk down the stairs, taking slow but determined steps, her unblinking eyes never leaving mine.

I turn back to the front door and yank the handle, almost falling backward as it flies open. I find my balance and run as fast as I can, out of the house and into the woods. Branches scratch my face, twigs shaped like bony hands claw at my body, while sticks on the ground constantly trip me up. It's uneven and boggy. I try to ignore the pain in my ankle, but it isn't long before I fall again. I land hard, slamming into an old tree stump. The impact winds me and I drop my phone.

When Catherine Kelly never came back to

412

school, rumors of her suicide started to circulate. They were started, of course, by Rachel. I think she worried I might tell someone the truth about what had happened, so there were some rumors about me too. I wish I *had* told someone. But before I could, Rachel slipped a naked photo of me inside my locker as a warning. I recognized her writing, scribbled in black felt-tip pen on the back of the picture, along with the date it was taken, my sixteenth birthday:

If you don't want the whole village including your mother to see copies of this, I suggest you keep quiet.

So I did.

But it wasn't enough.

I came home one day to find Mum crying in the sunroom. Kit Kat was missing. Despite buying the kitten for me, she loved it just as much as I did, and I had never seen her so upset. Not even when my dad disappeared. We did all the things other people did when their cats went missing in Blackdown. It happened so often that I'd never quite understood all those homemade posters people put up around the village — every telephone pole in the high street seemed to be permanently covered in them — but, as with so many things in life, it is different when it happens to you.

We searched the streets and the woods, asked neighbors if they had seen Kit Kat, and put up our own Missing posters all around town.

Then a parcel arrived with my name on it.

Inside, I found a black felt hat, with a gray fur trim.

I knew that Zoe had made it; I recognized the messy stitching. And the fur.

I only just made it to the bathroom in time before throwing up.

My mother didn't understand, thank god. She thought I was ill and let me stay home from school. As soon as she left, I got dressed and took the shortcut through the woods to Zoe's house. When nobody answered the front door, I walked around the back, but there was no one home. I had a crazy idea to break in, but didn't know how. There was an old shed, right at the very end of the garden, and I thought there might be tools inside that I could use.

I'll never forget the sound of cats crying when I got closer.

The shed door had a padlock and I had to use a rock to smash it open. When I did, the first thing I saw was that the wood inside was covered with scratch marks.

There must have been ten cats in there, all skinny and starving. I felt sick and a little unsteady on my feet as I realized that the fur coat Zoe had made for Rachel hadn't been fake at all. I recognized some of the cats from the Missing posters dotted around town, and suddenly the twisted pieces of the puzzle slotted together to reveal a very ugly picture. Zoe had been stealing people's pets, returning them if owners offered a cash reward, keeping them for her sewing projects if not. The horror of it was hard to conceive, but I knew I was right.

The cats ran out, leaving just one in the corner: Kit Kat.

She looked thin and scared, and had a bloody stump where her tail used to be.

I picked her up and carried her home, tears streaming down my face the entire time. I put her in the cat carrier, where she would be safe until Mum got home. Then I went up to my bedroom to write a letter.

I never stopped feeling terrible about what happened to Catherine Kelly. I thought it was all my fault; I invited her that night. I didn't know whether the rumors about her committing suicide were true, but I decided that if anyone deserved to die, it was me. I wrote it all down, everything that had happened, so that my mum wouldn't blame herself when she found me.

I planned to use my school tie to end it all, but I couldn't go through with it, so I tore up the note and threw it into the fireplace in my bedroom.

I did nothing but study for the next few months. I got straight As in my GCSEs, and won a scholarship to a boarding school far away. It broke my mother's heart, but the school had a fantastic reputation and she didn't try to stop me. I never told her the real reason why I wanted to leave.

My fingers frantically search for the phone I just dropped in the dark, feeling among the dead leaves and mud on the forest floor. When they find it, accidentally illuminating the screen, I see that I have one bar of signal. I stab the Contacts button and dial Jack's number.

"Pick up. Pick up. Pick up," I whisper.

I'm so surprised and overjoyed when he does, that I don't know what to say. Then the words rush out all at once.

"Jack, it's me. I'm in trouble and I need your help. I know who the killer is. The fifth girl in that photo is a woman called Cat Jones. She's a BBC News anchor, but we went to school together and something bad happened. It was twenty years ago, on my birthday, maybe that's why. There's a house, I don't know where, but I'm in the woods. I think she's killed him, I think she's killed them all and she's coming for me. Please hurry."

"Ms. Andrews, this is DS Patel. Jack is driving at the moment," says a voice on the other end.

Her words are obscenely relaxed, as though the person who spoke them didn't hear a thing I just said.

"I need to speak to Jack, right now."

I am shouting and crying at the same time. I hear a branch snap somewhere behind me, but when I spin around, all I can see is eerie darkness and the ghostly shapes of dead trees.

"I need you to stay calm," says the voice on the phone. "We are on the way, but we need a location. Can you tell me anything more about where you are? What can you see?"

I blink away my tears and peer into the darkness again, but there is nothing except the woods. I can't tell them exactly where I am, because I don't know. I wipe my face with the sleeve of my jacket, then I turn and see something else.

She is standing right behind me, dressed in white.

HIM

Thursday 01:30

"Anna hung up," says Priya.

"What? Where is she? What did she say?" I ask, driving as fast as I dare on dark country lanes in the middle of the night.

We've taken Zoe's car. I feel more comfortable being behind the wheel, and I still don't trust Priya. She grabbed my phone as soon as it started ringing, as though she didn't want me to answer it. Although that could have something to do with my speed — she's checked her seat belt several times.

"Anna mentioned the woods," she says, holding on to the side of the car as I take another bend more quickly than I should.

"Great, that's a big help in a town surrounded by trees," I snap.

"I'm just telling you what she said."

"Was it definitely her?"

"Yes."

"Call the tech team, get them to triangulate the signal from her phone right now. Then call Anna back."

Priya does as I ask, but I can only hear one side of the conversation she is having with someone at HQ. Her tone changes toward the end of the call.

"What is it? What's wrong?" I ask when she hangs up, but she doesn't answer.

I take my eyes off the road for just a second to look at her, and when I turn back, there is a stag standing directly in front of us. The deer's eyes shine in the headlights, its enormous horns look lethal, and it doesn't move. I hit the brake and only just manage to swerve in time to avoid hitting him. Seconds later we smash into an old oak tree instead.

For a moment, I think I am dead.

"Jesus Christ," says Priya, reaching for the back of her neck as though in pain.

"I'm sorry," I say, mentally checking myself for injuries, but finding none.

My chest hurts, and I'm still gripping the steering wheel so tight that my knuckles look as though they might burst through my skin. I notice the deer has disappeared.

"It's okay, I'm still in one piece, are you?" Priya asks.

"I think so."

She leans down into the footwell. At first,

I think she might be about to vomit, but she picks up her phone, and dials Anna's number. I decide that I was wrong not to trust her; she *is* trying to help me. Even now, when I almost killed us both.

"Anna's mobile is going straight to voicemail again," she says. "Maybe her battery died, or she lost signal —"

"Or someone turned it off," I say, finishing her sentence.

"The good news is, according to Google Maps, Catherine Kelly's old house is five minutes away on foot."

She unfastens her seat belt and feels the back of her neck again.

"Are you sure you're okay to walk?" I ask.

"Guess we'll find out."

We abandon the car, which seems wise given the dented hood and flashing warning lights on the dashboard. I don't even take the keys or bother closing the door; it feels like there is no time to waste. Priya is surprisingly fast. She navigates a path for us between the black branches of ancient trees, running ahead, almost as though she has been here before and knows the way. My chest hurts every time I breathe in. I slammed into the steering wheel when we crashed, and I suspect I may have cracked a rib. The volume of my wheezing, labored breaths seems to increase with every step.

Priya stops just ahead of me.

"Did you hear that?" she whispers.

"What?"

"Sounded like someone running in the opposite direction."

She stands a little straighter, her body poised and perfectly still, like the startled deer we saw a few minutes ago. But her head reminds me more of an owl's, turning slowly from side to side as her big brown eyes blink into the gloom. I don't hear anything, except the normal sounds of the woods at night, but I remember Priya is a city girl.

"It's okay," I say, trying to reassure her. "It was probably just another animal. We should carry on."

She reaches inside her jacket, pulls out a gun, and flicks the safety catch.

"Whoa!" I say, taking a step back. While I'm aware that some of my colleagues think all police should carry guns in the UK, personally, I'm glad we don't. I've never worked in a firearms unit, and neither has Priya. "Why do you have that?" I ask.

"Self-protection," she replies, looking over my shoulder.

When I turn — trying to keep one eye on the gun in her hand — I see the shape of an old wooden house camouflaged in the darkness. It's surrounded by pine trees, as though they are guarding the building from unwelcome visitors. There are lights on inside, and the shape of the door and windows almost resembles a face, with glowing yellow eyes.

As we get closer, I see Richards's BBC crew car. Then I see Rachel's Audi TT parked right outside.

"Isn't that Rachel Hopkins's missing car?" Priya whispers.

"I think it might be," I reply, knowing that it is.

We reach the house and Priya stares at the ancient-looking front door. I wonder if her fear has finally caught up with her, but it hasn't. I watch as she puts her gun down, before reaching up to her ponytail, to pull out one of the old-fashioned hair clips she always wears. She slides it inside the lock.

"Are you kidding me?" I say.

"Why don't you try around the back?" she replies without looking up.

She's got more chance of finding a one-ended stick in the woods than opening that door. We don't have any time to lose, so I do as she suggests, and head for the rear of the house, hoping I might have better luck. Most of the curtains are drawn, but there are definitely lights on inside. I try every door that I come across, but they are all locked. Eventually I find myself back where I started at the front of the house, but Priya is gone.

I stare into the darkness that surrounds me, waiting, watching, and listening for some sign of her, but she isn't here. Then I hear the creak of the front door slowly opening. I spin around, but can't see who it is at first. The relief I feel when I see that it is Priya produces a nervous smile from me, and a strange one from her.

"Seriously? You managed to get in using an old trick with a hairpin?"

"Old door, old tricks," she says, heaving the heavy door open, just wide enough for me to squeeze inside.

I'm surprised to see she is already wearing her blue plastic gloves, but then she never was one to waste time.

Smashing the glass of the kitchen door to let myself into the cottage earlier was unfortunate; I hate to make a mess. I'd forgotten to take the key. There is normally one hidden beneath the flowerpot at the front of the house, but that was missing, so I didn't have a choice. I've been far more careful breaking in and out of all the other homes I have visited, and cars, and public buildings. I always wear gloves and tidy up after myself, so that nobody would ever know I was there, let alone be able to prove it.

We tend to categorize people the way we categorize books: if they don't fit neatly into a genre, we're not sure what to make of them. I've always had problems fitting in, but the older I get, the less I care. Personally, I think being the same as everybody else is overrated.

I reach inside my pocket and feel the final friendship bracelet in my hand. I like to wrap it

424

around my fingers and wear it like a ring sometimes. I shall be sad to let it go.

There is a curtain we all hide behind; the only difference is who pulls it aside. Some people can do it themselves, while others need someone else to reveal the truth about who they really are. Those girls were not good friends, and they deserved to be silenced.

Forever.

Rachel Hopkins was a two-faced slut. She might have been beautiful on the outside, but on the inside she was ugly and rotten — a vain, selfish Barbie doll, who stole money from charity and men from their wives. I did the world a favor removing her from it.

Helen Wang was a liar, who spent a lifetime pretending to be someone she was not. The headmistress was addicted to drugs and academic admiration, always had to be the best regardless of the consequences, and did not deserve to be in charge of a school of girls.

Zoe was a monster. Even as a child. If she didn't get her own way, she would pull off all her clothes and run around naked, before kicking and screaming on the floor. She did this until she was seven years old, and not just at home. Everyone in Blackdown must have seen at least one of her tantrums. She was a horrible little girl and grew up to be a despicable woman, whose cruelty to animals could not go unpunished. When bad things happened, she always turned a blind eye.

The other one, well, they all got what they deserved, and she is no different in my book, I don't care what she did or didn't do. It might have been a long time since that night in the woods — twenty years, in fact — but she was there.

HER

Time stops as I stare at the woman standing in front of me.

My fear fades into relief before converting into confusion. She's wearing a white cotton nightdress covered in embroidered bees, and an old pair of bee-shaped slippers on her feet. In the middle of the woods. In the middle of the night. At first, I'm convinced I must be dreaming, but she appears to be real and looks as terrified as I feel.

"Mum? What are you doing here?"

She shakes her head as though she doesn't know, and looks so very small and old. I can see scratches and bruises on her face and arms, as though she has fallen. She turns to peer over her shoulder, as if scared of who might be listening, then starts to cry.

"Someone smashed a window in the kitchen, then broke into the house. I was so afraid, I didn't know what to do. So I hid.

427

Then I ran away into the woods, but I think they followed me," she whispers.

She's shaking, and looks more fragile than I have ever seen her. I try to stand, but my ankle gives way when I put any weight on it.

"Who is following you? Who was in the house?"

"The woman with the ponytail. I hid in the potting shed, but I saw her."

I don't know what to say. I don't know whether what she is telling me is true, or just another symptom of her dementia. Jack told me she'd been found wandering around Blackdown in her nightdress, even the woman in the supermarket mentioned it, but I didn't believe them. Sometimes we choose not to believe the things we don't want to. I do it all the time — hide my regrets inside boxes at the back of my mind, and choose to forget the bad things that I've done. Just like my mother taught me.

Denying the truth doesn't change the facts.

I was here the night Rachel Hopkins died.

In the woods.

I saw her walk along the platform after getting off the train, and I remember the sound that it made, because for some reason, it reminded me of her camera.

Clickety-click. Clickety-click. Clickety-click.

When I lost my presenting job, I went home and started drinking. But then I stopped. I got in the Mini and blew into my breathalyzer. I remember it turned amber, but that meant I was still safe to drive. I made the journey to Blackdown, because it was the anniversary of what happened — as well as my birthday — and I wanted to see *her*.

My daughter, not Rachel.

It was exactly two years since my baby girl died, and I needed to be close to her. It was Jack's decision to bury her here in Blackdown, and I still hate him for it, but it's a lovely cemetery with beautiful views. The church is on a hill, and the nearest parking lot is at the station. The only way to reach her grave is on foot, through the woods. I spent a few hours there, sitting in the dark, telling her all the stories I would have if she were alive. I still feel guilty about not saying something to Rachel when she walked straight past my car to get into her own that night. Maybe if I had, she wouldn't be dead.

I hear something in the distance and it snaps me out of whatever melancholy I had slipped into. I don't know whether Catherine Kelly is still following me, but I don't plan to wait around to find out. I need to get myself, and my mother, away from the woods and somewhere safe.

"Come on, Mum, we need to go. It's cold and it's . . . dangerous out here."

"Are you coming home, love?"

She asks the question with such happy optimism.

"Yes, Mum."

"Oh, good. We'll be there in less than ten minutes, I promise. Then I'll put the kettle on, make us some honey tea, just the way you like it."

"We're only ten minutes from our house?" I ask.

She points confidently through the trees, and although it all looks the same to me — especially at night — I believe her. My mother might be forgetful, but she knows these woods better than she knows herself. I take her hand, surprised by how small it feels inside my own, and we walk as fast as we can. I hear every rustle of leaves, every snapped twig, and can't stop myself constantly looking over my shoulder. Even if someone *was* there, following us, it would be too dark to see them.

"I think she knows," says Mum, clearly confused again.

"Let's try to be as quiet as we can, just until we get home," I whisper.

"She has a badge, so I had to let her in."

"Who?"

"The woman. She knows and now I don't know what to do."

My mother looks over her shoulder as though she hears something, and it does nothing to calm my nerves. We take a few more steps in silence, and I can't help replaying her words. She's mentioned a ponytail and a badge now, and it makes me think of the female detective working with Jack. The same one who just answered his phone.

"What do you think she knows, Mum?"

"I think she knows I killed your father."

I'm so aware that someone is chasing us, but my feet stop working and I can't move.

"Do you remember that day when you came home from school, and found me on the floor underneath the Christmas tree?" she asks. When I don't answer she carries on. "Your dad had come home early from a work trip. He was drunk and hit me for no reason other than I'd been letting him do it for years. It started after you were born, but I thought I had to stay with him, for you and for money. I didn't have any of my own, and no qualifications to get myself a decent job. I told myself I could put up with it until you were old enough to leave school. But

431

he beat me so badly that day I thought I might die. Then he threatened to hurt you. Something snapped inside me when he did that, and I hit him back for the first time. It turned out to also be the last time, because he was dead."

I can't process her words; there seem to be too many of them. They are getting jumbled inside my head, and I can't straighten them out into sentences that make any sense. People tend to see what they want in the people they love. They reshape them inside their heads, twisting them into the people they *wish* they were, instead of the people they are. But this isn't real, it can't be. My mother is not a murderer. This is the dementia or the drugs talking. But Cat Jones being Catherine Kelly *is* real, and I don't doubt she is out here in the woods right now looking for me.

I take both of Mum's hands and try to pull her along. But she's stronger than she looks, and digs her bumblebee slippers into the ground.

"You didn't kill Dad, I would have seen his body. You're confused," I tell her, but she just stares at me and refuses to budge.

"I hit him in the face with a cast-iron Christmas tree stand. I kept hitting him until he was dead, so that he couldn't hurt you the way he hurt me. Then I buried him in the garden. I stuck him beneath the vegetable patch, and planted carrots and potatoes on top the following spring. I thought if I never moved house it would be okay, that he would never be found. But I think she knows, and if you are going to find out the truth, I want you to hear it from me."

My emotions collide inside my head, getting bigger and taking on a new shape, like liquid mercury. I don't want to believe her, but I think I do. Whatever she did or didn't do all those years ago, we still need to get out of here now.

"Mum, it isn't safe and we need to get home."

"What if she's there, waiting for us?"

"Who?"

"The woman who knows."

The trees around me start to bend and melt out of focus. I feel dizzy and sick.

"Mum, you said the woman who came to the house had a badge. Do you remember what it said? Just try to picture it."

She squeezes her eyes closed like a child, trying to look back at a past that frequently seems to escape her in the present. Then she opens them and whispers the name:

"Priya."

HIM

"Priya, how do you know how to pick locks?" I ask.

She shrugs, still holding her gun, I notice, before closing the solid wooden door behind me.

"I watched a video online; it isn't difficult."

"You understand, strictly speaking, what you just did isn't legal, right?"

"Do you want to find Anna or not, sir?"

I don't answer. I'm too busy taking in the sight of the house we are in. It looks like the set of a horror movie: gothic furniture, ancient wallpaper, creaking wooden floorboards, and a huge elaborate staircase in the middle of the hallway. All of it covered in a theatrical blanket of dust and cobwebs. I don't think I'm someone who scares easily, but this is creepy.

I follow Priya down the hall, both of us

434

walking as quietly as possible, before stepping into a huge formal living room. The furnishings look like they might have been borrowed from Windsor Castle, and the ancient-looking light fittings on the wall flicker a little. I glance at the pictures on the mantelpiece, but don't recognize any of the faces. Then I trip over the fireside tool set, catching it just before the whole thing can clatter onto the stone floor.

"Perhaps we should split up?" Priya says. "Why don't you look upstairs while I finish checking the rooms down here?"

"Good idea. Think I'll take this with me," I reply, picking up the metal poker.

To say that I climb the stairs with caution is an understatement. If whoever killed Zoe and the others is here, I'd rather they didn't see me coming. The house is completely silent now, except for the sound of my own rushed and labored breathing. My chest still hurts where I slammed into the steering wheel, and that isn't the only thing bothering me. I've learned to trust my gut over the years, and this all feels wrong.

I scan the elaborate red-carpeted landing, and see that all the doors on the first floor are closed, except for one at the very end. I check each room, my heart thudding inside my chest every time I open a door, unsure what I might find behind it. Most of the rooms are completely empty — except for dust, dirt, and cobwebs — but one of them is spotless and I see something I wasn't expecting. There are two small beds side by side, covered in pretty pink sheets, and a nightlight casting a constellation of moving stars over the walls and ceiling. I notice the dolls on the pillows, two glasses of water on a little table, and a copy of *Little Red Riding Hood.* There were children here tonight, but they're not here now.

I try not to think of my own little girl as I step back out on the landing and turn to face the final door at the end of the hall. The floorboards seem to get louder with every step that I take toward it, as though trying to warn me to stay away. An iron poker doesn't seem like adequate defense right now. I hesitate when I reach the door, then kick it fully open, not wanting any unexpected surprises. I get one anyway. The cameraman is dead on the floor, lying in a pool of his own blood with his head bashed in.

I stare down at him, it's impossible not to, then check the rest of the room until I am certain nobody is lurking in the shadows.

"I need you to drop the weapon, sir."

I spin around and see Priya standing in

the doorway.

Despite the combination of noisy floor-boards and perfect silence, I still didn't hear her coming. At first, I feel relief. But then I notice her gun — the one she said she carries for self-protection — pointing in my direction.

"Priya? What are you doing?" She looks down at the dead cameraman, then at the iron poker I'm still holding in my hand. "Now, hang on a minute —"

"I said drop the weapon, and put these on."

Without taking her eyes off me, she reaches inside her pocket with her free hand and produces a set of handcuffs.

"Priya, I don't know what you think —"

"Last chance," she interrupts. "I'm not going to ask you again."

HER

Thursday 01:40

It's as though Mum can no longer hear me, so I ask her again.

"When did the policewoman come to the house, and what did she want?"

"Lots of times. Asking questions."

"About what?"

She squeezes my hand and stares up at me.

"You."

"Me?"

Tell a person they're wrong and they'll cover their ears. Tell a person they're right and they'll listen to you all day long.

"It's okay, Mum. I believe you, but we have to get home now."

She nods and we carry on walking, navigating a path through the woods. I drag her along as fast as I dare over a forest floor full of obstacles. Giant roots and fallen trees can be dangerous in the dark, but then so

438

can Cat Jones. And I fear she's still out here somewhere, hunting us down.

Every few steps I check my phone for a signal, hoping I can call Jack. But then I remember that Priya Patel is with him.

It's impossible to know who to trust.

HIM

Thursday 01:40

"Priya, it can be very difficult to know who to trust in these situations —"

"I mean it, sir. Put the weapon down."

She stares again at the lifeless body of Richard Jones on the floor and then the iron poker in my hand. I see things the way she must be seeing them right now, and it makes me want to run.

"I didn't do this!"

"Put the weapon down."

"Priya, I —"

"It's over, sir. When I asked the tech team to triangulate Anna's phone, they told me that someone had canceled the same instruction I had placed on Rachel Hopkins's mobile yesterday. They just confirmed it was you. Boots that match the prints left by her body were found in your trash can, you have links to all the victims, and witnesses have described seeing a car that sounds a lot like

440

yours, parked outside the school the night Helen Wang was murdered."

"I know how this looks, but —"

"There's no such thing as coincidence. You taught me that on my first day."

"Someone is trying to set me up —"

"Who?"

"I don't know!"

She takes out her phone.

"Backup are on the way, and the tech team are now trying to trace both mobiles. Rachel's has been turned on again. Shall I call it?"

She presses a button, and seconds later a phone starts to ring inside my pocket. I try to talk over the sound of it ringing.

"Yes, I have her phone because someone planted it in my car. They've been sending me cryptic messages ever since. Think, Priya. Catherine Kelly was the fifth girl in the photo. Turns out she is now Cat Jones, a journalist who works with Anna, is married to the dead man on the floor, and owns this creepy fucking house. You're right, there is no such thing as coincidence, so where is Cat Jones now?"

She hesitates, but then her face twists out of shape again.

"Please drop the weapon, sir."

If this situation wasn't so deadly serious, I

would laugh at the fact she is still calling me "sir." I know the killer is still out there, and I know Anna is in danger, but I can't see a way through this. Then something catches my eye. Something light in the dark, and I'm sure I see someone move in the distance outside the window. I try to get closer and Priya snaps.

"Jack Harper, I am arresting you on suspicion of murder. You do not have to say anything. But it may harm your defense if you do not mention when questioned something which you later rely on in court. Anything you do say may be given in evidence —"

"There is someone outside. I can see them through the trees."

"It's probably backup —"

"We both know they wouldn't have got here that quickly. I'm aware how this looks, but I'm telling you the killer is still out there. Anna is in danger and I'm going to try and save her. You can shoot me if you want to, or you can help me catch whoever did this."

She shakes her head and looks so sad.

"I want to believe you, but I don't think I can anymore. I don't think you know what you've done, but that doesn't mean you didn't do it," she says.

442

"You *do* know me, Priya, and deep down I think you know I'm telling the truth."

She doesn't lower the gun, but I can see her eyes filling with tears. I take a step toward the door, unable to tell which way this is going to go. All I can think about is Anna. I let her down before and I can't do it again.

Priya flinches just as I am about to pass her. I've been trained for situations where a gun is being pointed in my face, and I know what to do. I just didn't want to have to do it. I grab Priya's wrist so fast she doesn't have time to react. She pulls the trigger, though, making a hole in the wall before I slam her into it. I step back as she slides down onto the floor. Her eyes are closed and I can see she has hit her head, but she'll live. Backup will be here soon and they'll take care of her. There isn't time to wait.

"I'm sorry," I whisper, before leaving the house, and heading into the woods.

I love the woods at this time of year.

The sounds, the smells, the screams.

Especially in the dark.

Everyone has a place they run to when the world gets too loud; this is mine.

There is nothing more satisfying than crunching over dead leaves, breathing in cool country air, and knowing that you are on a journey from one moment in your life to the next. Sometimes I think where you are going is far less important than the fact that you are going somewhere. You have to learn to enjoy the ride, not just the destination.

People frequently talk about what it is like to have "made it," but it is far better to be on your way than to have arrived. If you succeed too soon, or arrive too early, that just means there is nowhere else left to go. Success is like love — it's not something everyone can appreciate, even when they have it. And life is about moving forward and moving on. Never look back; that way only leads to feeling lost.

Which is how I feel now, because I'm running out of time to find her.

Things have mostly gone according to plan so far. I dumped Rachel's car here a couple of days ago. It was fun to drive, and this seemed like as good a place as any to hide it. I'd never driven a sports car before. It made me think of all the other things I haven't done, things that some people probably take for granted. It was tough financially when I was growing up, and I had to work for everything I've got. It was hard but I think it made me stronger.

Now I just have to finish what I started, which means finding her before anyone else does. She was supposed to be dead by now.

Finding people is surprisingly simple once you know how, even those who do not wish to be found. Police and journalists use a lot of the same tools to trace people. You'd be amazed how easy it is, not just to find someone, but to find out everything about them. All the things they would rather nobody knew.

My job made it almost too easy.

People trust people like me.

But they don't know who I really am, what I've done, or what I am capable of.

I said at the start of this journey that I was

going to kill them all, and I meant every word.

HER

"Everything is going to be okay, Mum," I say, not believing a single word of my own lie.

Then I hear what sounds like a gunshot in the distance.

I can see from the look in her eyes that she heard it too.

"We need to hurry — are you sure we are going the right way to get home?" I ask, dragging her along beside me.

"I think so," she whispers, finally seeming to understand that we are in danger.

We only manage a few more steps before I hear the sound of someone running in the woods behind us. The night is so silent that the noise of branches snapping travels through the trees. It's impossible to tell how far away they are, or see anything in the darkness, but I know they're getting closer. The possibilities of what happens next play

447

out in fast-forward in my mind. None of them are good.

We won't be able to outrun them.

The best we can do now is hide.

I duck down and pull my mother onto the ground with me.

"Sorry, Mum, but you have to stay still and be quiet. Okay?" I whisper.

She nods as though she understands. The sound of someone running stops a short distance from where we are. I hold my breath, willing them to turn back or run the other way. But I don't get my wish. They keep getting closer. I try to think of a way to defend myself and Mum, my fingers searching the forest floor for a rock or a stick at least, but they find nothing of use. As much as I don't want to give up, I think this might be it.

I see the flashlight then, shining between the trees, and it isn't long until the beam finds us. I'm blinded at first and can't see who it is.

"Anna?" a voice says in the darkness.

I shield my eyes, then blink away tears when I recognize the person in the distance.

I have never been happier to see my ex-husband.

"Anna? Is that you?" he calls again.

"Yes! Jack, thank god you're here!"

He smiles as he makes his way toward us through the trees. We're *safe*. The relief that floods through me is overwhelming. I know that Jack will get us out of here, and that we're going to be okay now.

Then I see the shadowy silhouette of someone behind him.

He turns to see what I'm looking at, but it's too late.

The sound of gunfire echoes through the woods and Jack falls to the ground.

Everything is silent and still for a second, maybe two, maybe three, as though life itself has paused to see what will happen next. Then some kind of primal survival instinct kicks in. I pull Mum up and use the only word left in my vocabulary.

"Run."

She does and so do I, but I've no idea if we are running in the right direction. She's surprisingly fast for her age, quicker than me thanks to my twisted ankle. Whoever is out there is gaining on us; I can hear them not too far behind. Branches and leaves slap me in the face as we scurry through the woods. Moonlight breaks through the canopy of trees in places, but the forest floor is mostly cloaked in darkness, and I struggle not to trip and fall. I follow my mother, constantly trying to keep her in sight, but she soon gets ahead of me. Fear can make runners of us all.

When I realize I can no longer see her, I stop. I'm too scared to call her name. I don't want to attract attention, so I spin around, completely disoriented. Lost. Then I hear them. Despite instinct urging me to run in the other direction, I rush toward the sound of my mother and another woman screaming at each other. Their high-pitched exchange is impossible to translate, simultaneous shrieks canceling out any discernible words. I find them just in time to see my mother fall to the ground. Cat Jones is standing over her, holding a bloody knife. She stares at me with those huge eyes of hers, then shakes her head and starts to cry.

"You ruined my life," Cat says in my direction, sounding hysterical.

She takes a step toward me, the knife still in her hand. I can't speak. I can't move. I just stare at my broken mother on the forest floor.

"You pretended to be my friend," Cat says between strangled sobs, getting closer. "You ruined my childhood. You followed me to London, pretended not to know who I was, so I pretended too. But then you tried to steal my job. And then you tried to steal my husband, and now —"

I hear another gunshot behind me. Someone is shooting in our direction, but when I spin around I see nothing but darkness. When I turn back, Cat has gone. I rush over to Mum and cry tears of relief when I see that she is still alive.

"I'm okay," she whispers, but there is blood on her nightdress and her hands.

I put my head under her arm and lift her, then we hobble together as fast as we can, away from the sound of twigs snapping in the distance behind us. I think I must be hallucinating when we literally stumble across a road and see a car. The driver's door is open, and the key is in the ignition, as though someone just got out and left it here for us to find. But then I see the old oak tree it has clearly crashed into.

I gently lower my mother into the passenger seat, and fasten her seat belt before getting in myself. She presses on the wound on her stomach, trying to stop the bleeding, but there is a lot more blood now than before.

"Can you drive it?" she asks.

"I guess we'll find out."

I manage to turn on the engine, and when it starts, I feel a rush of hope. I slam the gearstick into reverse, and the car slowly rolls backward, away from the tree. I change gear, ready to drive away, then I hear sirens in the distance. I look at Mum and can tell that she hears them too.

"It sounds like help is almost here; shall I wait?" I ask.

Her hopeful expression changes into one of horror, and she screams.

When I follow her gaze, I can see why.

Cat Jones is standing right in front of the car, illuminated by the headlights like a ghoul.

There is blood on her white dress, a knife in her hand, and a crazed look on her face.

It all happens so fast.

There is no time to think.

In my desperation to get away, I hit the pedal, forgetting that the gearshift is now in drive, not reverse. There is a loud thud as the car slams into Cat, knocking her backward, before pinning her body between the bumper and the tree.

"Oh my god," I whisper. "What have I done?"

The years fall away and all I see is Catherine Kelly in the woods that night, twenty years ago. She must have hated us all very much to have planned a revenge like this. I can't help feeling responsible for everything that has happened, and I open the door.

"Stay in the car," says Mum, but I ignore her.

Cat's eyes are closed. There is a trickle of blood leaking from the corner of her mouth, but I might still be able to help her. I make myself walk toward her broken body, then reach out to feel for a pulse.

Her eyes open. She grabs my wrist with one hand, simultaneously raising the knife with her other. I try to get away, but her nails claw into my skin, pulling me closer. The knife seems to fly toward my face in slow motion, and I close my eyes. Then I hear another shot. When I turn around, I see Priya Patel standing behind the car, still pointing a gun in our direction. When I look back at Cat, a dark red stain is spreading across her white dress. Her eyes are still open, but I know she is dead.

HER

Friday 14:30

I open my eyes and see Jack standing at the end of my hospital bed.

"Apparently I missed visiting hours, but they said I could say hello," he whispers.

"You're okay," I say.

"Of course; it takes more than a bullet through the shoulder to stop me."

I hate hospitals. Apart from the twisted ankle and a lot of scratches, I'm fine. I worry someone else needs the bed more than I do, but the doctors insisted on keeping me here for twenty-four hours. Jack takes my hand in his and we share a silent conversation. Sometimes there is no need for words, when you know someone well enough to know exactly what they would say.

"Is Mum —"

"She's fine, promise," he says. "They've stitched her up and moved her onto a dif-

454

ferent ward. She's doing really well, considering." He pauses. "There's something else. I'm not sure how to tell you this, and maybe you already know, but I didn't. Something came up on your mum's medical records when they brought her in."

"If this is about her dementia, then I know she's a lot worse than before —"

"It's not that. I'm so sorry to be the one to tell you, but she has cancer. It was diagnosed a few months ago. I don't know why she didn't tell me — us, I mean. I think maybe she didn't fully understand it herself. But I've spoken to two different doctors here now, who have both confirmed it's an aggressive variety. I'm so sorry."

I don't know what to say. My relationship with my mother has been strained since I was a teenager, but I still struggle to come to terms with her keeping something like this from me.

"She probably just didn't want you to worry, or frankly forgot — you've seen how confused she gets now," Jack says, as though reading my mind.

I haven't forgotten what she told me in the woods about my dad.

Now that I've had a little time to think about it, I do believe she might have killed him all those years ago. He was a violent man, and if she did do it, then I believe it was as much about protecting me as saving herself. My mother isn't the only one who is good at keeping secrets. I am too, and there are some I'll never share with anyone. Not even Jack.

"What is happening to Priya?"

"She did everything she should have."

"She shot you, Jack."

"I know she shot me. I've got a hole in my shoulder to prove it. But if the roles had been reversed I might have done the same. Priya also saved you and your mum."

"About that . . . Mum said that she came to the house, asking questions."

"If she did, then she was just doing her job. Cat Jones was very good at covering her tracks and trying to make other people look responsible, but evidence was found at her house linking her to each of the murders. Including childhood diaries, in which she went into quite graphic detail about how much she hated you all. Especially you. She seemed to think you pretended to be her friend then betrayed her. Priya witnessed her attacking your mother, and it was lucky she was there again before Cat could hurt you. They still can't find the knife — which is frankly bizarre given all three of you saw Cat holding it — but every inch of the

456

woods where it happened is being searched, so I'm sure it will turn up. Forensics think the same weapon was used in all four attacks, and I'm pretty confident she carried out the murders alone."

I can't stop thinking about it.

The idea of Catherine Kelly growing up to be Cat Jones is one thing, but her plotting such horrific revenge on girls who bullied her at school is another. It's hard to believe, but everyone else seems to. I feel the weight of Jack's stare and snap out of it.

"I'm so sorry about Zoe," I say.

He looks away and his face crumples a little.

"How did you know? It hasn't been released to the press yet . . ."

"I guess doctors and nurses gossip just as much as journalists. I overheard."

He nods.

"I don't know how I'm supposed to tell my niece that her mum is dead."

"You were a wonderful father and I'm sure you're a brilliant uncle. Olivia is lucky to have you in her life. It will be hard, but you'll get through it."

He can't look me in the eye, and I know we are both thinking about our daughter.

"I've thought about it a lot, and I'm going to move back to London," he says. "I don't want to stay here. I'll sell my parents' house, go back to the Met, but maybe ask for a part-time role so I can be there to take care of Olivia. I don't have it all figured out yet. But . . ."

"Sounds like you do."

"Well, she's the only family I have left."

His thought triggers one of my own.

"You were right about Mum — she needs more help, especially now we know how unwell she is. I'm sorry, I should have listened to you."

"Wow, can I get that on the record, please?" he says, and I try my best to smile.

The apology was served a little cold, but he swallowed it anyway. Sometimes when you are hungry enough for forgiveness from someone you have loved, the tiniest morsel will do.

"I'll look at that care home you suggested and try to pay for it myself. That way she won't have to sell the house, which was always what she was most upset about," I tell him.

"Because she'll miss her garden and her bees?"

I pause for the briefest of moments.

"Exactly."

He takes my hand in his and it feels so good to have him hold it. Such a small thing and yet it makes me cry. Not sad tears; hopeful ones.

"Maybe we could help each other," he says.

"I'd like that."

"You know I —"

"I know."

I don't need him to say that he never stopped loving me. I feel the same way too.

Him

Friday 14:45

She lets me hold her hand, then starts to cry.

Seeing Anna in a hospital bed reminds me of when our daughter was born. It's as though the years and hurt and pain fall away, and we're back. Perhaps not where we started, but to a place before we got broken.

The truth is, although it sounds like I have a plan, I don't really know what happens next. But maybe I don't need to. Maybe life already has a plan for us all, and we only get lost when we shy away from it, through fear, or pain, or heartbreak. Charlotte's death broke us, there is no doubt about that. But sometimes when things get broken, they can be fixed. It just takes time and patience.

I let go of Anna's hand because I'm confused by what this is. She stares at her

460

fingers, as though I might have hurt her by holding on too tight, and I wonder if maybe I always did. I haven't slept for days, and I don't want to make anything worse than it already is for anyone, by saying or doing the wrong thing.

"I should go," I say, and she looks confused. "Visiting hours, remember? I'm already breaking the rules."

She nods, but can see straight through me. Just like she always could. Anna avoids my eyes as though afraid of what she might find there. Then she asks a final question. So simple and yet loaded with meaning for us both.

"Will you come back later?"

"Of course."

I kiss her ever so gently on the forehead, then leave without looking back. I didn't need to think about it before I answered, but that doesn't mean it was true.

HER

I watch him walk away, then dry my face and press the little red button by the side of my bed. A middle-aged nurse comes in to see me within a couple of minutes, and I'm glad; I don't have any time to waste. She has a pixie haircut and big green eyes, accentuated with lashings of liquid liner that has smudged a little. I notice that she looks at least ten years older than the photo on her badge.

"Is everything okay?" she asks.

"I need to leave the hospital."

Her face pauses while her mind plays catch-up, processing what I've just said.

"I don't think that's a very good idea."

Her patronizing tone makes me like her less than I did a moment ago.

"Probably not, but it's what I'm going to do. Thank you, for everything, but I really need to go now. Are there some forms you

462

need me to sign to say I'm discharging myself?"

It isn't the first time I've done this; I know the drill. I can't stand being in hospitals — the stench of death and despair — and there are things I need to do that can't wait.

"Let me go and get the doctor," the nurse says.

The doctor will try to persuade me to stay, no doubt, but it's pointless. Once my mind is made up about something, there really isn't anyone who can change it. Including myself.

Plus, I could *really* use a drink.

As soon as the nurse is out of sight, I reach for the locker next to my bed and take out my bag. I know there isn't any alcohol left inside, but that isn't what I'm looking for.

I'm pleased to see that the knife that killed them all is still there.

It was important to make myself look like a victim, in order for everyone to believe my story, but the facts speak for themselves. I was in the woods the night Rachel died, I was at the school when Helen was killed, I was in the house the day Zoe was murdered, and I was there when Richard was bludgeoned to death. Cat Jones being crushed between a car and a tree before being shot was not part of the original plan, but it did the job. There is no such thing as coincidence, and yet they all believed me.

I was so convincing in the hospital, I almost believed myself.

The lies we tell ourselves are always the most dangerous. I think it's instinct; self-preservation is a fundamental part of our DNA. We are a species of liars, and sometimes we deliberately connect the dots in the wrong order, and pretend to make sense of what we see. We stretch the stories of our lives to fit our own desired narratives, presenting a prettier picture for those around us. Honesty loses every time to a lie less ordinary, and truth is overrated. Far better to make it up than to make do.

The world of make-believe isn't just for children. Like shoes, the stories we tell about ourselves get bigger with age. When we grow out of one, we make up another.

I did what I had to do.

■ ■ ■ ■

SIX MONTHS LATER

■ ■ ■ ■

HIM

I'll admit that looking after a toddler on my own was far harder than I ever anticipated, but I'm coping. I think. Just about. I relied quite heavily on neighbors and the kindness of strangers those first few weeks. There were people who knew my niece far better than I did, through nursery and various classes my sister used to take her to. They were a huge help, but it was still difficult. Things are getting easier, and the new normal is starting to feel like a good fit.

The first thing I did after Zoe's funeral was sell my parents' house. It wasn't easy; buyers weren't too keen on a rural family home where someone was murdered in the bathtub. But it sold eventually — for far less than it was worth — to a development company who will no doubt knock it down. I can live with that, though. Sometimes starting again is the only option.

Work was pretty understanding. I was

given compassionate leave and then allowed to apply for a part-time position in London. A new role I suspect my old boss might have created just for me. Human beings are most empathetic when bad things happen to people they know. Perhaps because when the unthinkable happens to friends or family, it makes you realize it could happen to you. I just knew I had to get away from Blackdown, for good this time, and I'm pleased that they managed to find such a wonderful replacement to head up the MCT unit in my absence. Priya will do a great job, and she deserves the promotion.

It isn't all good.

I have my fair share of dark times, and there are things I have seen that will haunt me for the rest of my life.

I try not to think about what I've lost.

For now, all I can do is take one day at a time, and try to hold on to what I've got left.

Sometimes you have to lose a lot to remember how much you have.

HER

"A reminder of our main news again this lunchtime. The former president has been seen in public for the first time since leaving the White House, scientists warn that bees may face extinction in less than a decade, and we'll leave you with some pictures of the baby panda born at Edinburgh Zoo this morning. You can see more over on the BBC News Channel, but from all of us on the *One O'Clock News* team, good afternoon."

I smile for the camera, tap my papers on the desk, and wait for the little red light to disappear. As soon as we're off-air, I swing by the debrief and listen politely to the rest of the team as they talk about today's show. I'm so happy to be back where I belong, presenting the lunchtime bulletin. Nobody cares who you used to be; it's only who you are now that counts. Like yesterday's news, old versions of a person are easily forgotten.

These people really are my surrogate family, but after everything that has happened, I've remembered that I do have a real one too.

As soon as the debrief is over — it's Friday afternoon, so I'm not the only one keen to get away — I grab my bag and head out the door. I take a cab to save time. Home isn't where it used to be and I can't walk there anymore. I've started to think that home might not be a place at all, more of a feeling. You don't always have to cross a bridge when you come to it. You can plan ahead, tunnel underneath, or even learn to swim if you have to. There is always a way to change sides if you make up your mind to do it.

I sold the apartment near Waterloo, and bought a little house in north London instead. It feels strange sometimes, living north instead of south of the Thames, but it felt like I needed a fresh start. And a house with a yard. And a driveway for the brand-new SUV; I sold the Mini too.

I pay the cabdriver, then head toward the porch, my key already in my hand so as not to waste even a moment. Once inside, I close the front door, then freeze when I hear footsteps behind me.

Someone is here.

But that's okay, because they are supposed to be.

"Anna, Anna, the bees are alive, come and see!"

My niece takes my hand and drags me toward the kitchen window. I stare out at our little yard, looking at the white wooden box she is pointing at. My mother's beehive was the only thing I kept from her house. Something to remind me of her.

I had to hire specialists to help me move the bees from Blackdown to London. They said winter was the best time to do it, while they were sleeping, but even then — and despite considerable cost — there was no guarantee they would survive.

But now it's spring. Six months have passed and there are cherry blossoms on the trees, a little girl living in my house, and sure enough, there is activity around the old beehive. It's far from a swarm, but there are definitely more than a handful of buzzing black shapes dancing to and from the wooden slats. They went through a life-changing journey, it was difficult and dangerous, but they survived. Now they are starting again in a brand-new home. Not unlike us.

Jack walks into the kitchen carrying a suitcase.

"You're back!" he says, kissing me on the cheek.

It's early days for us too. Jack and Olivia only moved in with me a few weeks ago. He got a new job in London, still with the police, but part time and office based. We were all spending so much time together that moving in seemed to be the logical next step. Jack and I feel like a family again. While nobody could ever replace our daughter, Olivia is a beautiful little girl, and I feel proud to be playing a part in raising her.

"We should get going if we want to beat the rush-hour traffic," he says.

"Well, I better go and get my things then," I reply.

I stop in the doorway and turn to look at them both as they point at the bees on the other side of the glass. Together we've created a little sanctuary in the city. What happened before doesn't matter anymore. I did what I had to do.

Choosing to forget can be a lot less painful than choosing to remember.

HIM

It is not my choice to go back to Blackdown today. The idea fills me with the heaviest variety of dread. But I know it's important to Anna, and it won't be for long. Just a quick pit stop to check on things before we carry on toward Dorset and the coast. A weekend away from it all, just Anna and me and our niece, who feels more like a daughter every day. Olivia loves the seaside.

Us getting back together again was what I always wanted.

Sometimes, when something terrible happens, people fall apart. We've definitely experienced that before, but this time we seemed to fall together.

When I look at Anna sitting next to me in the car, I see the only woman I've ever really loved. I let her down once, but I'll never do it again. We have it all now. Almost everything we ever dared to dream of, and more. I would do anything to make her happy and

475

keep her safe.

Anything.

We pull up outside her mother's old house in Blackdown. Despite the look of dread drawn all over her face, Anna insists that she wants to go in by herself. There is a FOR RENT sign up outside already and the viewings start tomorrow. I think she just wants to check everything is as it should be, and say good-bye to what was once her home.

Anna has been down here, alone, the last few weekends, busy packing up all her mother's things and redecorating the whole house. She even cleared out the backyard a few months ago, so there are no more bees, or potting shed, or allotment-style chaos. Then she laid a new patio, completely covering what used to be her mother's vegetable patch. Anna did it all herself. Why she wouldn't just pay someone else, I'll never know.

I wait ten minutes then decide to follow her inside, hoping to hurry her along.

The house still smells of fresh paint. The kitchen is brand new, and the place looks almost unrecognizable from before. I find Anna out back, sitting on the little wooden bench her mother used to love so much, staring at the new yard. The patio is a circular shape of dark gray bricks, with a single perfectly round piece in the middle. There is a bee carved into the stone. A few pots with hardy plants add a splash of color, and a newly laid lawn leads down to the woods in the distance.

"It looks really good," I say, gently closing the kitchen door behind me.

She shrugs, and I pretend not to notice her wipe away a tear.

"It's better for the rental market. A low-maintenance yard that will be easier for tenants to look after," she says.

"Exactly. You've done a really good job."

"It's just that it doesn't look like our home anymore."

"That's the whole point, it isn't supposed to. Another family is going to live here now, but it will always mean something special to you. Nothing is going to change that, and it meant so much to your mum that she didn't have to sell the place."

"You're right, I'm being silly. It's just a pile of bricks."

"It will be okay, I promise," I say, kissing her forehead. "Besides, you have a new home now, with Olivia and me."

HER

I never thought I'd see my mother move out of her home.

She said she'd rather die than leave our old house, but once I understood the real reason why, I knew what I needed to do about it. I don't know if I really believed her about killing my dad, until I dug up the vegetable patch and started finding bones. Nobody is going to find anything they shouldn't buried in the garden now, at least not in my lifetime. What happened is all covered up with a brand-new patio, the past buried underneath for good.

I don't feel bad about it.

My father got what was coming to him, and my mother did what she did for me, as well as for herself. The things we will do to protect those we love know no bounds.

The retirement village Jack managed to get Mum into is quite beautiful. It costs a small fortune, but I had a little money left over from the sale of the Waterloo apartment, which helped secure her a place. Plus the rental income on her house — now that tenants are about to move in — will just about cover the monthly payments. Besides, her cancer is an aggressive variety. In many ways she seems well, and certainly happier than I can remember seeing her before, but the doctors say she doesn't have long.

"Wow!" says Olivia from the backseat.

It's one of her new favorite words, and also appropriate as we make our way up the long private driveway.

The communal gardens are immaculate, with a series of little fountains and subtle lighting among the pretty, color-coordinated flower beds. The reception looks like a five-star hotel, and the facilities include a choice of restaurants, a library, a swimming pool, and even a spa. Mum has her own ground-floor apartment and, most importantly, she has her own private yard, with a view of Blackdown Woods. Albeit from the other side of the valley.

"Hello, Mum," I say, holding her close, breathing in the smell of her familiar perfume.

She looks well and has put on a little weight. I can see that she has had her hair done, and her clothes are clean and ironed just like they always used to be. Someone else cleans for *her* now, something I still don't think she's gotten used to. So many years of letting herself into other people's houses, to do their dirty work while they were out doing something else. I found a drawer full of keys in her old bedroom when I was clearing out her home; she must have had one for almost every house in the village.

Someone else pops by to give her medication twice a day now too, although I'm not convinced she always takes it. There are emergency buttons and cords in every room, so that if she feels unwell, or needs anything at all, help is close by. She can choose to eat in the restaurant, or they deliver fresh, organic food along with recipe cards for her to cook herself. Mum took a little convincing, and it's obvious she misses her beloved vegetable garden, but I think she's adjusting to her new life well. Albeit slowly.

The apartment is decorated in neutral tones and it's all very minimal, but I can see some of her old familiar things from home. There are pictures of me when I was fifteen for starters, but also a more recent framed photo of me, Jack, and Olivia, which makes me happy. She isn't holding on to that teenage version of me anymore; she sees me as I am today and seems to love me anyway. Parents spend their youth trying to understand their children; children spend their adulthood trying to understand their parents.

My mother insists on making us some tea. She disappears into her little kitchen and we hear her opening the cupboards and drawers. I enjoy the familiar sound of cups being put on saucers, and metal teaspoons on china. We wait for her old-fashioned kettle to boil on the stove, and I experience a brief involuntary shudder when it screams.

She shuffles back in a few moments later, a pretty silver tray rattling in her shaky fingers. I notice that she has bought some organic honey in a squeezable bottle, as well as a jug of milk and bowl of sugar. It makes me smile. She's doing well, but still has moments of confusion.

"The bees are alive!" squeals Olivia, on seeing the honey. We've been reading Winnie-the-Pooh stories to her, and she's become a little obsessed with the stuff. "Your bees live with us in London now, Nanny Andrews, and they came out of the hive today!" she says, beaming at my mother.

"They survived the trip?" Mum asks, staring at me.

"Yes, Mum."

"Did they find the knife inside the hive?" she asks.

I hid it there after leaving the hospital; I didn't know what to do with it. I should have known she would find it — she's the only person I know crazy enough to stick their hand in a hive. Luckily everyone else presumes it's the dementia talking.

I smile and pick up the knife on the table to cut the cake we bought.

"No, Mum, it's here, see? Bees don't need knives to spread the honey, they can do that all by themselves. Now, who wants a slice of chocolate cake?" I ask, starting to unwrap the big white box from the bakery.

"Me!" shouts Olivia.

Mum asks for the tiniest sliver of chocolate sponge, and I can tell that she doesn't really want to eat it. I should have taken it out of the box, and pretended to have baked it myself, so she wouldn't have thought it was shop-bought and filled with poisonous additives.

"The woman with the ponytail came to see me again," she says, putting down her fork.

My own hovers in midair while I try not to look as worried as I feel.

"Do you mean Priya? The detective?" I ask.

"Yes. She likes to ask me questions."

"Why would Priya be visiting Mum?" I ask Jack, and he shrugs, oblivious to my concern.

"She's a nice person. Probably just wants to check up on you, make sure you're doing okay after everything that happened," he says.

"I'm sure that's all it is," I agree, trying to reassure her.

I can tell she doesn't believe me. I'm not sure I do either.

Mum smiles and puts down the uneaten cake, then takes a sip of her tea instead, before adding another squeeze of honey to her cup.

"Don't you worry about me. I can take care of myself."

483

There are at least two sides to every story; yours and mine, ours and theirs, his and hers.

I always prefer my own.

But maybe it's for the best, that no one else ever knows the truth about what happened. I doubt they would believe me anyway. Nobody suspects a little old lady with dementia of killing people.

I've never really had a problem with my memory. If there are things I've forgotten over the years, it's because I chose to forget them. But the cancer diagnosis was real. Which meant I would be leaving that house one way or another, and someone else would move in and find my past mistakes buried in the garden.

The idea of people knowing the truth about what I did to my husband all those years ago was almost too much to bear. Bad stories about people stick like honey, and I didn't want to be remembered that way. Most of my life was spent being and doing good. He was a violent man, and I've always thought of it as self-defense, not murder. Of course I wish things could have been different, but regret is not the same as an apology. I am not sorry for what I did; I just never wanted anyone to find out.

Burying my husband beneath the vegetable patch seemed like such a clever idea. It was somewhere I thought nobody would ever think to look. I found his wedding ring one day, while digging up potatoes. He was the real reason I could never leave that house, but I know Anna has taken care of things for me now.

For years, I thought she left home when she was sixteen because, deep down, she knew what I had done. Anna found me covered in blood, as well as mud from the garden, on the afternoon I killed him. She decided to leave Blackdown as soon as she finished school the following year, and rarely came back. I thought it was my fault; that she hated me for taking her father away from her.

I made myself content with looking at old photos of my only child, then a few years later, made do with watching her on my TV screen, reading the news. She looked so happy and healthy without me in her life. So I accepted the rare visits and infrequent phone calls, grateful whenever she did get in touch.

It was Jack's idea to let me look after Charlotte for the night, so that he could take Anna out for her birthday. I'd hardly spent any time at all with my baby granddaughter, so I was delighted when Anna agreed to it. I thought it might bring us closer together; Anna having a daughter of her own, and knowing how it feels to be a mother. But Charlotte died. It wasn't my fault, but it felt like she blamed me anyway.

The drinking started again after that. It numbed my pain. When people in town confused me being drunk with me having dementia, I had an idea. A good one. It brought Jack back into my life, which I hoped would mean Anna would come home out of pity too. All I had to do was pretend to be a bit forgetful, and wander the streets a few times in my nightdress. Jack insisted on me seeing a doctor; that's the only reason I found out about the cancer, not that I told him or anyone else the truth about that.

When I started clearing out the house, I left Anna's room until last. I'd kept it exactly the same as it was when she still lived there. I noticed some soot around the bottom of the fireplace, which was strange given it hadn't been used for years, not since she left.

I got my cleaning kit out, and reached up inside the chimney to brush away the grime that had gathered. That's when a dirty, singed, torn-up letter fell down into the grate. I stared at it for a while, before picking up the pieces of paper covered in Anna's familiar handwriting. She'd obviously tried to burn them, but they had got sucked up into the flue instead. I knelt down on her bedroom floor and arranged the pieces like a puzzle.

It was a suicide note.

I don't know how many times I read it, but day turned into night outside the window, and the thoughts inside my mind were just as dark.

She described the terrible things that had happened on the night of her sixteenth birthday, and I felt sick with disgust and mad with rage all at once. I read about the drugs Helen Wang had given her, the men Rachel Hopkins tried to make her have sex with, and how Zoe Harper mutilated our cat as a warning not to tell anyone.

It was a long time ago, but I remembered that night.

We rarely had guests, but I agreed to leave Anna alone with those girls from St. Hilary's, thinking that they were her friends. She was so excited that I couldn't say no. I watched her spend every evening for a week making friendship bracelets for each of them, and even gave her the red-and-white thread from my sewing basket.

I still had the photo of them all together that night. Rachel gave me a copy a couple of weeks after the party, when I was cleaning her mother's house. She asked me to give it to Anna. I knew that they'd had some sort of falling-out — having been inseparable, they hadn't seen each other at all — but I did give it to her. I found the picture in the trash the next day. I've always had a habit of holding on to things — birthday cards, diaries, photos — and I was glad I held on to that one.

I knew who they all were once I found that picture.

And I knew where they lived; I'd cleaned all their houses.

I might have retired, but I still had the keys, and people rarely change their locks. I finally knew the real reason why my Anna left Blackdown. It was because of them, not me.

They had to pay for that.

And they weren't the only ones.

Jack left Anna when their little girl died, and I hated him for it. I hated him even more when I followed Rachel Hopkins from the station and saw the two of them fucking in his car. I decided there and then that, despite all the kindness he had shown me, he had to be punished for leaving my little girl and sleeping with that whore.

I fully intended to pin all the murders on him

after that. I even borrowed his Timberland boots to wear in the woods. They were too big, of course, but nothing a little cotton wool in the toes couldn't fix, plus it saved getting my own shoes dirty. I started planting evidence in his car and home, and followed him whenever I could. Shortcuts rarely lead to success, but knowing the woods so well made it easy for me to get from one part of the village to another, quickly and undetected.

But then I saw them together again — Jack and Anna — and I knew there was something still there between them. They just needed a little help to find their way back to each other, that was all.

When I let myself into Anna's hotel bedroom — I cleaned that place for years — she looked like a little girl, fast asleep in her bed. It made me feel sad to see her drinking so much, but I understood why. Alcohol was always my drug of choice too. I tucked her in just like I used to, tidied away her rubbish, and put a bottle of water by her bed. It felt so good to take care of her, even if she didn't know I was there. She reminded me of a bird with a broken wing. I wanted to fix her, and I knew that if my plan worked it would be good for Anna's career too, as well as her personal life.

Catherine Kelly was the only one of those girls who had left town. When I let myself into her parents' old house in the woods, looking for clues about where she might be, it was a shock to see a newsreader I recognized in the family photos. The same one who stole Anna's job.

Killing Rachel brought my daughter home to me.

Killing Helen and Zoe helped me to keep her close.

Killing Cat Jones meant Anna could get her job back on the *One O'Clock News,* and I would be able to watch my little girl on TV every lunchtime again.

Anna called me on her birthday this year in floods of tears, because she had lost her presenting job. I hardly said a word, and I think she thought I didn't understand. But I did. And it made me so happy that I was the one she called. For the first time in years she needed my help, and I was not going to let her down again. That's when I understood that by punishing the people who hurt her in the past, I could give her a happier future. I had to kill them all. I did it for her.

Cat Jones came straight to Blackdown when I asked her to. Admittedly she thought the text I sent was from her husband. I stole Richard's mobile from his unlocked car when he and Anna were filming in the woods. Then I used his phone to contact his wife. The message was simple enough:

I know what you did with those men in the woods twenty years ago. I've seen the photos, and I fear everyone else at the BBC might see them soon too. If you want to save our marriage, bring the children to your parents' house tonight so we can talk.

I ignored all the desperate texts she sent him, the calls and voicemails. Sure enough, a couple of hours later she arrived at the old house in the woods, with a worried expression on her pretty face and two beautiful little girls by her side.

The rest was easy. When Cat put the children to bed, I took them. I would never have hurt them, but she had no way of knowing that. When she realized they were gone, I listened while she turned the place upside down searching for her girls. She screamed her husband's name the entire time, as though he had stolen them. It was only when she reached the main bedroom that she was quiet. I'd left some old photos and a note:

Richard isn't coming and I've taken your children. He doesn't really know what you did twenty years ago and he doesn't need to. Neither do they. As long as you do the right thing. The pictures on the bed will be destroyed and your girls will be returned to your husband — all you have to do is kill yourself

491

using the school tie hanging from the beam in the ceiling. If you call the police, if you call anyone, your children will not be found until it is too late. The longer you take to do as I ask, the longer they will be in danger. Whatever happens, you'll never see them again, but if you kill yourself you have my word that they will live.

She took out her phone but it didn't work. I already knew it was impossible to get a signal anywhere near that house, and that she'd never leave her girls. I listened to her pacing back and forth for a while, then she searched for them again. When she accepted that they could not be found, she burned the note and Rachel's photos in the fireplace downstairs, before returning to the bedroom. I wasn't sure if she'd do it or not, but most mothers will do anything for their daughters. I did.

I wanted Catherine to kill herself, because then I knew everyone would blame her for the murders. She had the best motive, after what those girls did to her. I hid beneath the bed and waited, with my knife in my hand just in case I might need it. I could hear everything she did — arranging the chair, removing her shoes before climbing onto it, crying — but I could not see. It took a long time for her to put the noose around her neck, but it wasn't until afterward I discovered she had changed the knot. Something her father taught her how to do when they went sailing, apparently.

As far as I knew then, everything was going according to plan. I heard her step off the chair and the sound of the ceiling beam creaking as she swung from it. But then Cat's husband arrived unexpectedly — the greasy cameraman — so I had to kill him too. He screamed like a girl when he saw Cat swinging from the ceiling. So I stabbed him before he had a chance to turn and see me. Then I smashed his skull with a cast-iron paperweight I'd seen on the dresser. He wasn't supposed to be there. Neither was Anna. I had to hide again when she came upstairs. The only reason I canceled their hotel rooms was because I thought she would come home to me. That was all I ever wanted. For her to come home.

I stared up at Cat after I killed her husband. The noose was still around her neck, her eyes were closed, and I was convinced she was dead too. But I guess she was a good actress. Willing to do whatever it took to save her children, just like me. She must have seen my face without me realizing, because she recognized me a little later.

I'll admit that I was scared when I ran into her in the woods. Cat could have told Anna and the police what I had done. Instead, she started screaming like a madwoman, demanding to know where her little girls were. She stabbed me with my own knife when I wouldn't say. Her daughters were fine, of course. Just a little drugged and sleeping it off in the shed; the police found them not long after. I'd never hurt a child; I'm not a monster.

Sometimes I think Anna knows that I killed those women as well as her father. I can think of no other reason why she picked up the knife Catherine dropped in the woods and hid it in her handbag. I think she must have recognized it. I borrowed it from Jack's house, after all, from a set I gave them as a wedding gift.

"What are you making?"

Olivia comes into my bedroom and I realize that I had been daydreaming. My mind does wander when it wants to, but not because I have dementia, just because I am old. I don't take the drugs the doctors give me; I plant them in the soil instead, like seeds. When my time comes I will go gracefully, but not before. Priya Patel coming to ask me questions is nothing to do with kindness. Nor is it a coincidence; there is no such thing. Loose threads should always be dealt with; they can make things untidy.

The child walks over, then climbs up to

sit on my lap. She stares at the friendship bracelet I've been making.

It's almost finished.

I make a fist around the red-and-white cotton strands to hide them from view, surprised as always by the age spots and paper-like quality of my skin. Then I slip the bracelet inside the old wooden jewelry box that used to belong to Anna. I am aware that Olivia saw it. Children always see far more than we'd like or know.

"That was pretty," she says.

"It was, wasn't it?" I reply.

"Is it a present for me?" she asks with a cheeky grin.

"Oh no, it's for someone else next time they come to visit."

Olivia looks sad.

"Don't worry, I have something for you too."

I take the bumblebee costume out of the closet and she squeals with delight. Anna and Jack also look pleased as the child hurtles out of my bedroom, through the living room, and into the garden, running around in circles. I made it myself in the textiles class they have here. I'm rather good with a needle and thread.

"I miss my busy bees," I tell Olivia, watching her from the doorway.

She laughs and dances and sings the same sentence over and over.

"I'm a busy bee! I'm a busy bee! I'm a busy bee!"

Her words translate into something else entirely inside my ears.

Happy family. Happy family. Happy family.

I smile at them all then, because I've finally got what I always wanted.

ACKNOWLEDGMENTS

Books are a bit like children for authors; you're not really allowed to have a favorite, but I am rather fond of this one. I wouldn't have been able to write it without the following amazing people in my life.

Forever thank you to my agent, Jonny Geller, for taking a chance on me and always knowing the right thing to say. Agenting is a funny business, and far more complex than I ever imagined. It requires one person to perform many roles: reader, editor, manager, therapist, surrogate parent, boss, and friend. Thank you for being so good at all of them.

Amazing agents are rare, so I feel incredibly lucky to have more than one. If Mary Poppins had decided to become a literary agent, she would be Kari Stuart at ICM. Thank you to Kari for being (actually, not practically) perfect in every way. Thank you to Kate Cooper and Nadia Mokdad for selling my books around the world. Thanks to these two brilliant women, stories written in my little shed have been translated into more than twenty languages. It is nothing less than magic, and I'm so grateful. Thank you to everyone else at Curtis Brown, the best agency in town, with special thanks to Ciara Finan.

Thank you to Josie Freedman and Luke Speed for making a dream I didn't even dare dream come true. Because of them, I get to see my characters come to life on-screen. Thank you to Sarah Michelle Gellar, Ellen DeGeneres, and Robin Swicord for believing in my debut novel. It's been a real roller-coaster ride and very exciting.

Publishers come in all shapes and sizes, and I'm so grateful to be working with the best. Huge thanks to Manpreet Grewal, my editor extraordinaire. Editors don't just edit — they do everything, and Manpreet is Wonder Woman. We'll always have kitchen foil and ants in ice cream. Thanks also to Lisa Milton, Janet Aspey, Lily Capewell, Lucy Richardson, and the whole HQ team at HarperCollins. Thank you to the equally brilliant team at Flatiron Books in the United States, with extra special thanks to Christine Kopprasch (who I will always picture sitting in a tree while reading two books — because one is never enough!). Huge thanks also to Amy Einhorn, Conor Mintzer, Bob Miller, Nancy Trypuc, and Marlena Bittner. Thank you to all my other publishers around the world for taking such good care of my books.

Thank you to the booksellers and everyone else who has helped put my books into the hands of readers. Special thanks to Hatchards in London for a fairy-tale launch I will never forget, and to the Mysterious Bookshop in New York for making the first time I saw my books in America so magical. I spend most days in a shed with my dog and my laptop, so seeing my stories out in the world will never stop being special.

Writers are nothing without readers. Thank you to all the bloggers, bookstagrammers (I love seeing your pictures of the books), librarians, book reviewers, and journalists who have been so kind about my novels. I hope you continue to enjoy my stories, and I'm forever grateful for your support. Special thanks to Brian Grant for being a wizard with a camera, and to Lee Fabry for all his advice about police procedure in the UK. Any mistakes are my own.

Thank you to my friends for being my family. This has been a difficult year for me, with a variety of grief so heavy it sometimes felt impossible to stand. Thank you to the people who pulled me up. You know who you are.

Last, but never least, thank you to Daniel — my first reader, my best friend, my best everything.

ABOUT THE AUTHOR

Alice Feeney is a writer and journalist. She spent fifteen years with BBC News where she worked as a reporter, news editor, arts and entertainment producer, and *One O'Clock* news producer. Alice has lived in London and Sydney and has now settled in the Surrey countryside, where she lives with her husband and dog. *Sometimes I Lie,* her bestselling debut novel, is being made into a TV series by a major film studio. *His & Hers* is her third novel.